D0233066

'Rozenn, I would swim to England for *your* kiss.'

Ben could not have said that, and in so *serious* a tone. He had to be teasing her. And then thought fled as he whirled her around so she had her back to the audience on the bridge. He lowered his lips to hers.

His kiss began light as thistledown, so light that she could barely feel it. Her body went quite still, as if it was curious, as if it wanted to know what kissing Benedict Silvester would be like.

We shouldn't be doing this, her mind protested, while her body hung limp in his arms and experienced what it was like to kiss him. Achingly gentle. Warm lips, despite the swim, lips that moved softly over hers and made her want to melt into him. He tasted of heaven, he tasted of everything she had ever dreamed of, he tasted of…Ben.

Pulling back with a shaky laugh, she smoothed his hair from his face. Hands firmly gripping her waist, Ben smiled down at her, eyes warm.

I would swim to England for your *kiss.*

What a tease.

'You're all wet,' she said, clearing her throat. She gave him a little shove. 'Go, go! You have a wager to win.'

Author Note

In 1066 William, Duke of Normandy, seized the English crown. Many Franks came with him, including knights from Brittany and elsewhere in France. The hero of my last novel was one of these, and I wondered how it might have been for the family and friends he left behind.

This novel opens in Brittany in the summer of 1067. Politically, the Breton Duchy is in chaos. Rival counts are jostling for supremacy and allegiances change like lightning. What if William also attacks neighbouring Brittany? In AN HONOURABLE ROGUE two young Bretons are drawn into this political maelstrom. A lute-player, Benedict Silvester, is one. He carries out secret missions for the Duke of Brittany—which means a journey to turbulent England. Rozenn Kerber, Ben's childhood friend, is another. Knowing that Rose is ambitious, Ben arranges for her to receive a 'proposal of marriage' from a knight in England, and together they set off…

Minstrels would both sing and recite the ancient epics, stories in which heroes and heroines are tested to their limits. On his travels Ben recites *The Romance of Tristan*. He also sings a version of *The Song of Roland,* originally made famous by a renowned minstrel known as the dwarf Turold. Turold can be seen on the Bayeux Tapestry.

I hope you enjoy reading about Ben and Rose as they embark on their journey, a journey which will put them to the test…

AN HONOURABLE ROGUE

Carol Townend

™MILLS & BOON®
Pure reading pleasure™

First published in Great Britain 2008
Large Print edition 2009
Harlequin Mills & Boon Limited,
Eton House, 18-24 Paradise Road, Richmond, Surrey TW9 1SR

ISBN: 978 0 263 20652 4

Set in Times Roman 16 on 17 pt.
42-0109-82859

Printed and bound in Great Britain
by CPI Antony Rowe, Chippenham, Wiltshire

Carol Townend has been making up stories since she was a child. Whenever she comes across a tumbledown building, be it castle or cottage, she can't help conjuring up the lives of the people who once lived there. Her Yorkshire forebears were friendly with the Brontë sisters. Perhaps their influence lingers…

Carol's love of ancient and medieval history took her to London University, where she read History, and her first novel (published by Mills & Boon) won the Romantic Novelists' Association's New Writers' Award. Currently she lives near Kew Gardens, with her husband and daughter. Visit her website at www.caroltownend.co.uk

To Mick, with thanks
for the Bosham connection,
and Tim for help with the horses

Chapter One

Quimperlé, Brittany

Even though it was Witches' Night, the first time the door latch rattled Rozenn was not alarmed. The sun was yet to set, and she was expecting her young friend, Mikaela.

In any case, Hauteville, the quarter of Quimperlé in which Rozenn lived, was scarcely the town slum. At the top of Quimperlé, built on the edge of a rocky outcrop overlooking the main town and castle, Hauteville remained a reasonably safe place in which to live—even the lawlessness that followed the recent killing of Duke Conan had not reached Hauteville. However, this was 1067 and the times were uncertain, so just in case it wasn't Mikaela, Rozenn shoved the silver coins she had been counting back into their pouch and draped some sewing over them. Her little hoard—except that now it was not so little—was growing.

Perhaps today was the day to tell Mikaela she planned to leave Brittany, possibly for ever....

As she expected, it *was* Mikaela outside; she was busily fastening a garland to the door in the fading evening light. Overhead, screeching swifts traced arcs in the sky; house martins darted in and out of their nests under the eaves.

'You've come straight from the tavern,' Rozenn observed.

'Mmm.' Mikaela's fingers were busy with the garland, tweaking, adjusting. 'How did you work that out?'

'No veil.'

Mikaela and her father ran the local tavern, the White Bird, and since a veil was not practical for cooking and cleaning, Mikaela often dispensed with it and forgot to put it back on when she went out about town.

Rozenn glanced at the garland, a Midsummer's Eve garland. Yellow St John's wort gleamed against glossy bay leaves; corn marigolds winked out from between trailing strands of ivy; yarrow and elder flowers nodded in the warm breeze that was drifting up the narrow street from the river and port below....

'Pretty.' Rozenn smiled. Mikaela was using the

same rusty nail she had hung her garland on the previous year, and the year before that. Mikaela was a creature of habit. And very superstitious.

Mikaela shoved her plait over her shoulder and threw her a look. 'Pretty's not the point, Rose. This is meant to protect you.'

'Against witches.' Rozenn managed not to laugh.

'Of course. Don't roll those brown eyes at me. This—' Mikaela flicked at the St John's Wort, dusting her fingertips with the heavy pollen '—will see you safe till the feast of St John the Baptist on the morrow and this—' she indicated a sprig of bay '—wards off witches and evil spirits—'

'Oh, Mikaela...' Rozenn shook her head with a smile '...you're wasting your time. I don't believe in the old tales.'

Mikaela gave the garland on Rozenn's door a final tweak and stepped back to admire her handiwork. 'Maybe that's your problem,' she murmured, wiping pollen on to her skirts.

'I beg your pardon?'

Mikaela shrugged. 'Too serious, that's your trouble. You could come down to Saint Columban's tonight, find out who your true love is.'

Rozenn's lips tightened. 'Midsummer madness. No.'

'Please, Rozenn. Nicole and Anna are coming.

It would do you good to join in. See it as a bit of fun. Your time of mourning is over, there's no need to feel guilty.'

'I don't feel guilty,' Rozenn said. 'I simply think it is folly, a waste of time and sleep. Walking seven times round a church at midnight, for heaven's sake. As if that will tell you your true love. It's utter lunacy.'

'You don't have to believe in it, it's *fun*.' Mikaela took her hand and squeezed it gently. 'Per wouldn't mind. He'd want you to be happy, to find someone else. And if the spell does work—' she grinned '—you'll learn who your true love is.'

'But I already know that,' Rozenn said, before she could stop herself.

Mikaela's jaw dropped. 'What?'

Rozenn could have bitten out her tongue; she had planned to be subtle when she told Mikaela her plans, not blurt them out like a fool. Abruptly turning her shoulder, she fingered the gold cross she wore on a chain round her neck and gazed down the cobbled street as it ran down to the quays and the castle in Quimperlé proper. Overhead, the house martins threaded back and forth across a pink-streaked sky.

'Nothing.' Rose wiped her forehead with the back of her hand and sighed. Young Anton was toiling up the hill, pulling a hand cart laden with bales of cloth, destined doubtless for Mark Quémeneur, the town's main tailor now her husband was dead. 'That boy will have to hurry if he wants to get to Mark's workshop before he locks up for the evening.'

'Rozenn Kerber, don't you dare change the subject!'

Rozenn sighed. 'It was nothing, Mikaela, I spoke out of turn. It was so hot in Countess Muriel's solar today, my brain must have addled.'

As Anton and the cart rumbled by, Mikaela tugged at her hand, trying to make her meet her eyes. 'No escape, Rose. You said something extremely interesting. You said you already know who your true love is, and it didn't sound to me as though you were referring to Per.' Mikaela's voice was light and teasing, but she was frowning. 'I know you were fond of him, but you were hardly starry-eyed when you married. You didn't mean Per, did you? Is it someone I know?'

'Leave it, Mikaela, I spoke without thought.'

'Tell me, Rose,' Mikaela said, softly wheedling. 'Tell me who you love.'

'No.' Rozenn tossed her head and laughed at her friend's persistence. 'In truth, I was going to tell you some time soon, but since this has you in such a fever, you have to guess. I'll share my supper with you if you guess his name.'

'Not fair, since you were going to tell me anyway.'

'It's more fun teasing you! And did my ears deceive me, or didn't you just say I needed to have more fun?'

Mikaela narrowed her eyes. 'That, Rose, is a low blow.'

'Go on, *guess!* I went to the castle bakehouse and Stefan gave me a chicken pie that would feed a giant. There's far too much just for me.' She moved to the threshold, and pulled her garlanded door fully open. 'Come in, please. Your father will know where you are.'

The house that Rozenn had shared with her husband was, like most of the merchants' houses in Hauteville, a two-roomed dwelling, wattle and daub on a wood frame. The room at the front, facing the street, had wide shutters that Per used to fling open to display the shop and its wares. The shutters were pulled to now, and the shop was stuffy and full of deepening shadows. A further door led through to the room behind the shop, the living room where Rozenn and Per had cooked and eaten and slept. Light glowed there and the girls moved towards it, long skirts rustling. The shutter on the far wall was open, and the back of a neighbour's house was dark against a purpling sky.

As they passed through the shop, Mikaela's gaze

fell on the shelves, half of which were empty. Her frown deepened. 'Your stock, Rozenn? Where's all the cloth?'

'Sold most of it.'

'To Mark Quémeneur?'

'Yes.'

'Will it pay Per's debts?' Mikaela asked, knowing how upset her friend had been to discover that her husband owed several of the townsfolk money.

'I pray so.'

Mikaela indicated the remaining stock. 'And what happens to this lot?'

Rozenn smiled. 'I plan to sell it on market day. Mark offered me a reasonable price, but you know what a huckster he is. These fabrics should sell quite easily, and I think I can make more money myself.'

'You'll still take in sewing, though?'

Rozenn murmured something noncommittal and turned away, not quite ready to reveal her plans to leave the Duchy. 'Mark was pleased to have the damasks and the Byzantine silks. Oh, and before I forget, I saved you a length of that blue velvet you were so taken with.'

'Did you?' Mikaela's eyes lit up. 'My thanks but, Rose, I do have a little money. I can pay you.'

'Don't be silly. Per may have left debts, but I am not so encumbered that I can't give you a gift.'

'You are generous. But what will you do without your shop? You will keep on with your sewing? Rose, you must. You're so clever with a needle, you'll never want for work.'

Leading the way into the living room, Rose smiled and bent to add a log on to the fire in the central hearth. Taking a taper, she lit a couple of candles and waved Mikaela to a stool. 'Aye, there's always needlework.' She picked up the sewing and her heavy money pouch and dropped them on the bed by the wall. It was such a relief to know that soon she would be able to pay off Per's debts.

At the table, Mikaela leaned her chin on one hand and airily waved the other while Rozenn hunted out wooden cups and plates. 'Enough of work,' Mikaela said. 'Let's get to the main business of the evening. I have to guess who Rozenn loves? Who can it be?' She tapped her lips with her forefinger. 'You say I know him?'

'Ye…es, but you won't have seen him for a while.'

'Hmm.' Abruptly Mikaela straightened. 'Oh, this is like stealing sweetmeats from a baby! I know, I know exactly who it is!'

Rozenn took a wine-skin down from its hook, drew the stopper and reached for Mikaela's cup. 'You do?'

'Yes, yes, of course I do! It's Ben, Benedict Silvester!'

The wine-skin jerked in Rozenn's hand. Rozenn stared blankly at a dark pool of wine that had somehow splashed on to the table. 'B-Ben?'

'Yes! The lute-player.'

Rozenn snorted and shook her head. 'I wouldn't love Benedict Silvester if he were the last man on earth.'

Mikaela raised a brow. 'You wouldn't? I always thought you adored each other. You played together as children whenever he was around—inseparable, you were.'

'Children are extremely uncritical.'

'But you do like him, Rose, I know you do!'

'Yes, yes, of course I like him,' Rozenn said, a touch impatiently. 'How could I not? He's kind and witty and amusing.'

Mikaela's expression grew dreamy. 'Handsome, Rozenn. Don't forget that. Those eyes—dark as sin—'

'He's a rootless charmer—'

'Those long eyelashes…hair like ebony. And he plays the lute like an angel.'

'That last is true.'

Mikaela's bosom heaved. 'And as for his body…'

Rozenn scowled. 'What would you know about Ben's body?'

Mikaela's lips twitched. 'I thought that would

sting. I know I'm right, it *is* Ben! Rozenn loves Ben Silvester…'

'I do *not!*' Rozenn thumped Mikaela's cup down on the table and turned to the hearth where Stefan's pie was warming in a dish. Honesty compelled her to add, 'At least, not in the way you mean. I love him as a brother, in the same way that I love Adam.'

Mikaela tipped her head to one side. 'I thought at one time you would marry Ben, you and he seemed so well suited, but you married Per and—'

'Ben and I? Well suited? You link me with a feckless lute-player who has seduced half the women in Brittany! You flatter me…'

Mikaela did not respond. Her finger tapped on her mouth.

'Besides,' Rozenn said, frowning, 'I haven't seen Ben in *two years.* Not since that quarrel that flared up between him and Adam.'

'Yes, that was odd. Until then they had been very close. I wonder what it was about?'

'I have no idea, Adam would never say.'

'So there has to be someone else who hasn't been in Quimperlé for some time,' Mikaela said thoughtfully. 'Someone else whom you love?'

'Yes. And it really is *not* Benedict Silvester. Think again.'

Mikaela sipped at her wine and eyed Rozenn

over the rim of her cup. 'This is good. Did you buy it from Father?'

'Countess Muriel gave it to me. Come on, Mikaela, guess again.'

Setting her cup down, Mikaela shook her head. 'Lord knows, if it's not Ben. Mark?'

'Mark Quémeneur? No, he's more of a business associate.'

'One of Adam's cronies then? Didn't you have word from him a week back?'

'Yes and yes. Your aim is improving!'

'So, this paragon is a knight? Aye, you would have it in mind to marry a knight…'

Setting the pie on the table, Rozenn pulled up a stool opposite Mikaela.

'Not that knight who gave you that gold cross, the one with a lute like Ben's? Not Sir Richard of Asculf?'

With a flourish, Rozenn cut a large slice from Stefan's pie. 'The very same, well done! You, dear friend, have won yourself some of the best chicken pie in Quimperlé.'

Later that night, Rozenn lay in the bed by the wall in the living room, unable to sleep. Sticky and hot, she thrust back the bedcovers and stared through the blackness at the rafters. Next door, baby Manu was crying. Someone ran past the house, their boots ringing loud on the cobbles. She heard a soft murmuring, the baby stopped crying, and then silence settled over the street. She tugged at the chain round her neck and pulled the cross out of her nightshirt. A gold cross. *Gold.* Sir Richard had given her a gold one because he held her in high regard.

The heat was stifling. It was an August heat rather than a June heat, and it seemed to rise up like a fog from the port and linger in Hauteville's narrow alleys. More wind, they needed more wind to carry off the heat. From the bottom of the hill, from Basseville, other sounds drifted in the air: a snatch of a drunken soldier's ditty, a howl of laughter. Men from Count Remond's garrison most likely, returning to the barracks after a session in one of the port taverns.

After Mikaela had left, Rozenn had smothered the fire down as much as she dared without putting it out completely. It glowed softly in the hearth, the only light in the room. It gave out too much heat, heat that was not needed tonight, but Rozenn liked warm water to wash in in the morning and it took too long to start a fire from scratch.

Mikaela. Rozenn smiled into the gloom, and as she shifted, the straw in the mattress rustled. Her friend had long been fascinated by the thought that Rozenn's gold cross had been a gift from Sir

Richard and not from her husband. It had been easy to divert her, and then the conversation had moved on, and suddenly the evening had passed and Rozenn still hadn't told Mikaela of her plans to take her 'mother' Ivona to England to find Adam and Sir Richard. Since Rose had been a foundling, and had been put into Ivona's care nineteen years ago, Ivona was not Rose's blood-mother any more than Adam was her real brother. But Rose loved them both as family. She was lucky to have them—not all foundlings were treated half so well.

What had been the exact wording of the startling message that Adam had sent her?

While Rose racked her brain to recall the precise words, she drew an image of Adam's messenger in her mind as, travel-stained and weary, he had caught up with her by the town well...

'Mistress Rozenn Kerber?'

'Yes?'

'Your brother, Sir Adam Wymark,' the messenger had said, 'sends loving greetings. He has asked me to inform you that he has important news for you and your mother, Ivona—'

'What news—he is unhurt?' she had asked, pleased at this evidence that Adam still considered her his sister.

'He is perfectly well, mistress. He requests that

you and your mother prepare to journey to England later in the year.'

Rozenn had rubbed her forehead. 'Ivona and I are to leave Brittany! But…but…'

Her mind had whirled, and two thoughts emerged from the maelstrom. The first was that her adoptive mother would be thrown into utter confusion by Adam's request, and the second that she herself was interested, *very* interested, in this idea. 'Adam must have said more…?'

'Indeed, mistress, and this is the meat of it: your brother has received an offer for your hand in marriage.'

'An offer, for me?'

'Yes, mistress. His friend Sir Richard of Asculf has asked if you would marry him.'

Rozenn had blinked, absently reaching for the cross at her neck. 'Sir Richard wants to marry me?'

The messenger had nodded. 'Your brother would like you to consider this offer most carefully. But in any case, whatever your decision regarding Sir Richard, he would be pleased to welcome you to his new holding. Sir Adam has some business to put in hand before he can send you an escort, but by early autumn he should be in a position to do so.'

'So soon? We are to join Adam this autumn?' Adam must have taken leave of his senses! Ivona would never agree to leave the castle that had been her home for so many years, *never*. And as for Sir Richard wanting to marry her—a knight, a *knight*… It was beyond anything she had dreamed of.

The messenger had simply nodded. 'Yes, mistress.'

Yes, mistress. As if it were a little thing, an everyday thing, for Adam to summon Rozenn and his mother across the sea to England and for her to receive an offer of marriage from a Norman knight.

'B-but I've never even left Quimperlé…'

The messenger had given her a strange look and he had sighed. He was holding himself in such a way that told Rose his back was aching. His throat had to be parched, he must be longing to put his feet up in a tavern. 'I'm telling you all I know, mistress,' he had said. 'Make preparations, your brother will send you an escort… Sir Adam also stressed that if anything were to happen to him, you must put your trust in Sir Richard, who has your best interests at heart.'

Rose could scarcely believe it, but it must be true. *Sir Richard has your best interests at heart.* Would Sir Richard have given a gold cross to a woman who meant nothing to him?

'H-how did Adam find out that I have been widowed?'

'I do not know.'

Shortly after that, having attempted with a fair degree of patience to respond to a barrage of questions, the man had bowed and had made his escape, leaving Rozenn staring after him, her thoughts in turmoil. Adam had done well in Duke William's service, apparently. For rallying fleeing troops at Hastings, England's new king had given Adam lands and a new wife—one Lady Cecily of Fulford.

As Rose had watched Adam's messenger limp towards the nearest tavern, an idea—no, it was more of a dream—had flashed into her mind.

Sir Richard has your best interests at heart...at heart. She had fingered the cross Sir Richard had, rather shockingly, given her even while she had been married to Per. Sir Richard had offered for her!

Once she would have thought such a thing impossible. But was it so incredible that Adam should wish to foster an alliance between his family and his good friend Sir Richard? After all, Adam was only the son of a horse-master, yet he had risen through the ranks and become a knight. And if that had happened, why should Rose not become a lady?

So now, on Witches' Night, Rozenn smiled into the dark, twirling the gold cross while she wildly embroidered her dream. Not for her the life of a cloth merchant's widow in Quimperlé where everyone thought of her as a foundling. She wouldn't have to depend on Countess Muriel for work, she would marry a knight! Lady Rozenn of Asculf…

England beckoned. Tomorrow she really must reveal her plans to Mikaela. And if Adam's mother refused to leave, she would simply have to travel on her own.…

First, Rozenn would pay off Per's debts, and then she would go and search out the place Adam's messenger had mentioned—Fulford, near Winchester. She wasn't about to wait for Adam's escort, life was too short. Why wait till the autumn? She would go as soon as possible—this month, maybe even this week! Somehow she would find a way.

King William had granted Adam lands in England!

How pleased Adam must be, to have lands of his own at last. But if only Adam had got a scribe to write a proper letter. Of course, Rozenn couldn't read herself, but England was a long way to go on the word of one exhausted messenger.

Coming briefly down to earth, Rozenn grimaced into the dark. She prayed she could persuade Ivona to accompany her. For if she could not, Ivona was bound to object to her setting off without Adam's escort. Having something in writing would have backed up her decision.

But…in England, she would have the chance of a new life. Once in England—Rozenn's lips curved—there would be no debts, no ignominious past to shame her. No one in England would realise why she had been christened Rose. No one in England would ever think, 'there goes that girl whose mother abandoned her by the rosebush outside the White Bird'.

In England Rose would meet Adam's new Anglo-Saxon wife—what had the messenger said her name was? Cecily, Lady Cecily of Fulford. And after that, Adam would direct her to Sir Richard…

Ben Silvester, wandering minstrel? Hah! She was aiming higher than that, she was aiming for a *knight.*

Turning over, Rozenn thumped her pillow, and determinedly cleared her mind of the image of Ben Silvester, Breton lute-player with the roguish smile, and instead set about conjuring up the face and features of Sir Richard of Asculf, Norman knight.

Down by the Quimperlé docks, at the confluence of the two rivers, some of the customers in the Barge were getting rowdy.

Benedict Silvester was wearing his dull brown cloak, the one he wore when trying to blend into the background. His lute was stowed in its leather bag and slung over his shoulder, hopefully well out of harm's way. Keeping the hood of his cloak up and his face in the shadows, he nevertheless seemed to have attracted attention. He didn't like the look in the eyes of the men hunched over their cups at the next trestle, particularly the one in the greasy leather jerkin. That broken nose matched the man's general air of belligerence. Doubtless, the man was a brawler. Had he observed Ben's interest in their conversation? Had the man marked his features?

He hoped not, but it was possible. Ben shrank deeper into his hood, and gazed into his wine. He'd not been back in Quimperlé above two hours, and if he was to remain useful to Duke Hoël, he must not court trouble.

When the man glanced Ben's way for the second time, Ben realised events could take an ugly turn. Wishing he had left his lute in the care of the stable boy guarding his horse, Ben dropped a coin on the table and edged to the door. His lute must not get damaged. It had once belonged to his father and it gave him good cover, cover which was vital because it drew attention away from his real work, his work for the Duke of Brittany.

Outside, the River Laïta gleamed like pitch in the moonlight, and a couple of longboats rocked gently at the quayside. This was the point where two rivers met, just downstream from the Isle du Château. Encircling the island like a moat, the rivers formed the perfect natural defence for Count Remond's keep before fusing into one and flowing on to the sea. Taking a moment to breathe in a lungful of warm night air, Ben found himself glancing uphill, towards the merchants' quarter.

Hauteville. Where Rose had lived with Per.

Two years, it had been two years. And now with the current unrest reaching into every corner of the Duchy, no lesser person than Duke Hoël himself had commanded that Ben put aside his quarrel with Rose's brother. So far everything was going according to plan. Adam had done his bit, and Rose had received her summons to England. It was time for Ben to make amends with her if the second part of his plan was to stand any chance of success.

A small smile lifted the corners of his mouth. As ever he must be careful. Rose knew him well and she was not stupid. But he had rehearsed his part, he would even affect surprise when she told him of Per's death. If she caught wind of the fact that she was being manipulated, she would kill him.

The tavern door creaked. Yellow light spilled onto the quayside, and the silhouette of a man with a broken nose loomed in the doorway. Ben turned, slipped into a dark alley between two rows of wooden houses, and began running swiftly uphill towards Hauteville.

Chapter Two

The second time the door latch rattled on Witches' Night, Rozenn's breath froze. It had to be well past midnight, Mikaela and her friends would have made their way home from Saint Columban's long before this. Rising from her bed, Rose groped through the dark and bumped a knee against a stool. Grabbing it, she held it aloft and edged her way through the shop.

Heart pounding, she put an ear to the front door. Breathing—surely that was someone breathing on the other side? No, no, she was imagining things. Mikaela's talk of witches and evil spirits had set her off. It was only the wind rustling through the flowers in the garland.

When the latch clicked, she leaped backwards, gripping the stool leg for all she was worth. She prayed the bolt would hold.

A shout in the street. Footsteps. Several people

running and, since they were making no attempt to be covert, they had to be Count Remond's men. The chilling rasp of steel being drawn.

'Christ!' This from the other side of her door. The door latch clacked back into place. More running.

'That way!'

'He went that way!'

A scuffle, a grunt, and the disturbance moved off. Rozenn remembered to breathe.

Lowering the stool, she leaned her head on the door and waited for her heartbeat to settle. It must have been a thief, and the count's men had likely scared him off—she hoped they had caught him. Some distance away, a dog barked. Yes, they were moving away.

Even here in Hauteville, Rozenn thought ruefully, a woman alone was not safe. Perhaps Countess Muriel was right, perhaps she *should* take up residence in the castle until she left. There was plenty of room in the solar with the other ladies. But, no, Rozenn did not want to sleep with them. She saw disdain and pity in their eyes every time her name was mentioned. Rose, the girl who was left outside a tavern and given to Ivona Wymark to bring up. It was true that Ivona's care of her had been good, she had treated Rose as well as she had treated Adam, but the pity and the disdain remained. Rose did not wish the other ladies' eyes to be the last thing she saw before she fell asleep at night.

She was padding back to bed, the wooden stool dangling from her hand, when something thudded against one of the shutters. Someone let out a grunt. Her heart thumped.

Oh, God, the thief was back! He, whoever he was, must have found out that she was a widow and had singled her out as defenceless. Well, she would show him…

Renewing her grip on the stool, Rozenn faced the shutter.

Wood creaked. Another grunt. The darkness seemed to shift, and a whisper of warm air across her skin warned her that the shutter was being forced. A sliver of silver flashed as a dagger slipped through from outside. Metal scraped on wood. The latch gave with a pop, and moonlight streamed in.

A black shape took form; it thrust an object through the opening and dropped it carefully on the floor. Other objects followed. He was trying to be quiet.

Taking a shaky breath, Rozenn raised the stool. She was trembling all over and every instinct was screaming at her to run, but the back door of the house was bolted fast, and by the time she reached it and struggled with the bolts, the intruder would be upon her. Whoever he was, she must face him here.

The draught of warm air increased. Breath frozen, she heard movement. A dark shadow shifted…

There!

No, there!

Breathing…

Behind her!

About to whirl about, strong arms caught her by the waist, her hair was nudged aside and a warm kiss was pressed to the nape of her neck.

'Guess,' came the soft murmur. 'Guess who it is.'

The relief—she knew the voice after one word— weakened her knees. Dropping the stool with a crash, Rozenn gripped the arms wound about her middle. She didn't have to see the long fingers that moved to cover hers; she didn't have to feel the calluses the lute-strings had formed on the pads of his fingertips; she didn't have to look into his brown eyes and see those tiny grey and green flecks to know who was holding her pressed so closely to him.

'Ben!' Her voice cracked, and to distract him from reading too much into that, for his hearing was subtle and he knew her so well he could read all of her moods, she thumped at his forearm. He winced, but she ignored this and let her body relax against his. 'You *fool,* Benedict Silvester, you scared me half to death.'

Another warm kiss was pressed into her neck. Since it had been so long since he'd sought her out, and she really was very fond of him, Rozenn did not object.

'Sorry, little flower, but I was in something of a hurry. No time to send out the heralds.'

Twisting round, she grasped his shoulders. 'Some poor cuckold of a husband after you, I expect,' she said lightly. It was too dark to read his expression, but he stepped back.

'Ah, Rose, you cut me to the quick. Always you think the worst of me.'

'Isn't there reason?'

Silence. Then, gently, 'Rose, I won't stay if I'm not welcome.'

Impulsively, guiltily, she found his hand in the dark and lifted it to her cheek. 'No, Ben, I am sorry, you are welcome. It has been too long.' She softened her tone. 'My house is yours. Treat it as your home.'

'I don't have a home, *chérie,*' Ben said, adopting what she termed his flirtatious voice. He carried her hand to his heart. 'But if I did, you would be its flickering flame, toasting a man's toes on a winter's night.'

Rozenn shook her head, smiling at him through the dark. 'You're a rogue, Benedict Silvester, to try to flatter me. Haven't you learnt I'm proof against your wiles?'

'I live in hope, I live in hope. Rose?'

'Mmm?'

'May I stay here while I'm in Quimperlé?'

'Won't you be bedding down at the castle?'

'I'd rather not; there's never much rest to be had for a minstrel in the hall of a castle.'

Forgetting he could not see her in the dark, Rozenn nodded. She knew how it was—he would be constantly in demand at the castle, as a musician, a singer, a drinking companion and… No, she would not think about *that*. It warmed her to think that Ben could relax in her house, but then, they had been friends for ever.

'Of course. You don't need to ask.' The words had slipped out before she had time to question the wisdom of letting Ben—a man with the most appalling reputation—stay in her house now that her husband had died. Moving past him, Rozenn led the way into the private family room. Fumbling for a taper, she lit a candle and mocked him. 'Do enter, kind sir.'

'My thanks, little flower.'

Ben fetched the things he had tossed through the shutter and, as the light strengthened, Rozenn recognised his lute bag among them. She ought to, having stitched it herself years ago. It was the first and the last thing she had ever made in leather, and by the time she had finished it, she had gone through two thimbles and her fingers were pricked to the bone. Never again, she had sworn, vowing to stick to fabric thereafter.

Ben tossed his cloak on to a stool and frowned at her empty bed. In the candlelight she could see that his hair was cut in the fashion favoured by the Normans—shaved short at the back. It was longer at the front though, so long that his dark fringe flopped into his eyes. With an impatient gesture, he shoved it back.

He has been running, Rozenn reminded herself, deliberately turning her attention to his clothes to stop herself staring at his face, like just another of his lovestruck women. But even a furtive glance had told her that Benedict Silvester remained more handsome than a man ought to be. It wasn't fair, but Mikaela was right, those dark looks, especially his eyes and the way they appeared to soften when they regarded one, were almost irresistible. His face was leaner than it had been; it was no longer the face of a boy, but that of a man coming into his prime. He needed a shave and this gave him a faintly disreputable air that hinted of danger, but typically, since it was Ben, this was not unattractive. His looks were as much his stock in trade as was his talent with a lute.

Shaking her head, Rozenn forced her attention to his clothes, assessing them with the eyes of a woman used to judging the quality at a glance. Under that unremarkable cloak that was surely too dowdy for Ben and far too hot for a night like tonight, they were showy. This was more like it, this was the Ben she knew. Ben's clothes had always been fit for a prince—they were the clothes of a man who earned his bread by entertaining noblemen. And, a little voice added waspishly, by pleasing noblewomen too. The candlelight shone on a tunic that was a rich kingfisher blue. It had the sheen and drape of silk. Both the tunic and the belt at Ben's waist flattered his form—wide shoulders, slim waist. A silver buckle glinted. Ben's chausses were of fine grey linen, and the leg bindings matched the blue of his tunic. His boots…

'Rose…' he was looking around, apparently puzzled '…where's Per?'

Rozenn took a deep breath and looked into Ben's eyes and wished the night was not so hot and airless; it was very hard to breathe.

'Oh, Ben, there is so much to tell you…'

Thus it was that Ben found himself sitting at Rozenn's board, tasting rich red wine and chicken pie while he pretended her news was new to him.

Ben listened while Rozenn talked about Per's death, about how swiftly the sickness had taken him, about how she had tried to nurse him, all to no avail. He watched the sadness enter her eyes, shoved aside his empty plate, and reached for her hand.

'You'd come to care for him very much, hadn't you?'

Rose's hair was unravelling from its braid, a glossy, dark mass of curls. She bent her head and wound it loosely at the nape of her neck. Her voice, when she spoke, was muffled. 'Naturally, I cared for him. He was my husband.'

'Rozenn...' gently Ben turned her face back to his, and reclaimed her hand '...there's more, isn't there?'

She sighed. 'Per had debts.'

Knowing how punctilious Rose was and how shamed she must have felt, Ben made his voice light. 'Don't we all?'

'Ben, I'm not talking about the odd penny here and there, but substantial amounts. After the funeral, half the town came knocking on the door, demanding payment.' She gave him a rueful smile and Ben caught his first glimpse of her dimples. 'Ironic, isn't it? I chose Per because I wanted—no, *needed*—security, and he turns out to owe money to the world and his wife. I tell you, if I ever catch so much as a glimpse of a tally stick again, I'll jump on the next horse I can find and gallop out of the Duchy.'

Ben smiled. 'They have tally sticks in Normandy too, *chérie.*' He rubbed his thumb against the back of her hand. Her fingers were clinging to his as though she'd never let go. Her breasts were something of a distraction, rising and falling as they were, under that flimsy nightgown. Rose thinks of me as a brother, he reminded himself, and kept his eyes fixed firmly on her face. It struck him that her dimples were surprisingly kissable and her mouth too looked inviting…

No. *No*. What was he thinking? Abruptly he released her hand and reached for his wine-cup. This was Rose, who openly admitted she wanted stability, the security he could never give her. Thank God, she seemed unaware of the temporarily lustful direction his thoughts had taken.

He indicated the money pouch at his belt. 'I've a few deniers with me, if that will help, *ma belle*. Don't mention it to Countess Muriel, but I was in Rennes recently with Duke Hoël. He paid handsomely to hear Turold's new "Song of Roland".'

When she nodded, Ben knew he did not have to expand. Rose might not know of his secret work for the Duke, but it was common knowledge that while Duke Hoël was titular Duke of Brittany, many of the barons, Count Remond of Quimperlé included, merely paid lip-service to his authority. The nobles made, and broke, other alliances every day. Deals were struck with Bretons, with Normans, with anyone—nothing mattered but that the arrangement gave a temporary advantage. Frankish noblemen had about as much honour as court whores.

Rozenn laid her fingers on his arm. It was the lightest of touches, the friendliest of touches, but it had muscles clenching in Ben's belly, sensual muscles that had no business clenching when she touched him. He frowned.

'That's sweet, Ben, but not necessary. Fortunately Mark Quémeneur offered a reasonable price for most of Per's stock. I hope to sell the rest on market day.'

Sweet. Now there was a novelty. 'So you can settle Per's debts?'

'Yes.'

'I am glad of that. Rose?'

'Mmm?' She smothered a yawn.

'If you ever did need me—for anything—you only have to ask. I am—' he raised her hand to his lips '—yours to command.'

Her brown eyes danced, her dimples winked at him. 'I know that, but you're not often around to ask, are you?'

Ben's heart contracted as guilt took him. Was he wrong to think of using Rose as cover to get him to England? Rozenn was no more suited to the wandering life than his mother had been—few women were. Rozenn craved security, Rozenn craved position. Ben understood, of course, but privately he wondered if she would for ever be making up for being a foundling. If it were not for the fact that the Duke vitally needed to establish a line of contact with his men in England, he would abandon the entire plan….

'Rose, I must ask, have you heard from Adam since he left? When I heard of the great battle at Hastings, I prayed that he would survive.'

'He did. Word came via a messenger bringing news to Count Remond. Adam distinguished himself at Hastings and Duke William—that is, the new King of England—has rewarded him with lands and a wife.'

'A *wife?*'

'Aye, her name is Cecily of Fulford,' Rozenn said, with a little yawn. 'And very soon I am going to visit them.'

'You are?' Ben said, affecting disbelief. 'My Rozenn leave Quimperlé—impossible!' She shot him a strange look and, deciding it was probably best not to overdo the disbelief, Ben shook his head and continued. 'But Adam—remarried—I can scarcely believe it. Poor woman, he will never love her as he loved Gwenn.'

'How could he? But Adam is kind. He will be a considerate husband, I'm sure, and that will be enough.'

'Will it? Was your marriage with Per like that? Was Per a considerate husband?'

Anger flared in her eyes. 'Ben, you go too far, even for an old friend.' Then her shoulders slumped and just as swiftly, the anger was gone. 'Per was *not* considerate, as you now know. How could he have just borrowed and borrowed?' Sighing, Rozenn leaned on her hand and stared into the fire.

There was more, he knew. Ben waited, but Rozenn continued to gaze blindly into the flames. There was a time when she would have trusted him with all of her secrets. His heart ached. He needed to know more about her plans to visit Adam, he needed to know her reaction to Sir Richard's 'offer', but she was tired and melancholy, so he held his tongue. Tomorrow would be soon enough.

'Sorry, little one.' Leaning forward, he touched her cheek. 'Don't be sad. You drive those dimples away, and they are very beautiful.'

'Beautiful dimples?' She roused herself and covered his hand with hers. 'You fool.'

'It's true, they are beautiful. I dream of those dimples; I sing songs about them; knights have jousted over them…'

'Idiot. Oh, Ben, it *is* good to see you. I… I've missed you.'

'And I you.'

She smothered a yawn.

Ben pushed himself to his feet. 'Has Countess Muriel asked for you on the morrow?'

'Aye, at first light.'

'I'm keeping you up. We can exchange more news tomorrow.' He made his voice as brisk as he might, to hide an inexplicable wave of longing that Rozenn might lie in his arms till dawn. 'Shall I sleep in the shop?'

'What? Oh, no. Make your bed over there, if you like, on the other side of the fire.'

Once the candle had been snuffed out and there was only the flicker of the fire to see by, she fell asleep quickly. She lay on her side on the bed, facing him, cheek pillowed on her hand, lips slightly parted. She was, Ben hoped, relieved to have him there. Happy, as he was to see her. He had always been content in Rozenn's presence, even when they had been children. And every time he and his father had worn out their welcome at the castle, every time they had decided to move on, it had been a wrench to leave her behind. So it would be again, no doubt—she was a good friend.

Ben lay on the pallet she had found him, wrapped in his cloak, and watched the dying flames burn till they were little more than a soft glow. Then at last, his eyelids drooped, and he too found sleep.

* * *

Rozenn woke when the first fingers of light were edging round the shutter. She was conscious that her mood was lighter than it had been in months, if not years. Hazy with sleep, she rolled on to her back. She dare not linger long because her neighbour's cockerel was crowing and Countess Muriel had commanded her presence in the solar at first light.

The Countess and her ladies were working on a wall-hanging intended for the Great Hall, above the dais. Rozenn had been commissioned to design it and, though the designing was done and the Countess and her ladies were perfectly capable of embroidering it without her, the Countess liked her to be present when they sewed.

This was another reason why Rozenn had not made public her intention to journey to England to find Adam and Sir Richard. If she feared upsetting Mikaela and Adam's mother, she was twice as worried about Countess Muriel. As a rule the Countess was even-tempered, but when crossed she could be spiteful and vindictive. And since the wall-hanging was her current obsession… Oh, Lord.

Eyes firmly shut, Rozenn stole a few more moments in bed, her thoughts drifting. When complete, her tapestry—half-a-dozen yards long and as many deep—would dwarf the other castle wall-hangings. At her first sight of the unworked linen unrolled on the trestle in the solar, the Countess had been delighted.

'Rozenn Kerber…' The Countess had smiled, lightly fingering the charcoal figures Rozenn had sketched on to the fabric. 'You are a wonder. Our hall will be the envy of Brittany. This figure riding out to hunt before all his men, is it Count Remond?'

'Yes, *Comptesse.*'

'And this, the lady in the orchard by the castle—is this me?'

'Yes, *Comptesse.*'

'You have done well, Rozenn. This will indeed enhance my husband's prestige.'

And that, more than decoration, was the purpose of the wall-hanging. Luckily Rozenn had been quick to realise this. That was why she had designed the hanging with her two powerful patrons in pride of place. Count Remond was ambitious, his Countess was ambitious and the wall-hanging was a visual representation of their aspirations. Rozenn understood about ambition; she had ambitions of her own—she was going to marry a knight. A man of honour, Sir Richard would never have given her the gold cross if his liking for her was not strong.

Sighing, Rose stretched and opened her eyes. Her heart gave a crazy lurch.

Ben.

Fast asleep on his stomach on the pallet on the other side of the room with his face turned to the wall. His dark hair was tousled and he must have pulled off his tunic and *chainse*—his shirt—in the heat of the night, for his torso was bare. He was not as large as her adopted brother Adam or her husband Per, but he was beautifully formed, with wide muscled shoulders and a narrow waist…

One arm was trailing over the edge of the pallet on to the floor. She looked at his hand, the hand she knew so well, with its slender musician's fingers relaxed and still. She wanted to touch him. How silly. She must have missed him more than she had realised.

Rozenn's gaze wandered down Ben's length to the cloak twisted at his waist, to the curve of buttocks concealed beneath it and finally to the naked foot sticking out at the bottom. Ben was no warrior, no Sir Richard of Asculf, and yet his body was strong, well muscled and athletic, like the tumblers and dancers that had visited Castle Hellon last month. But then Ben, she remembered, could tumble and dance along with the best of them.

She swallowed, and a disturbing sensation of longing made itself felt in her belly. Shaking her head, Rozenn flung back her sheet. No, not longing. It was not longing that she felt when she looked at Benedict Silvester. She, Rozenn Kerber, whose first marriage had been contracted on the grounds of practicality, and whose second would, like Countess Muriel's, be one of ambition, did *not* feel longing for men. It was only pleasure that she was feeling, the simple pleasure of seeing a dear friend again.

The cockerel had gone quiet, but the wood pigeons were cooing on her roof and above the town the martins were screeching....

Rozenn scrambled up. Quickly, she breathed life into the fire and put some of yesterday's water on to heat for washing. Then, dragging her gown over her head—a new one she had made a month ago out of the best blue linen in the shop—she slipped out for fresh water from the well in the square. At the tavern she bought a loaf of warm bread from Mikaela. She was careful to make no mention of Ben's reappearance because she was already late and there was no time for lengthy explanations. Half a loaf already lay in her bread crock, but Ben would appreciate a fresh one.

Back at the house, she set the loaf on a platter with a small round of goat's cheese and a couple of apples. Digging Per's house key out of the strongbox, she placed it on the table next to the food, where Ben would be bound to find it.

Then, picking up her workbag, she slipped out. The martins were swooping and diving for flies.

Young Anton was ahead of her, trotting down the hill in front of his cart. She had better hurry, if she was not to incur Countess Muriel's wrath.

When Rozenn entered the solar, Countess Muriel was pacing up and down in front of the fire that she insisted should burn day and night, winter and summer. The wall-hanging was still rolled in its protective covering to one side of the trestle, and several ladies were taking their ease on the window seat, murmuring softly to one another.

Countess Muriel strode up, full skirts swishing through the rushes. 'Rozenn, there you are!'

A tall, slender woman with narrow shoulders and a slight build, the countess nevertheless dwarfed most men. Her forthright manner could be intimidating, but Rozenn refused to be intimidated. She tipped back her head and met the Countess's gaze directly. 'Good morning, *Comptesse.*' Wondering why they could not have made a start without her, Rozenn put her workbag on the trestle and set about unrolling the tapestry. It occurred to her that though the Countess might command her person, she could not command her mind. Her heart lifted. Today, her happiness made her impervious to Countess Muriel's impatience. It must be because she would be leaving soon.

Countess Muriel made an irritable gesture. 'No, wait.'

Rozenn's hands stilled on the cloth. She ought to tell the Countess of her plans to leave Quimperlé as soon as possible. It was most odd, but this prospect did not unnerve her as much as it had last week. Giving only half an ear to what was being said, Rose wondered when the best moment would be. Perhaps she ought to wait until after market day, when she was absolutely sure she had enough money to settle Per's debts...

'Rozenn!' The Countess drew her dark brows together. 'Are you attending?'

'Y-yes, of course. My pardon, *Comptesse*.'

'So? You know where to find him?'

'Find who, *Comptesse*?'

Countess Muriel tutted. 'Really, Rozenn! I was talking about the lute-player, Benedict Silvester. My husband tells me he was seen last eve and I recollect you know him. Do you know where he might be?'

Rozenn's cheeks warmed. The thought of the Countess and her ladies learning that Benedict Silvester was staying at her house was disconcerting to say the least. Ben's reputation was such that they would never believe her relationship with him was innocent. Since she would soon be leaving Quimperlé, she should not really care what anyone here thought, but…

'B-Benedict?'

'Wake up, girl, for heavens' sake! You know perfectly well who I mean. The man's the best lute-player in the Duchy. I recollect he used to be a friend of your brother, so you should know his usual haunts. Do you know where he is? This morning I want him to entertain us while we sew.'

'I…I know where he might be, *Comptesse.*'

'Good, you may fetch him. Tell him he may have his usual fee, unless he'd rather settle for food and lodging.' Another imperious wave sent Rozenn hurrying to the door.

'Very well, *Comptesse,* I'll see if I can find him.'

The front door of her house in Hauteville was shut up when she got back, which probably meant that Ben had already left. Unlocking the door with the key she kept on the chain at her waist, Rose pushed it open and went in, stomach tightening. Ben had not said how long he was planning on staying in Quimperlé. But surely he would not come back for just one night? Not when they had so much more to talk about… No, no—vaguely she recalled him saying they would talk again later.

'Ben? Ben?'

A large bluebottle was blundering about the shop, but other than that the house was silent. In the living room, the bread on the table had been cut, one of the apples had gone, and the goat's cheese had been covered with a cloth. Flipping back the cloth, she smiled. He'd left her half. And Per's key was no longer there.

One of Ben's packs sat neatly on the pallet; there was no sign of his lute.

She huffed out a breath. Where might he have gone? He might be visiting old friends in the White Bird, but he could just as easily be in one of the dockside taverns. Or he might be singing in the market square, or playing dice in Count Remond's guardhouse; he might even be watching the hawks in the mews—he was fascinated by their speed and strength and ferocity. Resolving to walk back via the market square and the guard-house, Rozenn left her house and locked up.

Benedict Silvester was a will-o'-the-wisp. It was entirely possible that she might not run him to earth at all. Countess Muriel and her ladies might have to entertain themselves.

Chapter Three

At that very moment Ben was in fact in the castle stables, climbing into the hayloft to meet Alis FitzHubert. He was wearing his second-best tunic, the green linen one that was edged with silver braid at the neck, cuffs and hem, for he planned to win work in Count Remond's keep later that day. His lute, in its bag, was slung over one shoulder.

Lady Alis was the youngest, the newest and arguably the prettiest of Countess Muriel's entourage. A blonde beauty, she had arrived at Castle Hellon a few months ago and everyone in the keep had been led to believe she had come from Paris. That her status was relatively high was proclaimed by the deep dye of her pink gown, by the bright silks woven into her girdle, by the silver pins that kept her veil in place. Lady Alis was shod in neat white slippers, slippers that were fashioned for wearing indoors and looked completely impractical to Ben's eyes, even though he understood the importance of dressing as befitted one's station. White slippers were certainly out of place in a stable.

The air in the loft was warm and smelt of hay and horses. Shafts of sunlight slanted down through chinks in the slate roof. Outside in the bailey, where the count's men-at-arms were being put through their paces, the sergeant barked out an order.

'Christ, Alis,' Ben muttered, glancing askance at the mounds of hay covering the planked floor, 'you will have to be more circumspect when you choose the place for our next rendezvous. If we are seen, Sir Edouarz will certainly believe you are not the chaste fiancée you claim to be, and I am in no position to defend you. He could reject you.'

Shrugging off his lute, he set it carefully on a bale of hay. The hayloft was built on a platform to one side of the stables and the ceiling was so low that he had to duck his head to avoid hitting it on a beam.

Alis opened wide blue eyes at him. 'Sir Edouarz, reject me? I think not, Benedict. When I am done here, my dowry will be large enough to overcome any such scruples. The Duke said—'

'The Duke had no business asking a woman to undertake such a commission.'

Alis tossed her head and her veil quivered, giving Ben a glimpse of a honey-blonde braid. 'You think a woman incapable—'

He shook his head. 'Lord, no, it's not that, but I wonder if you fully understand the dangers.'

'I know the risks, Benedict.' Her voice grew hard. 'Better than you, I think. My father—'

'Your father is a fool, but he is blessed to have such a daughter. Jesu, I tell you this, if I were in your father's position—'

'Languishing in the Duke's dungeon…'

'Aye, if I were he, I would not permit my daughter to take such risks. Look what happened to my own father. Albin had years of experience in the field and three times your strength.'

Alis tipped her head to one side, and a spear of sun turned a strand of hair to gold. 'How noble, you think women are to be cherished,' she said, looking at him as though she were seeing him for the first time.

'Yes, yes, I do,' Ben said. Rozenn's features flashed into his mind. There was a woman he had once thought to cherish, but that was years ago. In any case, Rozenn had never shown the slightest desire to be cherished, at least not by him. Rozenn had chosen Per. Keeping a firm rein on his expression, Ben evicted Rose from his mind. As the Duke's special envoy, a secret and dangerous commission that was known only to a handful of people, he was never likely to be in a position to cherish anyone, let alone encumber himself with a wife. Not that he wanted to; such longings, thankfully, had faded.

Alis was watching him, a tiny smile playing about her lips. 'Your reputation belies you, Benedict Silvester—you are too much the flirt to cherish anyone.'

Ben shrugged, and forced his mind to the task in hand. He had lain awake half the night, startled by passionate thoughts that centred on Rose, but he would not let thinking about her interfere with his work for Duke Hoël. There would be no such foolishness where Rose was concerned. 'So, to sum up, you have learned nothing in the months that you have been here?'

'It takes time, Benedict, to build trust, as I am sure you are aware, but I believe I now have it. Last week the Countess asked me to walk with her when she attended Mass at the Abbey, and again this morning.'

Ben frowned. 'Surely *all* the ladies go with her to Mass?'

'Aye…' Alis's voice rose in excitement and Ben put his finger to his lips. She moderated her tone. 'You miss the point. We all go as her escort, but only one of us goes with her to the confessional. Usually, it's Ivona Wymark, the chatelaine. Ivona has been with Countess Muriel for years.'

Ben nodded. He knew Ivona. Thoughtfully, he

watched the dust motes drifting through a beam of light. 'Yes, that is well. The next stage—'

'I know the next stage, Benedict. I will watch, and I will listen. You may tell the Duke that as soon as I hear the slightest whisper about Count Remond initiating a Norman alliance, I will send word. They trust me now. This last week, a couple of strange knights rode in, claiming to have been waylaid by a gang of thieves on the highway.'

Ben stiffened. 'You think they are *Norman* envoys?'

Alis raised an eyebrow. 'I believe so.'

Ben had heard rumours that Anglo-Saxon refugees from England had been seen in this part of the Duchy. He wondered which was worse from the Duke's point of view: a pact between Count Remond and some of the Saxons dispossessed by William of Normandy, or an alliance with one of the great Norman barons. He ran his hand round his neck. It was not his place to reach any conclusions—the Duke had charged him with bringing information, not with planning his strategy. In any case, Duke Hoël was too clever to prevent agreements being made—particularly when most of them would amount to nothing. No, Duke Hoël employed Ben to inform him of any alliances, and to say how likely it was that one of the barons might actually mount a campaign against him.

With the peace and stability of the whole duchy at stake, it was important work.

'Which baron sent them, I wonder? Argentan? Lessay? Mortain?'

She sighed. 'Lord knows. But if some sort of a treaty is being made, it is only a matter of time before someone lets something slip.'

'Good. When I am in England, the Duke will be relying on you here in Quimperlé.'

'I won't let him down. The Duke holds my father, remember.'

Alis's laugh had a bitter edge to it and Ben frowned. Her father, Hubert, was a good man, and while Ben knew that the Duke must have his reasons for imprisoning him, it stuck in his craw that Hubert was kept under lock and key and that his daughter was being drawn into the shadowy world that he had been born to.

'Alis, before I go, I would ask if there had been any gossip lately among the ladies concerning Rozenn Kerber?'

'Rozenn Kerber? The seamstress?' Alis shook her head. 'What sort of gossip?'

'Has there been any mention of her making a journey?'

Again, Alis shook her head. 'Not that I have heard. I did hear she received word from Sir Adam, but no more than that.' She shrugged. 'I am sorry, Ben, I have heard nothing. Is she involved with your commission?'

'You might say that, though she, of course, knows nothing of my work for the Duke.'

The blue eyes opened wide. 'But Rozenn is one of your oldest friends—she must have her suspicions?'

Firmly, Ben shook his head. 'I have been more than careful. It is safer for her to believe I am simply a lute-player.'

'I understand.'

'And now the Duke has charged me with establishing links with his supporters in England. Since I have never been there, it struck him that suspicions might be raised at my sudden interest in William of Normandy's new kingdom. Escorting Rose would be the ideal cover.' Ben grimaced. 'Lures have been laid, but so far I am not convinced she is tempted.'

'There has not been so much as a whisper about her leaving in the ladies' bower. You might try the guardhouse.' Alis grinned. 'Don't look at me like that. Men are just as capable of gossiping as women. Rozenn Kerber has friends in the White Bird, and that is the tavern that Denez, the captain of the guard, favours. Denez and his men might know if Rozenn is planning on leaving.'

'My thanks.'

In the bailey, a young woman's voice rose above the tramping of the men-at-arms as she addressed one of the stable lads. 'In the *stable?*' the voice asked.

The stable boy laughed. 'In the loft, mistress. I saw him go up there.'

Quick footsteps approached.

'Hell!' Ben said. 'This is exactly what I was afraid of.' Taking Alis by the arms, he dragged her down with him into the hay.

'Benedict!'

Sweeping her veil from her hair, heedless of silver pins and satin ties, he covered her mouth with his hand. 'Shut up, Alis, for pity's sake.' Then, rolling her firmly under him, he buried his face in her neck.

'You saw him climb into the hayloft?' Rozenn repeated, standing in puzzlement at the foot of the ladder. She tipped her head back and looked up, but could see nothing save the edge of the wooden platform and a couple of greying bales of fodder, left over from the past winter. 'Are you sure it was he?'

The stable boy shifted the straw he was sucking from one side of his mouth to the other. 'I can't say I know Ben Silvester by sight exactly, but whoever followed her up there had a lute strapped to his back, so it must be him.'

Rozenn felt the unwonted happiness that had been with her since dawn drain away like so much water through a sieve. 'Ben f-followed *her* up there?'

'Yes, mistress.'

There was a lump in her throat the size of a hen's egg. 'Who—who did he follow?'

'That Norman lady, the one with the yellow hair.'

'Lady Alis,' Rozenn murmured, heart sinking to the floor. 'The pretty one.'

The stable boy's grin was knowing. He spoke through the straw in his mouth. 'Aye, that's the one.'

The muscles in Rozenn's face seemed to have gone stiff, and for the life of her she was unable to smile back. Since she had decided to marry Sir Richard of Asculf, she should not care—it was no business of hers who Ben Silvester tumbled in the hay. And since she already knew what Ben was like, this was scarcely a surprise. But unfortunately, this was one time she could not walk away and pretend to be unaware. This time the Countess had commanded her to fetch him.

How embarrassing.

Tucking the hem of her skirt into her girdle so she would not trip, Rozenn gripped the ladder and started to climb. Halfway up she paused, glanced down at the grinning stable boy and said, 'Thank you, Ivar, you may go.' No sense the whole world knowing….

Ivar picked up a nearby shovel and ambled out into the sunlit bailey. '*Holà,* Denez!' Ivar called a greeting, his voice fading as he engaged in conversation with Count Remond's captain and walked with him towards the barns.

As Rozenn neared the top of the ladder, hay rustled. Clenching her jaw, she forced herself up another rung. A low murmur reached her.

'Don't say I didn't warn you.'

Yes, that was Ben's voice. Rose felt sick, she actually felt sick. Then came a feminine giggle that tied knots in her belly.

'Let him think what he likes,' the woman hissed back. 'He will learn the truth when he marries me.'

Another rung. Another. Rozenn's feet were lumps of lead and her heart was thumping so loudly she could no longer hear the guards drilling in the bailey nor the horses stamping in the stalls below. Another rung and she was at the top.

And there he was, Benedict Silvester—that coal-dark hair was unmistakable, though his face was hidden since he was wrapped round Lady Alis FitzHubert, pinning her to the straw-strewn boards with his body. One of his long legs…

Jaw clenched, she stumbled on to the platform.

Ben lifted his head, and blanched. 'Rose!'

He was surprised to see her, that much was

plain. Pushing away from Lady Alis, he shoved his hair out of his face with that characteristic gesture that betrayed his unease more than words ever could. So he used to look when, as a young boy, he first fought his natural shyness to entertain the old Count and his household.

'*Holà,* Ben,' Rose said. The careless words she had prepared stuck in her throat; the loft blurred and wavered in a pointless rush of tears. Turning away, she blinked like a mad thing and fought for control. When she had composed herself, Ben and Lady Alis were both sitting up and he was picking straw from her back while she was placidly re-plaiting her fine blonde hair.

Rozenn tried to ignore the straw stuck in Ben's hair. 'Up to your old tricks, I see,' she managed. 'It didn't take you long.'

Ben's eyes met hers, and for a moment he looked as uncomfortable as she could wish. *Good.* She was glad she had interrupted them.

Suddenly, his eyes lit up and he grinned. 'You wanted me, Rozenn?' His voice was low, deliberately suggestive.

Damn the man! How was it that his responses were invariably laced with *double entendres?* Not that it would ever matter to her, she was far too sensible to be interested in a wastrel like Benedict Silvester, not in that way at any rate.

He pressed a swift kiss to Alis's cheek and, shifting away from her, patted the straw invitingly. 'Come on, Rozenn, you know you want to…'

Grinding her teeth at his effrontery, Rozenn stepped blindly towards him. In that moment, she wanted to clout him into next week.

Ben rose to his feet in one lithe movement and, reaching for her hand, drew her away from the edge of the platform. 'Careful, little flower, we don't want you tripping over that pretty gown, do we?' Gallant as any knight, may the devil blast him, while he gripped her hand so hard she could not free herself without making a scene.

Alis sat where Ben had left her, unconcernedly tidying herself. Taking her time about it. She had a contented smile on her lips, and a satisfied glow to her cheeks. She looked well and truly… Rozenn sought for a word… Loved sprang to mind, but it was easy to dismiss. Loved…by Benedict Silvester? A wandering minstrel who had more than his share of women in every town and castle in the Duchy?

The object of her anger nudged Alis gently with his boot. 'I'll see you later, *chérie.*' He swung Rozenn's hand to and fro and would not release her.

'Hmm?' Alis looked up, her blue eyes shifting from Ben to Rozenn and back again. 'Oh. You want to talk to Madame Kerber?' The girl had the gall to sound surprised, but she stood up, made a play of smoothing down her gown and reached for the ladder.

Rozenn tapped her foot until Alis had made it to ground level and the door of the stables had clanged shut behind her. The shadows deepened.

Ben eased his grip on her hand and raised it to his lips. 'I missed you this morning, *ma belle.*'

Rozenn snatched back her hand.

He recaptured it with a grin. 'You wanted me?'

'Yes! I…I mean, no, I wanted to *speak* to you,' Rozenn said, tripping over herself before she saw the laughter spring into his eyes. 'Oh, you wretch, Ben, you are incorrigible.'

He gave her one of his disarming smiles, but his eyes were serious. 'You are all right? Is something amiss?'

Rozenn shook her head. 'Countess Muriel sent me to fetch you, she'd like you to play for us in the solar. *Immediately.* Your usual fee, she said.'

In the solar, Rozenn stood with her back to the south-facing window seat. Here, where the light was strongest, Countess Muriel and the rest of the ladies murmured softly one to another as they sat round the table, working on the vast wall-hanging for the Hall. Some of the figures Rose had sketched on to the canvas had been smudged the previous evening when careless hands had rolled it away for the night. Rose had been re-drawing them, and her fingers were black with charcoal. Absently, she wiped them on her skirts.

She did not look at Lady Alis, but out of the corner of her eye she noticed Ben dragging a stool to one side of the great fireplace. He set about tuning his lute. The lute had once belonged to Ben's father, and it had been made to a Moorish pattern. It had a round body like the shell of a turtle, and the wood gleamed with a rich patina that owed much to years of loving use. The pegbox curved back on itself to resemble a leopard's head. She watched Ben's long fingers caress the leopard's head as he plucked each string and adjusted the pegs.

The fire crackled. It was warm outside the castle, but the fire that burned in the wide fireplace was a necessity. It would take more than a few days' sun to heat the keep's thick granite walls.

Catching Rozenn's glance, Ben threw her a grin, but Rozenn was nursing her anger with him and she hunched her shoulder and looked out of the window.

The Isle du Château sat at the junction of the Isole and the Ellé, like a boat anchored midstream. It was at this point that the two rivers became the Laïta before rolling on to the sea. Rozenn screwed her eyes up against a dazzle of sun, but she could still make out the marshes on the left bank. And on the right bank, just behind the port, the steep escarpment rose dramatically. She ran her eyes over the familiar jumble of houses running up from the port to Hauteville, the quarter where she had lived since her marriage to Per. Quimperlé. It was all the world she had ever known.

Was she wise to consider leaving? With Per dead and Adam gone and Ben hardly ever about, there was little reason to stay. Also, whenever the Countess tried to persuade her to move back into the Château where she had been brought up, she felt hemmed in and restless. In short, she didn't feel like herself. Quimperlé, much as she loved it, no longer felt like home.

As far as Rose was concerned, Sir Richard's proposal could not have come at a better moment. She thought about her adopted mother, Ivona, and chewed her bottom lip. Soon she must tell Ivona about Adam's wish that they should travel to England. Ivona would hate the idea and Rozenn was dreading discussing it, dreading the inevitable questions that would follow. *But* why *do you want to leave, Rozenn? Why not wait for Sir Richard to join you here?* She was also dreading the moment when she informed Countess Muriel of her departure. She frowned. The thought of neither interview filled her with joy, but she could not put them off for ever.

Behind her Ben began to play. A love song, naturally. The ladies cooed and sighed. Rozenn rolled her eyes.

Her cheeks burned as she recognised the song. Fighting the impulse to cool them with the back of her hands, she turned and glared at him. Before Ben had left Quimperlé, after his last, fleeting visit—the visit when he had quarrelled with Adam—he had sung this particular song one suppertime in the Great Hall. Those soulful brown eyes had focused entirely on her and she had not been able to think her own thoughts. He was such a flirt.

Why, the rogue still has a piece of straw stuck in his hair, she noticed, biting hard on the inside of her cheeks to stifle a smile. Dear Lord, why could she never remain angry with him for more than one minute at a time?

'Rozenn, dear...' Countess Muriel was scowling at her section of wall-hanging '...which colour had you in mind for this lady's gown?'

'I thought the sky blue, *Comptesse,* since most of the background will be green, but wouldn't it be best to work the darker wools first, as we had agreed?'

'Oh, yes, I remember.' Countess Muriel smiled and bent over the coloured hanks.

'Since Emma is working on the grass, you might like to work with that deep red. It would be good for those flowers. Or you could take that chestnut brown and work one of the deer.'

The solar door slammed and the flames danced in the hearth, as Rozenn's mother by adoption glided into the room.

'Ivona, welcome,' Countess Muriel said, looking up from the tapestry. 'Have you seen the children?'

Children. Rozenn's stomach knotted as a wave of longing swept over her. Children. Her marriage with Per had been childless and she worried that the cause might lie at her door. Would Sir Richard think it her fault? Two years married and no children? Would Sir Richard reject her lest she be barren as some in this town had been whispering before Per's death? A knight must have heirs…

In that unguarded moment she met Ben's eyes, and it seemed the link between them was as strong as ever. She read sympathy and understanding in his dark gaze—it was as though Ben understood what she felt, that he could read her mind. Which was nonsense. As children they had been close, but these days Ben was…just Ben…a footloose minstrel…a flirt…a devil who made his way by appearing to sympathise with everyone.

'The children are playing in the bailey,

Comptesse,' her mother said, 'now that the guards have finished their drill.'

'Good. Here, Rozenn…' the Countess patted the stool next to hers '…come and sit by me. You can help me do the background.'

Moving round the trestle, careful to avoid Lady Alis, Rozenn squeezed past Ben as he sat by the fire. He made no attempt to move his legs and as her skirt brushed his knees, her stomach fluttered. Brow creasing, she took her place by the Countess, conscious of Ben Silvester at her back, as his voice, his beautiful voice, floated over their heads, singing of true love, of faithfulness, of heroes winning their heroines though all the dice in the world were loaded against them.

Her heart twisted. She wished he had chosen another song, any other song, and must have muttered something under her breath as Ivona joined her at the trestle. Her adopted mother's eyes were too weak for close work these days, but she usually came to sit with the other women when her duties as chatelaine allowed.

'What was that, dear?' Ivona asked.

Rozenn jerked her head in Ben's direction. 'Ben's song, Mama—don't you think he's in good voice?'

Ivona pursed her lips. '"The Faithful Lover",' she murmured, repeating the song's title. 'Aye, he is—which is a wonder given the subject matter.'

'Mama?'

Ivona lifted her shoulders. 'Everyone knows that boy doesn't have a faithful bone in his body. But then…' Ivona shot Ben a meaningful glance '…he's paid to sing well, perhaps that helps him infuse the song with meaning.'

Rozenn found herself shifting away from Ivona, towards the Countess. 'Don't, Mama,' she muttered, at a loss to know why she felt compelled to rush to Ben's defence. She had never been able to fathom it, but in recent years Ivona seemed to hold Ben in dislike. 'It's not his fault everyone adores him.'

Her stepmother sniffed and picking up a hank of primrose-coloured wool, began winding it into a ball. 'It's his fault he acts on their adulation, though,' Ivona went on in an undertone. 'Particularly with the young women. Benedict Silvester has had more lovers than the whole of the garrison put together.'

Not trusting herself to comment, especially after what she had witnessed in the stables only that morning, Rozenn turned to the Countess to help her pick out some more thread.

The love song was finishing, which was a blessing because, oddly, it felt as though Ben had been directing it at her.

'Rozenn, dear?' Countess Muriel gave her a

strange look, a look that said she'd already addressed her and Rozenn had missed what had been said.

'Comptesse?'

'You really ought to move back into the keep. I hear there were disturbances last night. It's not safe for a young woman to live alone in the town.'

Rozenn stiffened. Not this again. Ever since Per's death, both the Countess and Ivona had been asking for her return. But, like Ben, Rozenn had no particular liking for sleeping in common. She had enjoyed the privacy her marriage with Per had given her; it was rare and precious and she was *not* about to give it up. And, in any case, it would not be for much longer.

'With respect, *Comptesse,* Hauteville is perfectly safe.'

Countess Muriel looked down her nose at her in the way she always did when she was displeased. 'Why is it, Rozenn, that when you answer me with one of your "with respects" I have the suspicion that you do not respect my views in the least?'

A choke, swiftly smothered, came from the fireplace and, a heartbeat later, Ben struck up another tune.

Ivona leaned forwards, surreptitiously digging Rozenn in the ribs. *'Comptesse* Muriel, Rozenn has ever been independent, she did not mean any disrespect.'

'No, indeed,' Rozenn murmured agreement. 'But I must say that Ivona is correct. I do enjoy living in the town. I have friends there, *Comptesse,* and I would miss them if I moved back to the keep.'

'You have friends here,' Countess Muriel said softly.

Rozenn caught her breath. 'I know, but—'

'Friends who are, I think, your best patrons…'

The Countess's insistence was unnerving. Thoughts racing, Rozenn concealed a sigh. She had hoped a simple refusal would suffice, forgetting how Countess Muriel liked to get her way. But if the Countess knew that she intended leaving, perhaps even she would not be so insistent. Rozenn glanced at the ladies clustered round the great canvas. This was not the time to break the news, either to her mother or to the Countess, not when they were surrounded by a roomful of women.

'Yes, *Comptesse,*' Rozenn said. 'I am grateful for that, but—'

'Friends whom you may be loathe to lose, Rozenn.'

Rozenn swallowed. The warning was clear. This might not be the moment to discuss her proposal and Adam's summons, but she was not about to be bullied. 'Indeed, *Comptesse,* but—'

'Your husband left debts, I understand. Have you cleared them?'

Rozenn relaxed; here she was on firmer ground. 'Almost. One more day at market should see the tallies set straight.'

'Good.' Countess Muriel smiled. 'Then you can concentrate on your sewing—a much better occupation for a young woman than hustling at a market stall. Besides...' another smile, this one directed at Ivona '...I should not like to see Quimperlé's best seamstress arraigned at my husband's court for debt.'

Wishing the Countess would focus on someone else, Rozenn squirmed on her stool. A ripple of notes drew all eyes as Ben finished the song with a flourish. Rozenn blinked. Surely he'd missed a couple of verses?

'Excuse me, *Comptesse,*' he said. 'What would you like me to play next?'

Bless you, Ben. Glancing over her shoulder, Rozenn flashed him a smile.

'I should like a story this time, Benedict,' the Countess replied. 'Tell us the one about Tristan and Isolde.'

'Oh, yes,' Lady Alis breathed, blue eyes wide. 'Tristan and Isolde, I *adore* that one.'

Rozenn gritted her teeth and stared blindly at a knight on the wall-hanging, so she would not have to see Ben exchange smiles with the girl he had met in the hayloft. Then, unable to bear it any more, she turned her head and shot him a brief glance.

He had laid his lute across his knees. Opening his eyes wide—he was *not* looking at Lady Alis—he began to recite. 'Once upon a time, King Mark…'

As Ben's seductive voice filled the solar, conversations drew to a halt. Needles froze over the canvas. Heads turned in the direction of the fireplace, old heads as well as young. Rozenn pursed her lips. Was *no one* proof to his charms?

Ben's voice, she had to admit, was his chief asset—it had a way of reaching deep into your heart. At least, that was how it was for her, and, given Ben's success and popularity, she assumed others felt the same. Reaching for a length of sage-green wool, Rozenn threaded a needle and shuffled closer to the table. Her stool leg squeaked.

Countess Muriel tutted.

'My apologies,' Rozenn mouthed, and bent over the canvas.

Yes, his voice was perfect. It was clear, it was carrying and it was somehow caressing. Like his fingers. A memory of the previous night flashed in on her, when she and Ben had been talking to each other with only her table between them. He had held her hand and his fingers had moved gently over hers. So gently. She could almost feel the warmth of his fingertips as she would feel them if he were to lift her hand to his lips. Later, he might lean forwards across the table and reach for her…he might slide his other hand round her neck, he might bring his lips to hers, he might…

Her needle ran into her finger and she gasped.

'Rozenn, do be still.' The Countess frowned. 'And mind you don't bleed on the canvas.'

Nodding an apology, Rozenn blinked at the welling blood and lifted her finger to her mouth. What *was* she about? Just because Ben's voice had the power to seduce half of Brittany did *not* mean it had the power to seduce her.

He had reached the point in the story when the lovers were sleeping in each others' arms, deep in the forest.

With rather more of an effort of will than she would have liked—the picture of Ben's arms around her was worryingly compelling—Rozenn made herself think of another pair of arms.

Richard of Asculf's. It is Sir Richard I yearn for in that way. And then, for one heart-sinking moment, she was utterly unable to recall the colour of Sir Richard's eyes. Brown? Blue? No, brown. Or was it grey? Lord. A knight, he's a knight, she muttered to herself, trying to close out the distracting sound of Benedict Silvester's voice.

Lady Josefa—Rozenn's jaw clenched—had abandoned all pretence of embroidering, and was sitting with her hands resting idle on the wall-hanging, gazing at Ben as though he were her only hope of salvation.

Hunching her shoulder—really, Josefa was embarrassing—Rozenn sneaked a look in Ben's direction. It was just her luck that his eyes were open and he happened to be facing her way. He didn't falter in his telling of the story, but his voice did soften as their eyes met. A curl of awareness unfurled in her belly. Damn him. Huffing out a breath, she turned back to her work.

As the story unfolded Rozenn held the image of Sir Richard in the forefront of her mind. The last time she had seen Sir Richard he had been riding out of Quimperlé at her brother's side. Two knights, one Norman and born to his station, with lands and a proud ancestry, and the other but newly knighted and with not one acre to his name. How kind Sir Richard was to have given me a gold cross. How kind he was, Rozenn thought, deliberately blocking out the beguiling sound of Ben's voice, to befriend Adam when he had been but an eager squire. Not many knights would bother with the son of a lowly horse-master. Firmly, she squashed the urge to turn to see if Ben was returning that idiotic smile Lady Josefa was sending his way.

Where was she? Ah, yes, how *kind* of Sir Richard to have sponsored Adam, to have seen him knighted. Yes, she had chosen a kind man, an *honourable* man. When Sir Richard and Adam had ridden out in response to William of Normandy's call to arms, they had looked so fine. She had been proud of her brother. And of Sir Richard, naturally. Rozenn frowned. But the colour of his eyes? Brown, surely, like Ben's?

She wriggled on her stool and again the legs screeched on the floorboards. Countess Muriel glared.

Sir Richard was taller than Ben, much broader, larger all over. Big hands. She had noticed that particularly, on the day he had challenged Ben to a lute-playing contest. The size of his large, battle-scarred fingers—her lips curved in a smile—Sir Richard could never hope to match Ben on a lute. But he had done astonishingly well, considering.

She sighed. Ben was... No—*Sir Richard*. It was *Sir Richard* she was thinking about, not Ben. Sir Richard was taller, very handsome with his brown hair and his broad shoulders. A man indeed.

Sneaking a sidelong glance under her lashes at Ben, Rozenn felt again that unsettling tremble in her belly. Ben was not as tall as Sir Richard, but he was, she had to confess, perfectly proportioned—strong shoulders, narrow waist, as ever accentuated by a wide leather belt. Ben knew how to make the best of himself, that green tunic matched those tiny flecks in his eyes *exactly*.

Needle suspended over her work, Rozenn did not notice that it had been some moments since she had set a stitch.

But Ben did. He intercepted her gaze and a dark eyebrow quirked upwards.

Hastily, Rozenn focused on the canvas, damping down that irritating flutter of awareness that only he could elicit. Even her idol, even Sir Richard never had that effect on her. Thank goodness. It was far too discomfiting.

She, Rozenn Kerber, would marry Sir Richard, on that she was determined. She was going to be a *lady*. One day she would have a solar of her own, and other women would join her there to work on the tapestries and wall-hangings that would decorate *her* hall. Perhaps, like Countess Muriel, she would hire a lute-player, maybe even Benedict Silvester himself if he was lucky, to entertain them while they sewed.

Chapter Four

That afternoon, Mikaela came to the Isle du Château to ask for Rozenn's company. As was her custom when entering the castle precincts, she was wearing her veil. She came directly to the solar, where the Countess, having tired of sewing, was happy to wave Rozenn away.

It was a Friday, a fish day, and every Friday since Per's death, Rozenn had got into the habit of accompanying Mikaela to the fish market, which was held in Basseville on the quayside. There she would help her friend choose fish for the tavern and load them on Anton's cart. In return for her assistance, Mikaela usually sent Rozenn a portion of whatever dish resulted such as baked cod, or mussels in wine.

Leaving the keep, the girls walked through sunlit streets towards the Pont du Port. Count Remond's guards stood sentry at the gateway that led from the castle to the quays. Ben was with them, hip propped against the wooden rail of the bridge, dark hair ruffled by the breeze. He was apparently deep in conversation with Denez, the guards' captain. Rozenn thought she heard her name mentioned, but at that moment Ben noticed her and turned her name into a greeting so smoothly, she wondered if she had imagined it.

'Mistress Kerber!' Ben's brown eyes were laughing as he straightened and swept her a bow worthy of a duchess. 'Good afternoon to you. And Mademoiselle Bréhat.'

'*Holà,* Ben.' Mikaela smiled. 'Distracting the sentries from their duties?'

'Naturally.' Ben resumed his position propped against the handrail. His lips drew Rozenn's gaze, and, as she looked, they twitched upwards. Colouring, she met his glance, gave her head a slight shake, and made to step past him. Had he been talking about her? She must be mistaken— why would Ben have been talking to Denez about her?

Ben put out a hand. 'Want to earn a couple of deniers, Rozenn? Mikaela?'

'How so?'

'I propose a race—swimming versus running.'

Rozenn gave Ben a level look. She couldn't swim—all her life she had been terrified of water—but Ben swam like a fish. He was pointing to where the jetty in the marshes was sited, lost in the tall reeds on the east bank.

'I reckon I can swim to the jetty and back in the time it takes Jerome here to run to and from St Michael's in Hauteville.'

Captain Denez snorted. 'You take us for fools, Silvester, but we know you of old. You'd cheat, and since we can't exactly see the jetty from here, what's to say you never actually reach it?'

'Me? Cheat?' Ben puffed out his chest and affected to look affronted, but Rozenn knew he was no such thing. He was teasing Count Remond's troopers, enjoying it almost as much as they were. 'As if I would…' He winked at Mikaela, who flushed prettily and gave a little trill of a laugh. 'But in case you are worried, I have an idea. One of your men can run round to the marshes and wait for me on the jetty. Jafrez, be my witness?'

Denez rubbed his chin. 'You have to actually touch the jetty, mind.'

Mikaela stirred. 'I set some eel traps by the jetty,' she said thoughtfully.

Ben gave Mikaela a soft smile. 'You wouldn't want to check them, would you, *chérie?* Then you could be my witness since these disbelieving oafs won't accept my word. They will accept yours, won't you, Denez?'

'Aye.'

'I thought we were going to the fish market,' Rozenn put in, her voice sounding more disgruntled than she had intended.

Mikaela shrugged. 'Eel counts as fish, you know that. If we've caught some, I could smoke them or make a pie.' To Rozenn's dismay, Mikaela slanted Ben just the sort of look that Rozenn would have expected Lady Alis FitzHubert to give him. It startled her coming from her friend.

She tamped down a flare of anger. It was one thing for Ben to flirt with Lady Alis who ought to know better, but quite another to flirt with Mikaela. He should not encourage her in this way. Mikaela was very young and she might not realise that Ben's smiles were just another of the tools of his trade, they did not necessarily mean anything. She hoped Mikaela was not taken in.

Mikaela was smiling happily up at him. 'We'll go—we'll witness you reach the jetty, won't we, Rozenn?'

Brown, thick-lashed eyes looked her way. He cocked a brow at her. 'Rozenn?'

'Oh, yes. I suppose so.'

Ben laid his hand on his heart. 'My thanks, *mesdames*. And if you'd care to lay a wager of your own…'

'Certainly not!' Rozenn said tartly. 'We can't afford to be throwing hard-earned money around.'

'Your money's not at any risk.' Ben's smile was confident. 'I'll reach the jetty and be back before Jerome even makes it to St Michael's, never mind returns. And, I must say, talking of witnesses, how do I know I can trust Jerome to run all that way without cheating? He might turn back early and who would know? Fair's fair, I demand a witness too. Any volunteers?'

One of the guards stepped forwards. 'I'll go.'

'Good man.'

Mikaela walked boldly up to Ben and put her hand on his. 'I'll be wanting a kiss for my pains,' she said.

Denez whooped, Rozenn looked heavenwards.

Ben sent Mikaela a slow grin. 'It will be my pleasure, *chérie,* my pleasure.'

'When's the wager taking place?'

'As soon as you and Rozenn reach that jetty?'

Eyes alight with laughter, Mikaela grabbed Rozenn's arm. 'We're on our way.'

'My thanks. We should be able to see you standing on the jetty, but just in case we cannot, wave your veils when you get there. That can be our starting signal—agreed, Jerome?'

'Agreed.'

Mikaela turned Rozenn back to face the bailey, for the way to the footpath into the marshes lay back past Ste Croix and off the island via the East Bridge rather than the Pont du Port. As they stepped off the Pont du Port and back into the bailey, Mikaela grinned over her shoulder at Ben. 'A kiss, remember?'

Ben's smile was warm. '*Chérie,* how could I forget?'

Rozenn said nothing, nothing at all, but she couldn't help wondering if Ben was *ever* serious. A thought which saddened her for no reason that she could point to.

A few minutes later, with the sun on their backs, the girls stepped onto the jetty and looked back towards the Isle du Château. They had hurried all the way, picking up their skirts when they reached the wooden walkway through the marshes. Some of the planks were rotting and the walkway was springy underfoot, but they arrived without mishap, though the hems of their skirts were dark with damp. There was more breeze here in the marshes; it rattled the reeds and tugged at their veils.

'Look!' Mikaela pointed, screwing up her eyes.

Some years ago, Rozenn had discovered her friend's eyes were slightly weak. They were not weak in the same way that Ivona's eyes were weak, for seeing close to—no, it was distances Mikaela had difficulty with.

'There they are, on the bridge,' Mikaela went

on, still squinting. 'Ben's green tunic shows up really well.'

'Yes, that's Ben.'

The guards were clustered around him and his challenger, Jerome.

Mikaela stared towards the castle. 'What's happening, Rose?'

'Ben and Jerome are being spun round—Jerome is being pointed towards the town and Ben—Ben's... Oh! He's climbing on to the guardrail, oh, no...' Rozenn's voice trailed off as, with a dramatic flourish, Ben gave one of his dramatic bows.

'What, Rozenn, what?'

Rozenn sighed. 'He's playing to the gallery, as usual.'

Mikaela looked a question at her. 'You sound upset.'

'Upset? No. I just wish that, for once, Ben didn't have to be so...so...'

'Entertaining?' Mikaela grinned. 'But that's what he does, Ben's an entertainer.'

About to object, Rozenn snapped her mouth shut. Mikaela was absolutely right, Ben *was* an entertainer, which was why people loved him so. And it wasn't just women who loved him, she thought, as she recalled the expectant look in the guards' eyes and the grins that lit faces that, for the most part, had little to grin about.

The life expectancy of one of Count Remond's troopers was not good. Captain Denez, one of the oldest and longest serving, was only thirty, but he looked at least forty. At best life was harsh for these men, at worst, brutal. If Ben could bring a little light and laughter into their lives, then well and good.

Across the water, Ben was tripping light as a tumbler along the guardrail, using it as a tightrope, surrounded by smiling faces. A gust of laughter floated downriver towards them. Rose's sense of misgiving eased. She must not turn into a killjoy. This was what Ben did, it was his *raison d'être,* and what kind of a friend would she be if she could not accept him for what he was? And since Ben did not have her fear of water, there was no way he would drown.

It is just that, sometimes, it is hard to see him continually playing the fool; and sometimes it is hard to share him with so many others.

Aghast at the possessive nature of that last thought, she snapped her brows together. Where on earth had that come from?

'Oh, no,' Rozenn muttered, as Ben unbuckled his belt and lobbed it to one of the guards, its silver buckle flashing in the sun.

'What?'

Rozenn swallowed. 'He…he's taking his tunic off.'

'I should think so, such a fine tunic, it would be a shame to spoil it. Did you make it?'

'No.'

Mikaela kept her attention on the group on the Pont du Port. 'I wish I could see properly.'

Rozenn murmured something noncommittal, her own eyes fixed on the lithe figure balanced on the bridge guardrail. The green tunic was tossed carelessly aside and was immediately followed by a cream linen *chainse*. That she *had* made, some years before. She was touched he still wore it.

The guards let out a cheer.

Rozenn cleared her throat. It was at least a hundred yards to the bridge, but even at this distance the sight of Ben's naked back set curls of tension winding in her belly. Why that should be, she could not imagine, especially since she had already seen his naked back several times before when they were children. And this morning, she reminded herself, heat flooding her cheeks, she had last seen his naked back this morning. She could not seem to tear her gaze from those athletic shoulders, the curve of his buttocks…

Thank God he was keeping on his hose. Wasn't he?

Hopping on one foot—how on earth did he keep his balance on the rail?—Ben tore a boot off and tossed it at a guard. Its fellow followed. To her relief he made no move to remove his hose.

From the throats of half-a-dozen men at arms, a slow countdown began.

'Ready!' Mikaela cried. She snatched her veil from her head and waved like a mad thing. 'Steady!' She jumped up and down, her enthusiasm shaking the entire jetty. *'Go!'*

Ben turned to face them, grinned across the water and dived into the river with barely a ripple.

At the same moment, Jerome hared off across the Pont du Port and up the hill towards Hauteville. In a moment, he had run out of sight behind the houses that clung to the escarpment on the other side of the river.

Ben's dark head remained visible as, sleek as an otter, he cut his way through the water with the swift, clean strokes that Rozenn remembered from their childhood.

'It's easier this way, he's swimming with the stream,' Mikaela said. 'He will find it harder on the way back.'

Absently, Rozenn nodded, holding her breath lest she lose sight of that dark head, of those strong, well-formed arms… If Ben drowned, if Ben drowned… Though she reminded herself that, unlike her, Ben swam well, the fear remained. Ridiculous. Ben would not drown.

Reeds rustled by the jetty, and she caught a flash of red as a water-rail squealed. A dragonfly darted.

The sun was hot, it was shining in the water droplets falling in silver arcs from Ben's arms.

Mikaela tucked her veil in her belt and approached the edge of the jetty.

'Take care, Mikaela, that plank doesn't look very secure,' Rozenn warned, even as Ben reached the jetty and proved her wrong by hauling himself out of the river in one swift movement.

Shaking water from his eyes, Ben put his hands on his hips and grinned. 'A kiss,' he said, looking at Mikaela. 'I claim my kiss.' He was barely out of breath.

As Mikaela stepped up and offered Ben her lips a distant shout from the bridge reminded those on the jetty that there were men who had wagered their pay on Benedict Silvester winning the race. He had to get back…

'Hey, Silvester!'

'Shift yourself!'

Playing to his audience, Ben swung Mikaela dramatically into his arms—his wet arms, Rozenn thought waspishly—and gave her a smacking kiss on the lips. A piece of weed clung to one well-muscled shoulder like a hank of wet wool.

A pain in her breast, Rozenn jerked her head away and glared into the dark water drifting past the jetty. A rousing cheer from the Pont du Port told her that Ben's audience approved of what he was doing. Which she, most certainly, did *not*. She huffed out a breath. As for Mikaela, she should know better…

Releasing Mikaela, Ben looked her way. Mikaela's dress was dark with damp from breast to knee, not that she was looking. 'Rose?' Ben murmured and held out his hand. 'Your turn.'

Rozenn stumbled back a pace, but then, and she was not quite sure how he managed it, Ben stepped forwards and in a trice she was standing hip to hip with him on the jetty, gazing into those long-lashed eyes, so close she could see the green and grey flecks. Her hands were resting on his naked shoulders, his were on her waist. How had *that* happened? Her mouth went dry.

'Oh, no.'

He tilted his head to one side, eyes on her lips. 'No?'

She shook her head. 'Y…you've already had your kiss. From Mikaela.'

The crowd on the bridge screamed encouragement.

The hands at her waist were cool from the water and were drawing her closer. His eyes were dark as night and—surely not? Was there just a hint of uncertainty in his smile, a hint of vulnerability? No. This was Benedict Silvester, the showman who had never known a day's uncertainty in his life.

'Why settle for one kiss, when I might have two?' His voice went low and intimate, for her ears alone. 'Rozenn, I would swim to England for *your* kiss.'

No… Her ears must be deceiving her. Ben could not have said that, and in so *serious* a tone—he had to be teasing her. And then thought fled as he whirled her around so she had her back to Castle Hellon and the audience on the bridge. He lowered his lips to hers. Rozenn did not struggle, though her heart was pounding as though it was she who had swum from castle to marshes, not he.

His kiss began light as thistledown, so light that she could barely feel it. Her body went quite still, as if it were curious, as if it wanted to know what kissing Benedict Silvester would be like.

We shouldn't be doing this, her mind protested, while her body hung limp as a rag doll in his arms and experienced what it was like to kiss him.

Achingly gentle. How surprising. Warm lips, despite the swim, lips that moved softly over hers and made her want to melt into him and… A lock of his hair flopped forwards and the chill drip of river water ran down her cheek and into the bosom of her gown. He tasted of heaven, he tasted of everything she had ever dreamed of, he tasted of…Ben.

Her legs had gone all trembly. Her breath was uneven. Pulling back with a shaky laugh, she smoothed his hair back from his face. Her hand, it was irritating to see, was unsteady. That piece of weed was still stuck to his shoulder. She brushed it away. Firmly gripping her waist, Ben smiled down at her, eyes warm.

I would swim to England for your *kiss.*

What a tease.

'You're all wet,' she said, clearing her throat. She gave him a little shove. 'Go, *go!* You have a wager to win.'

Nodding, he released her, and dived neatly into the river.

Mikaela at her side, Rozenn watched him every stroke of the way. Irrationally, she felt as though, by watching him, she was ensuring he reached the bridge safely. A nudge in her ribs had her looking across to see a knowing smile lifting the corners of Mikaela's mouth. 'Rozenn Kerber, you are such a liar.'

'I… I beg your pardon?'

'Sir Richard of Asculf indeed! I was right first time, you love Benedict Silvester…'

Fiercely, Rozenn shook her head. 'No, as I told you, Ben and I are good friends. He's my oldest friend, that I won't deny.'

'Liar,' Mikaela said comfortably, and turned to squint towards the Pont du Port. 'Is he there yet?'

'Just about. Someone's throwing down a rope, he's going to climb up it.'

'And Jerome?'

Rozenn turned her gaze in the direction of Hauteville, as Jerome hurtled into view. 'Jerome's at the port, but he won't make it, Ben will win easily. We should have bet on him. In so far as Benedict Silvester is reliable, he is reliable in unreliable matters, like the winning of wagers.'

Mikaela sent her a strange look. 'I knew he'd win all along.'

And before Rozenn had a chance to question her friend about that look and the peculiar tone of her voice, Mikaela had turned away.

'Now,' Mikaela said briskly, 'where on earth did I leave that eel trap?'

Ben could have kicked himself. What the hell had he been about, making Rose kiss him and in public too? He hauled himself up the rope and back on to the Pont du Port and submitted to a barrage of back-slapping and congratulations from those who had wagered on him winning the race. Moments later, when Jerome ran up, red-faced and sweating, he smiled and gave the man his commiserations, offering to buy him a consolatory jar at the Barge, but his mind was elsewhere—it was back on that jetty in the marshes, reliving that kiss.

Hell. Kissing Rose had never been part of his

plan. It was vital she agreed to journey to England with him, and to that end she must trust him, she must feel safe with him as she always had done. Not in a million years did he want her to feel threatened by him. That would not suit him in the least. Drying himself on his linen *chainse,* Ben dragged it over his head and relieved a guard of his tunic and belt.

'My thanks,' he said, and, though irritated with himself, managed a grin.

'Any time, Silvester, you've doubled my pay.' The fellow grinned back. 'I'll stand you a drink before supper.'

If Ben was honest, it was not just that he needed Rose to choose him as her escort. His relationship with her was important and he did not want to spoil it. She was his fixed point, his guiding star in a world where much was chaos. His work for the Duke was vital, and he loved it, just as he loved his music. But proud though Ben was of these two interlinked aspects of his life, they doomed him to a wanderer's life—to the kind of life that was an anathema to a homebody like Rose. As the Duke of Brittany's special emissary, Ben must be eternally on the move between the courts and power centres of France. And now, apparently, England too. He must for ever be tramping the highways.

The point was that wherever his work for the Duke had taken him—and at times he'd visited some dark places—Ben had always known that, back here in Quimperlé, there was Rose. Even when she had married Per, he had known that. It was something of a shock to discover that even after all this time, even while he was hoping to lure Rose to England on false pretences, he did not want to put his relationship with her at risk.

Cursing under his breath, Ben shot a glance downstream towards the jetty, but Rozenn and Mikaela were not in sight. He could see them in his mind's eye, though, clear as day: they would be kneeling on the jetty, reaching down to haul the eel traps out of the water. Yes, he could see them clearly. Just as clearly he could see Rose's face while he had been kissing Mikaela. Her dimples had vanished.

That was where he'd gone wrong. With Mikaela in his arms, he'd glanced across at Rose and for an instant he'd imagined a flash of yearning in her eyes. Wrong, Ben, wrong.

She *had* hesitated, that should have warned him. She had taken a firm backward step. She had even said, 'Oh, no.' He should have heeded that. He sighed and shook his head. He'd been so caught up in the moment that he'd ignored the warning signals.

So much for priding himself on his sensitivity

and responsiveness to others. He hoped he hadn't wrecked his chances of persuading her to let him act as her escort. If, that is, she really was going to answer Adam's summons. Denez had heard no mention of Rose's plans, any more than Alis had done.

'See you in the Barge then, Silvester?' Jerome asked.

'What? Oh, yes, yes, right away.' Jerome might have heard something. He would ask Jerome. Hastily, dragging on first one boot and then the other, Ben draped a friendly arm around Jerome's shoulder and turned in the direction of the tavern.

Ben could not get Rose out of his mind. He hoped she wouldn't use the kiss as an excuse to deny him houseroom. He had kissed her on impulse and, whatever he might want others to think, in reality Ben's strength of will and his habitual rapidity of thought meant that he almost never acted on a passing impulse.

Then why start with Rose? It was madness given what was at stake, and he prayed she still trusted him. Rose didn't put her faith in many men these days, it seemed. As Ben walked towards the tavern with Jerome at his side, lines formed on his brow. Rose hadn't always been mistrustful of men. Something must have happened during the time she had been married to Per, something that had changed her, and it was more than the matter of a few debts.

He had thought she might confide in him, but that involved closeness and trust. From this moment, he vowed, he must be circumspect. The kiss had been a lapse of judgement, but if he took care it did not happen again, she would regain her faith in him. A reminiscent smile chased his frown away.

Rose—who would have thought it? The feel of her…the taste of her… The way he and, he would swear, she too, went still the moment their lips touched…

He shook his head; such a lapse must not happen again. It was vital that Rose should put her confidence in him. Lord help him if she ever found out that he was behind her summons to England. He must take care. Not that it mattered on his own account, naturally, it mattered because of the Duke and his mission. Rose was out of bounds.

Tossing and turning on her mattress that night, Rozenn waited for Ben to come in. She had not laid eyes on him since he had kissed her on the jetty and dived back into the Laïta to win his wager. He was very late.

A discordant howl cut through the night air. By the sound of it, a battalion of drunks were toiling up the hill from one of the port taverns, yowling like tomcats. Tensing, Rozenn listened for the sound of a key turning in the lock, but it never came. Of course not. Even in Ben's worst moments, he would never howl so discordantly. Drunk as a lord, Ben could hold a tune.

Absently she touched her fingers to her lips. Why had he kissed her? Their friendship had never been on that sort of footing, and, as far as she was concerned, it never would be. So why the kiss?

The answer came in a flash. As show. Both she and Mikaela had been but part of the show he had laid on for the entertainment of the Count's men; to him the kisses had meant nothing.

To her, though… Gently rubbing her lips with her finger, Rozenn closed her eyes against the glow of the banked-down fire. Ben's kiss had melted her bones; she had wanted to press close and closer still. She had wanted more, and when he had lifted his lips from hers, it had taken every ounce of will-power not to reach up and draw his head back down again.

I had no idea, she thought. No idea a kiss could be so…so compelling. With Per… She repressed a shudder. She would not think about kissing Per, not now, and soon, when she left Quimperlé, she need never think of him again. Once away from this town, there would be no reminders, nothing to point out that marrying Per had been the biggest mistake of her life.

Kissing Ben, though… Kissing Ben on the jetty had been nothing short of a revelation. Kissing Ben had been disturbing, but not in the way that kissing Per had been disturbing. No wonder women fell over themselves to gain Ben's attention…

She bit hard on her finger. Was Ben regretting kissing her? Was that why he was so late coming back? Could he not face her?

Perhaps he had decided to sleep elsewhere. If he had, she would have liked to know. She would have double-bolted the front door. Worrying about that unbolted door was what was keeping her awake. But tonight, lest he return, that door must remain unbolted. If Ben wanted to sleep here, she would hate to lock him out.

Turning her head, Rozenn peered through the dark in the direction of the street. The drunks' caterwauling was fading as they progressed up the hill; heading, she expected, for one final drink at the White Bird.

A log shifted. Rolling on to her side, Rozenn tried to compose herself for sleep. No sense waiting up half the night. Ben was most likely celebrating his winnings by the broaching of a few barrels himself. Unbidden, the features of Alis FitzHubert swam into her mind, with her pretty blue eyes and her yellow hair. Rose grimaced—please God, let him not be celebrating with Lady Alis.

Rose would think about Sir Richard of Asculf as she usually did when falling asleep; she would recall his kindness; she would think about the gold cross that he have given her; she would remind herself how strong he was.

But despite her best intentions, Rozenn's last conscious thoughts were of a dark-haired lute-player singing love songs. His eyes were tender and, impossible though that might be, he was gazing at her, and *only* her.

I would swim to England for your *kiss.*

He was such a flirt.

Chapter Five

When Rozenn woke the next morning, the light slanting through the cracks in the shutters told her that the sun had risen. There was no sign of Ben and his pallet did not appear to have been slept on. But she had things to do. Firmly suppressing any suspicions as to where he might have passed the night and in whose arms, Rose dressed quickly. It was market day, and she was determined to sell as much of her husband's stock as possible—nothing was going to distract her.

By the time Anton had arrived at the front of the shop, handcart in tow, Rose had broken her fast and had the cloth piled up by the doorway.

'Morning, mistress.' Anton indicated the heavier of the bales of cloth. 'These first?'

'If you please.'

After helping Anton load the cart, Rozenn accompanied him down the hill towards the Pont du Port, one hand resting on her stock to steady it.

Captain Denez was again on guard by the drawbridge. '*Holà,* Mistress Rozenn,' he said, his usually dour expression lighting when he saw her. 'Not with Silvester this morning?'

Rozenn gave Denez a searching look, but she could find no malice in his expression. She was pleased to be able to reply without a blush, 'Ben and I are friends, Denez, no more.'

'Aye, mistress, as you say.' But a fractional twitch to the man's lips told Rozenn that he was controlling a broad grin and that he disbelieved her. For a moment she seemed to hear a faint echo of the raucous cheering that had accompanied Ben's kiss on the jetty.

Lifting her chin, Rozenn gestured at Anton to continue and the cart, laden with her cloth, rattled over the bridge at her side. Passing through the gate in the castle's curtain walls, they stepped into the bailey.

Market Square was a small cobbled area squeezed in between the Abbey of Ste Croix and Count Remond's keep. The rest of Basseville, the part of the island where the ordinary townsfolk lived, lay behind the Abbey.

The keep towered over them. The window of the solar was high up near the top, only visible if you tipped your head back and craned your neck. As Rozenn and Anton rounded a corner, the bells of Ste Croix rang out, calling the monks to matins. The Abbey was still being built and it was bristling with wooden scaffolding, but Abbot Benoît insisted that the services should take place in their proper order.

Reaching her site in the market-place—they were early and there was hardly a soul in the square—Rozenn began heaving cloth on to the trestle.

'My thanks, Anton.'

'My pleasure.' Anton helped her offload the rest of the stock. 'Will that be all, mistress?'

'Monsieur Quémeneur wants you?'

'Aye, I'm carting for him next.'

'You may go.' Noticing the expectant light in his eyes, Rozenn bit her lip. 'Oh, Anton, my apologies, I shall be needing my small change. Would it be all right if I pay you at the end of the day?'

Briefly, Anton touched her arm. 'Pay me whenever you like, I trust you, Mistress Rozenn.'

Her eyes misted. 'You cheer me up, Anton.'

Grasping the cart handles, Anton trudged back towards the keep and the Pont du Port.

The church bells continued to ring. A couple of other stallholders arrived to set up shop, and an arrow of white light—a seagull—flashed by and landed clumsily where the butcher's stall would shortly be.

A small procession was winding down the steps of the keep, with Countess Muriel at its head. The Countess was followed by a handful of her ladies, their long skirts rich with the bright colours that only the wealthy could afford: fine linens dyed madder red in Paris, purple silks and satins from the east. They were heading towards Ste Croix to join the monks in prayer.

A soft giggle had Rozenn's eyebrows snapping together. A glimpse of blonde hair escaping a veil that was light as gossamer produced a clenching in her stomach. Lady Alis was among the ladies.

Two strange men brought up the rear—no, not strangers exactly, for hadn't Rozenn seen one of them yesterday in the bailey? That mop of red hair, unusually long, that nose, sharp as a blade… Yes, she had seen him before.

Rozenn was about to turn back to her stall when one last figure came down the steps of the keep and into the square; a dark-featured, handsome young man whose fine green tunic fit his wide shoulders to perfection, and whose silver buckle flashed in the sun. Her heart stuttered. Ben!

Another feminine laugh floated out through the great doors of the abbey. Deliberately pitched to carry back towards the keep?

Rozenn clenched her teeth as with sickening predictability Ben's head turned in the direction of the laughter. He frowned, and then he too was striding towards the Abbey.

Ben? Attending matins with the Countess and her ladies?

A lump formed in Rozenn's throat.

Ben and Alis. So. No need to worry whether Ben had spent an uncomfortable night in some dank corner of the Great Hall. No need to worry whether the kiss on the jetty had meant Rose's relationship with Ben was in danger of changing. She had been forgetting—this was Benedict Silvester, the man with ties to no one and nothing. Save to his music, of course. Ben would wander off again soon, as he always did, and Lady Alis would be left behind to weep. She could almost find it in her heart to be sorry for Alis FitzHubert. Almost. Wasn't the girl meant to be betrothed to some knight?

Turning away from the sight of Ben taking the Abbey steps two at a time, Rozenn stared at her stall and forced herself to consider how best to display the cloth. The striped Byzantine silk should go at the front. The red velvet on the left, while, on the right, the green damask. It was a struggle and her heart ached, but she made herself continue. The plain linens could be ranged behind; and the satin ribbons…

* * *

Market Square gradually filled with people and customers, but Rose was not too busy to miss Countess Muriel emerging from Ste Croix with her entourage. Nor did she miss Alis FitzHubert and the red-haired stranger. And Ben? Not that she was watching for him—she just happened to be looking at the workmen swarming up the scaffolding as they started their morning's work. Like Ben, they had a breathtaking sense of balance.

'Excuse me, mistress.' A woman at her elbow cleared her throat. 'How much for a dress length of that blue linen?'

Rozenn tore her gaze from the Abbey doorway—still no sign of Ben—and forced a smile. 'You have a good eye, mistress, that's the finest linen in town.'

She and the customer were haggling over the price when Ben sauntered out of the Abbey in the company of Abbot Benoît. Ben? In the company of the Abbot?

'But you'll give me a discount?' the woman said, drawing her gaze. 'If I ask my husband to drop off some lamb cutlets at your doorstep tomorrow morning? And this is not mutton, mind, but new season's lamb…'

Rozenn unhooked the shears at her belt. 'Agreed.' The shears crunched through the cloth;

she folded it carefully, put the money in her pouch and looked up. 'Who's next?'

For the next few minutes—it could have been longer—she was almost overwhelmed by the rush. Word had apparently got around that there were bargains to be had at Widow Kerber's stall.

Countess Muriel bought the entire length of striped green-and-gold silk. Her mother, Ivona, bought a fine cream lawn to make a summer veil. Even Lady Alis bought from her—several ribbons 'to make a headdress'—and from Lady Alis Rozenn was startled to receive a shy smile as the money, a couple of silver coins, was pressed into her hand. Lady Josefa bought some English braid for a man's leg bindings. In short, trade was brisk, very brisk.

Rozenn's heart began to lift. With luck, today would see the last of Per's stock sold off and his debts paid.

The sun climbed and the shadows shrank. Rozenn's stall began to look a little depleted, but she remained busy. When the angelus bell tolled, it set the pigeons fluttering from their perches. Noon already? Rozenn wriggled her shoulders, clipped her shears back on to her belt and surveyed her stall. There was not much left, which was pleasing, since experience had taught her that most sales were to be made in the morning.

Rootling through what remained, Rose refolded the cloth and straightened the odd bale. She wondered if she should lower her prices. No, not yet, some of it was too good to reduce further; she would wait until later in the day.

Countess Muriel and her ladies, having scoured every stall in the market, were making their way back to the keep.

'Rozenn?'

She gave a start. Mark Quémeneur stood beside her, his grey eyes regarding her gravely.

'Good morning, monsieur, I didn't see you.'

'You are in good health, I trust?' Mark asked in his slow, formal way. Mark Quémeneur was about ten years Rozenn's senior, and he was a trifle stout. His wife, before she had died bearing their fifth child, had liked to keep a generous table.

'My thanks, I am well. And you?'

While she exchanged greetings and comments with Mark on the success of the market so far, Rozenn caught sight of Ben threading his way through the stalls, slowly but surely heading towards her. Her heart began to thud.

'Did you get top prices as you had hoped?' Mark—always the merchant—asked.

'Indeed.'

Mark shifted closer, absently fingering a remnant of velvet that was too small to make even a short cloak. Sweat was beading his upper lip. Clearing his throat, he flushed. 'Enough to…ah…solve the problems Per left you with, perhaps?'

Mark's grey eyes fixed earnestly on Rozenn's. He was asking her this, she was sure, because if she could not settle Per's debts then he thought to persuade her to let him have her leftovers at a knock-down price.

'Remember my offer,' Mark Quémeneur continued, patting his bulging money belt. 'If you do find yourself short and unable to settle, it would not be a problem for a girl who had agreed to become my wife.'

Her gut twisted. 'Y-your wife?'

Naturally, Ben would have to draw level with her stall at that very moment. His hair gleamed dark as a raven's wing. One of his eyebrows shot sharply upwards, his lips twitched, but he drifted on, tugging at an earlobe while apparently intent on a piglet tethered to a post by the butcher's stall. Rozenn bit her lip. By tugging his earlobe as he had done, Ben was letting her know that he was eavesdropping on her conversation with Mark. It was an old signal from a game they had played as children.

Rose's mind was reeling at a second unexpected proposal, but she was thankful Ben was close. The tension in her gut eased and she produced a smile for Mark because the man was offering her marriage, even if, in the wording of his offer, he had made it sound as if he was hoping to buy her by way of paying off Per's debts. It would be convenient for Mark if she were to accept him. He would have a mother for his five children; he would have a housekeeper and cook, and a partner to assist him with his business. Mark would make a reliable husband. Unlike Per, Mark Quémeneur *always* settled his debts. He might overeat on occasion, but he never drank to excess. She need no longer be alone. How convenient. How sensible. How ghastly. Thank God, Sir Richard had offered for her…

'Monsieur, I… I thank you, but I have sold all I need. This day's work will see me setting the tallies straight, every last one. Your offer is kind, but I must refuse it.'

For a moment, emotion glimmered at the back of the grey eyes. Disappointment? No, Mark Quémeneur was a merchant to his core—he did not love her.

He inclined his head, formal as ever. 'I am sorry I cannot be of service to you in that way, *madame,* for I truly hold you in high regard.'

And then Mark Quémeneur shocked her—he looked at her lips. Slowly and deliberately, with such blatant sensuality that the hot colour surged in her cheeks. Jaw tight, Rozenn fought down a cowardly impulse to rush to Ben and grab his hand. She held her ground, but barely.

The grey eyes lifted. '*Ma chère,* you will not reconsider?'

'I…I… *No!* That is…' Her voice was too high; desperately she moderated her tone. She did not want to offend the man, but the thought of kissing him—it would be Per all over again. Praying he had not seen her revulsion, she waved vaguely at the remaining cloth on her stall. 'I—I thank you, *monsieur,* but I am not certain we would suit.'

'No?'

Again his eyes were on her lips.

Breath tight in her chest, she repressed a shudder. 'No.'

He stepped away from the stall. 'You need time to consider, I understand. Even a widow like you, encumbered by her husband's debts—'

'The debts will be paid off, I told you!'

The cloth merchant nodded, but his gaze was on the contents of her stall. 'You need time,' he repeated softly, before reverting to his more familiar, businesslike voice. 'Rozenn?'

'Yes?'

'If you want rid of these offcuts, I'll take them off your hands.'

'Offcuts? Those are good pieces!'

With a tight smile, Mark Quémeneur shook his

head. 'Remnants all, but I'll take them if you find you need an extra denier or two.' Bowing, he turned and walked away.

Rozenn glared after him. She was shaking from head to foot.

'Hello, little flower.'

Ben's brown eyes were warm and very welcome. Hauling in a breath, Rozenn had to steel herself not to throw herself into his arms. 'Oh, Ben.'

Rose's bosom was heaving with indignation and red flags were flying in her cheeks. No dimples. Ben smiled at her, and pressed a chaste kiss to her temple. The elusive fragrance of jasmine tangled with his senses. Surreptitiously inhaling, he draped a casual arm around her shoulders. She was glaring after Mark Quémeneur.

'Careful, *ma belle,* you can fell men with such looks.'

'I don't like him,' she said, glancing briefly up at him. 'I never have, but I never realised it until today.'

Ben shrugged. 'The poor man is desperate to have you in his bed—is that so great a sin?' Briefly he caught a glimpse of a dimple. Her anger was leaving her.

'It is when it is him.'

'You refused him?'

'Of course I did! Did you hear the way he asked

me? As though I'm an object and he's bartering for me, as though I can be *bought!*'

Realising that he was stroking her neck in a soothing manner, and remembering his decision to keep his distance, Ben released her and rested his shoulder on a post at the corner of the stall. 'You still surprise me, Rose. Even after all this time, I thought I knew you.'

She wrinkled her nose. 'I surprise you?'

Why was it he had only just noticed how long her eyelashes were? And why was it that every time he looked at her he suddenly wanted to kiss her? It had not always been like that. Ben was conscious of those melting brown eyes on him while she waited for his reply, and all he could think was that he was glad that he had got in one tiny kiss without her noticing, while she was fuming at Mark Quémeneur.

He sucked in a breath. 'You didn't like his proposal.'

'No.'

'It was too…?'

'Mercenary, like horse-trading.'

Ben narrowed his eyes. 'Many marriages are made that way. You've heard the stories, rich lord weds ugly daughter to ambitious young knight.'

Her eyes became stormy. 'You had better not be telling me I am ugly…'

Ben threw his head back and laughed. 'Don't fish, Rose. It is unbecoming, and besides, you are wilfully twisting my meaning. All I am saying is that many marriages are made after a little horse-trading has gone on. It is the way of the world.'

She glowered as fiercely as one of the gargoyles adorning Abbot Benoît's half-built church.

He held out his hand. 'Come on, Rose, you will frighten the sun away if you look like that.'

'I'm upset.'

'So I see.'

With a sigh, she picked up a stray length of cream ribbon and began weaving it in and out of her fingers.

'Your own marriage was carefully planned, was it not?' Ben went on. 'Did Per not fight off other suitors in his negotiations with Adam for your hand?'

Rozenn swallowed and, with a jolt, Ben saw that her face was a picture of distress. 'L-leave my marriage out of this, if you please.'

He tilted his head to one side, aware he was moving on to dangerous ground. Though they had indeed been friends for years—the closest of friends at one time or so he had assumed—the matter of her choosing to marry Per seemed to be the one subject that was out of bounds; he had yet to get her to discuss it.

Ben took a deep breath and focused his gaze on

the top of the church roof, where even now a workman was edging his way out on to the parapet at the top of the tower. He did not think this was the right moment to bring up the offer she had turned down, the offer that had, sadly, precipitated his falling out with Adam. 'I wonder…' he spoke casually, almost musingly, but was startled to realise that his every nerve was taut as a lute string, alert for her slightest reaction '…if you truly know what you do want.' He slanted her a look.

Her eyes glistened, tears looked about to fall, and her fingers were almost as pale as the cream ribbon, which was wound so tightly it threatened to cut off her circulation.

'Don't, Ben, please,' she said, in a choked voice.

Reaching for her wrist, Ben gently began un-winding the cream ribbon. 'Careful, little flower, you're tying yourself in knots.'

Ben's fingers were warm on hers. Careful fingers with calluses from playing the leopard's-head lute; fingers brown from the summer sun; fingers that belonged to a minstrel who called no place his home. A pain in her chest, Rozenn watched them untangle the ribbon and smooth it out.

And then Ben changed the subject and they spoke of inconsequential matters, of the heat of the day, of the lack of rain. Shortly afterwards, he wandered off, and Rose watched his lithe figure threading its way through the townsfolk until it was lost to sight.

Noticing Anton in the crowd, Rose thrust Ben from her mind and waved him over. 'Anton, there's extra money for you if you will man my stall for a minute. I need to speak to Mark Quémeneur.'

'Yes, *madame.*' Anton, who had helped Rozenn many times before now, took up his position.

'I won't be long.'

When Rozenn reached Mark Quémeneur's stall on the other side of the square, the crowd had thinned, which was a blessing. Mark's stall, like hers, was a tumble of silks and linens and wools, only his was much better stocked. Artfully arranged, the fabric looked as though there were bargains to be hand, but Rozenn knew, as indeed did half the town, that Mark Quémeneur charged full prices.

His eyes lit at her approach.

'*Monsieur,* my apologies if I was too abrupt.'

'Nay, *madame,* I was perhaps too blunt myself.' Mark looked pointedly through the arch into the castle bailey where Ben was to be seen in conversation with Lady Alis. Naturally. Nearby, the red-haired stranger with the sharp nose was lounging in the stable doorway. How odd, she was seeing that man everywhere.

'Unlike some,' Mark continued, nodding towards Ben, 'I'm out of practice when it comes to wooing graceful ladies.'

Flushing, Rozenn held up her hand. 'Please, I have not come about that.' She waved to where Anton stood guarding her stall. 'I have reconsidered your offer to buy the rest of Per's stock. Are you interested?'

Mark's grey eyes narrowed. 'You have that green linen?'

'Half a bolt.'

'And that brown wool, the fine weave, not the coarse homespun?'

'That's all gone, I'm afraid, but I have some of it in russet.'

'Half a length?'

'No, full.'

'I'll take it.' Mark named a price, not overgenerous, but fair.

'And the rest?' Through the arch, Ben took Alis FitzHubert's hand and, with natural gallantry, raised it to his lips. Rozenn gritted her teeth and struggled to concentrate on her negotiations with Mark. 'And the rest? You will take the rest?'

'Aren't you keeping any for your own use?'

Half her mind on the scene in the castle bailey,

Rozenn shook her head. 'No. I can't be burdening myself with heavy cloth. I shall be travelling—to England, in fact.' She had not wished to tell Mark Quémeneur of her journey before she discussed Adam's summons with her adopted mother Ivona, but Mark's proposal had forced it on her. She might not be in love with the man, but she did not wish to hurt his feelings. And to that end, she must supply Mark with a good reason for her refusal.

'You are leaving Quimperlé? You are going all the way to *England?*' Mark's eyes bulged. 'This is the first I have heard of it.'

'I am sorry…' She smiled. 'You caught me unawares with your proposal. It is a recent decision but I do indeed travel to England. The new English king, the Norman Duke William, has granted my brother an estate in the south, and I intend to join him.'

Mark looked thoughtful. 'Dangerous for a woman alone, a journey like that.'

Her chin went up. 'Nevertheless, I intend to go.' She softened her voice and touched his arm. 'I appreciate your other offer, *monsieur,* but for the first time in my life I feel truly free to choose my own way. I want to find my brother. Perhaps I'll make my home in England too.'

'It's that friend of his, isn't it, the Norman knight?'

Rozenn darted a glance through the arch, but Ben and Alis had moved out of her line of sight. The red-haired man still lounged by the stable door and by the direction of his gaze and the cynical twist to his lips, she knew that he was watching them. Were they kissing? It was *not* her business.

Ice in her guts, Rozenn managed a light shrug. 'Sir Richard has asked me to marry him. Mark, I am sorry.'

The icy feeling in her guts was telling her that she did not like Sir Richard enough, not nearly enough, but she ignored it. Yesterday Ben's kiss had disturbed her with its sensuality, a gentle sensuality she had known with no one, not even her husband. Especially not with her husband. However, while Ben's kiss had unsettled her, it was not nearly as unsettling as the thought of the pedlar's life that would be hers if she gave in to such impulses and followed them to their natural conclusion. Ben was not steady; Ben was not constant. But yesterday, when for the first time Ben had kissed her as a man kisses a woman, her mind had opened on an unexplored world of pleasure….

Mark's gaze was not hurt as much as openly curious. Noticing it, Rozenn gave herself a little shake and ejected Ben from her thoughts. Smiling, she spread her hands. 'Lord knows what the journey may bring, *monsieur,* but I intend to make it.'

Astonishingly, as she spoke, her heart lifted and the sun seemed to shine a little brighter. Yes! She would definitely go to England, whether or not Ivona chose to accompany her. She would find Adam and Sir Richard and would see how they suited. Suddenly her rash confession of intent to Mark Quémeneur did not seem quite so rash.

Murmuring her thanks, Rozenn took her leave of Mark. Since gossip travelled faster than the flight of a swift, she had to discuss her plans with Ivona at once. Ivona must be told of Adam's invitation for them both to go to Fulford, and she must hear it from Rozenn's lips and no one else's.
And if Ivona decided against accompanying her? Well, Rose could not force her; Ivona must make her own decision.

And once she had discussed it with Ivona, Countess Muriel would have to be told.

Chapter Six

Ben was talking to one of Count Remond's grooms, Ivar, when he saw Rose leaving the market square. Nodding farewell to Ivar, Ben slung his lute over his shoulder and left the stables.

He fell in step with Rose as she was crossing the Pont du Port. It was late afternoon and the port was in shadow, the sun having dipped behind the cliff on which Hauteville was built. Rozenn's purse was bulging, leading Ben to conclude that she was on her way home and that her day at market had been successful. He had earned a few pennies himself that afternoon and hoped to buy her supper at the White Bird. It was past time for him to learn if her plans to answer Adam's summons were really taking shape.

It was time for him to become involved. Discreetly, of course. It would not do for Rose to learn that she was being manipulated....

She sent him a vague smile. She seemed oddly nervous. Distracted. He wondered why.

'Anton not carting the cloth back for you?' Ben asked, almost, but not quite, regretting his impulse to kiss her on the jetty the previous day. He had wanted to know what kissing Rose would be like for some time and now that he had kissed her, he could not regret it, except that it seemed that he wanted more, every time he looked at her. Rose had felt right in his arms, right in a way that all the Alis FitzHuberts in the world would never feel. But at this moment Rose's pretty mouth was set in a straight line. He hoped the kiss was not the cause of it. Ben's chest tightened. She stepped off the bridge and turned left, heading for Basseville. It was as though she hadn't heard him.

Ben blew out a breath. If this awkwardness between them was the result, kissing her had been a mistake. He needed to be on good terms with Rose. Hell, the Duke needed him to be on good terms with Rose. But maybe it was not the kiss that was bothering her; perhaps she was angry about his comments regarding her marriage with Per. He leaned forwards, the better to catch her gaze. 'Rose?'

'Sold all the stock,' she mumbled, continuing to walk on.

Damn. He liked it when things were easy between them, but if this was to be the way from now on…

Touching her arm, he was appalled when she jerked aside, as though he'd stabbed her with one of her needles. 'Rose, *chérie…*'

'Mark Quémeneur bought it,' she said brightly. 'Got quite a good price.'

Ben recognised a cue when he heard one. A slight belligerence in her eyes and a tilt to her chin warned him to follow her lead. Something was making her nervous. 'Really? He's not usually so generous.'

'Hmm.' Her nostrils flared. 'Most likely he thinks he can persuade me to marry him.'

Ben's boot caught on a loose cobble. 'You would not accept?'

Finally, thank God, Rose paused mid-stride and turned to face him, grinning with something of her old familiarity. 'Won't have to. Sold enough myself at the full price today.' With a slight smile, she tapped the purse at her belt. 'Going to see Ketill to pay him off.'

'Ketill?'

'Ketill Saffell, one of Per's suppliers. He is a Norseman—from Scandinavia, I think. He has a couple of trading ships.'

'I'm coming with you,' Ben said firmly. 'Some of these men are pretty brutal characters.'

'Not Ketill.'

'Nevertheless…' Breathing easier because she did not gainsay him, Ben casually linked his arm with hers and they proceeded towards the port.

They passed Denez on his way to the gatehouse. '*Holà,* Ben.'

'Captain.'

Denez threw a grin Rozenn's way and raised a brow.

Rozenn's cheeks reddened and she fixed her gaze on the flag fluttering on the tallest of the masts by the docks. The ducal colours, Ben noticed, his attention sharpening. Abbot Benoît, a distant cousin of the Duke, was standing by the ship, supervising the unloading of some huge blocks of stone destined, doubtless, for the church. Ben was careful not to look at him.

Several other vessels with furled sails were moored at the quayside. They had heavy oak rudders and sat low in the water, like a fleet of Viking longboats. Curved wooden prows pointed to the sky. Carvings had brought the prows to life—twisting snakes, smiling mermaids and writhing sea-monsters—but these seemed out of place in the shining calm of Quimperlé's placid river. And instead of being crammed with Viking raiders, the ships were stacked with barrels of wine from the south; with jars of oil from the

East; with pottery packed in straw-filled crates; with cloth wrapped in oilskin…

Ropes creaked. Winchmen on the boat from the ducal quarry shouted orders. Swifts were feeding high in the sky, black arcs against blue.

Rozenn shot Ben an odd look and attempted to extricate her arm from his.

'Nay, *chérie.*' Ben held her gently but firmly in place. 'I have my reputation to think of.'

Melting brown eyes looked up at him, a dimple winked out. 'You have a reputation? What about mine? I'm a respectable widow here in Quimperlé, while you, you…'

Unabashed, Ben grinned, well aware she had been about to name him a womaniser, or worse. 'But, Rose, you have been a widow such a short time, while I… I have been a wandering minstrel, doomed to wander the country for ever. It's hard…but I must insist. I have to maintain my reputation—I need to be notorious.'

'Oh?'

He lifted a brow. 'Certainly, notoriety guarantees a crowd for every performance. People come to hear me because they think me a devil.'

'I see, very well.' Her tone was light, but at the back of her huge brown eyes, he could see shadows.

Rozenn let Ben keep one arm while she gathered up her skirts with the other. They picked their way to the end of the jetty, past stacks of crates and heaps of fishing nets to where Ketill's ship was docked at the last mooring.

At this, the southerly end of the port, the smell of gutted fish was strong and the planking slippery. Noses wrinkling, they trod warily.

On the deck of the ship, the protective canvasses had been rolled back and Osgood, Ketill's youngest son, was using the deck hoist to rearrange the cargo. He had tied his fair hair back at the nape of his neck like a Saxon, and was rolling a barrel into the cradle, brawny biceps bulging.

Rozenn waited while Osgood finished with the barrel before attracting his attention. Her heart was leaden in her breast, which was not what she had expected to feel on this, the day she had longed for—the day she was repaying the last of Per's debts.

While the barrel was being manoeuvred into place, Rozenn looked up at the cliffs towering above them, to the highest point where the White Bird stood just out of sight. Wondering what Mikaela would be serving for supper, she ran her gaze down the slope, down along the line of little houses that stopped at the port. Hauteville. Rose's throat tightened. She would shortly be leaving—was that why she felt as though her heart was breaking? *No,* a little voice said, *be honest, it is not entirely that. You are sad because the night Ben came back, you made a point of telling him of your plan to leave Brittany, and he did not so much as blink. You expected a reaction from him, but you did not get one. You think he no longer cares, as he did when you were children. And maybe you are right.*

The barrel safely stowed, Osgood hauled back the empty cradle.

'Osgood? *Osgood!*'

The fair head turned; Osgood flashed a practised grin in her direction and vaulted lightly over the ship's rail to take her hand.

At her side, Ben went very still. He looked startled and for some reason this irritated her.

'Mistress Kerber!' Osgood ran his thumb lightly up and down the back of her hand. 'I am right glad to see you. You look very well, the prettiest widow in all of Brittany.'

'Yes, yes, Osgood.' Ignoring Ben, Rozenn smiled into the trader's blue eyes. Osgood loved to flirt, but this was harmless flirting. The world knew that Osgood was blissfully happy married to a woman named Anki, who lived with their daughter in a place called Scarborough on the north coast of England. Osgood only ever flirted with women who knew this. The flirting had begun when Rozenn had been married to Per and it continued now because Osgood knew there was no chance of Rozenn reciprocating. If the trader thought for one moment that Rozenn really had her eye on him, he would untie that mooring rope and be off faster than you could blink.

Rozenn indicated the purse at her waist. 'I think your father will be pleased to see me too, for I have come to set the tallies straight.'

She unhooked her half of Per's tally stick from her belt, while Osgood called his father over. The tally stick was a record of the money Per owed the trader, the amounts being noted by the making of marks on the stick at the time the debt was incurred. As was the custom, the stick had been split lengthwise—Rozenn had kept one half and Ketill the other.

'Father! Father! Mistress Kerber is here with her husband's money.'

Out of the corner of her eye Rozenn spotted the red-haired man with the sharp nose, seated on a bollard near the Duke's quarry ship, whittling a stick. It occurred to her that he was uncommonly interested in the conversation that Abbot Benoît was having with the ship's master, but just then Ketill bustled up with his half of the tally stick, and the red-haired man was forgotten.

'Mistress Kerber.'

With much smiling and not a little relief,

Rozenn noted, on the part of the trader, she put the two sticks together. 'Here, Ben, hang on to these, while I count the money out.'

Moments later the money was counted out into Ketill's broad and callused hands. Ketill and Osgood checked the amounts marked on the tallies.

When they were satisfied, Ben shifted. 'May I?' he asked, holding the tally sticks aloft.

Ketill nodded. 'Aye, lad, you do the honours.'

Ben smiled, brought his knee up and the sticks smartly down. They snapped with a crack. 'I witness that this debt is settled in full,' he said, formally.

Free at last! The relief was as heady as strong wine. Per's debts were settled, to the last penny. Rozenn's purse felt lighter, but what of it? There was enough to do one last deal with Ketill. However, it wouldn't do to look too eager…

Pointedly, she closed her purse.

'My thanks, Ketill, for your patience,' she said. 'And now I have one last proposition to put to you.'

'One *last* proposition?' The trader frowned. 'Mistress Kerber, I had thought that you and I would be doing business for years to come.'

She shook her head. 'I'm afraid that's not likely. You see, I am planning to journey to England to join my brother, Sir Adam.'

At her side, Ben sucked in a breath. 'Rose—'

'And I may not return,' she continued firmly. 'I

was wondering how on earth I, who cannot ride, could get there. But then I remembered that your family is based somewhere in the north of England, and that you and Osgood must return there between voyages.'

Ketill's gaze had narrowed, but he smiled. 'You wish to book passage in my ship, yes?'

'Yes. For myself and, possibly, another.'

Ben had hold of her sleeve. '*England,* Rose? You *are* serious!'

'Yes, I'm going to join Adam.' She met Ben's dark eyes steadily, but a certain intensity to his expression gave her pause. He looked pleased, excited almost—how strange. 'But, Ben, I have already told you. I had word from Adam, and he has invited Ivona and me to join him.'

'Yes, yes, I remember that, but…but you really mean to go?'

Rozenn put her hands on her hips. 'I cannot speak for Ivona, but as for me, why, yes, I intend to go. Why shouldn't I?'

Ben ran his hand through his hair and sent her a crooked grin. Yes, he was definitely pleased. 'No reason.' He took her hand and steered her away from Ketill and Osgood.

She hung back. 'Wait a minute, my business with Ketill is not concluded.'

'It is for now.' A muscle twitched in his jaw, and,

with Rozenn firmly in tow, Ben continued down the quay, dragging her farther from Ketill and Osgood.

'I beg your pardon!'

'We will discuss this over supper,' Ben said, marching with her towards the street that led up to her house and the White Bird at the top of the escarpment.

Ben. Sometimes he was most odd. Rozenn found herself smiling at his back before she came to her senses enough to resist his pull. 'Ben, I will have supper with you, but I must book passage and with Ketill and Osgood while they are in port. Not only are they the most trustworthy of the traders, but they live in England, where I intend to go.'

Ben came to a halt so abruptly that she ran straight into him. Instinctively, they reached to steady each other. Ben's hands slid down to hers and they stood at the foot of the hill, holding each other's fingers.

'I'm the last to know, I suppose,' he said, twining his fingers with hers and loosing a disturbing *frisson* in her belly.

Rozenn frowned. 'Actually, I told you first, but—'

'Rose, I wasn't sure you meant it.'

She shrugged. 'Well, I do mean it. Ben, I will

have supper with you, but please release me so that I may speak to Ketill.'

He shook his head. 'You can't…'

Hackles rising, she glared at him. *'Can't?'*

A gentle fingertip touched the side of her face; again her belly tightened. His mouth edged up at one corner. 'Careful, little flower, your dimples have gone into hiding. All I meant was that you can't go that way, not by ship.'

She tipped her head back to look at him. 'Why ever not? Osgood told me their trade route takes them north. It skirts the coast of the Duchy till it reaches the Narrow Sea.'

'Yes, Rose, and England is on the other side of the Narrow Sea.'

'So?'

'Rose, you are *terrified* of water. A few moments ago you looked very ill at ease. I see why.' Ben gestured beyond the docks towards the Laïta. 'You've never so much as put a toe in the river and now you are contemplating a sea voyage—'

'I'll be on board Ketill's ship, I won't be swimming! Ben, this is the best way, given I can't travel on land. Ketill will look after me.'

Ben was shaking his head, and his dark hair fell into his eyes. 'I know you. You are likely be sick the entire way. No, there's nothing for it, you'll have to go overland.' He looked thoughtful. 'Even then there will be the Narrow Sea to navigate, but if we embark from one of the northern ports and land at Bosham, say, in Wessex—yes, that would be about right, a shorter crossing. I will have to make enquiries, but the less time you spend at sea with your fear of water, the better. You should have let me teach you to swim, Rose, but that can't be helped. Yes, we'll go by land, to one of the northern ports—'

'We?' Puzzled, Rose stared at him. Ben hardly seemed himself this afternoon. There was such a light in his eyes, such a determined light, as he attempted to take charge of her plans. Where had her frivolous lute-player gone?

Ben cleared his throat. 'Yes, *we.*' And then, abruptly, he was back to his old gallant, superficial self as he bowed over her hand and raised it to his lips. 'Rose, you are my lady fair. Surely you did not believe I would let you embark on such a dangerous enterprise on your own? If you are set on joining Adam in England, then I shall be your escort.'

'But, Ben, I can't ride, remember?'

'No matter, I'll teach you.'

'Ivona can't ride either.'

His lips curved. 'I will teach her too.'

'And what about horses?'

'We'll hire them.'

'Won't that be expensive?' Knights and squires

and ladies rode horses, noblemen rode horses, not ordinary girls like her. It was true that Rose was going to marry a knight, but the thought of riding right through Brittany was more than a little daunting. However, if Ben were to accompany her…

He gave her a smile that had melted sterner hearts than hers. 'Little flower, I have money, I told you.' His brown eyes danced. 'It seems I was not the only one who was not listening the night I came back. If you don't have enough to stand the hire fees, I have.'

She snorted. Was it likely that Ben would have *saved* his money, even if he'd earned it? Rozenn threw a glance at Ketill, who was standing where they had left him, watching them. 'Ben…' Her voice trailed off.

Dear Lord, he knew her too well. The thought of the voyage *had* been troubling her, and the thought of making the journey with an old friend like Ben was tempting indeed, even if it meant she would have to learn to ride. Earnestly, she looked at him. 'You would travel with me?'

He shrugged. 'I have long had a yearning to travel to England, to play in London or Winchester.'

'Truly, Ben? You would be my escort? The *whole* way?'

He swept her one of his extravagant bows. 'I

am, as I have told you a thousand times, yours to command. I'll have you and Ivona riding within a week.'

'You will change your mind.'

'Not a chance.' Offering her his arm, he started up the hill.

Rozenn was smiling from ear to ear, but she could not help herself. Ben would accompany her to England!

He grinned down at her. 'Anyway, I have no choice.'

'How so?'

'Adam would have my hide if he knew I'd let you set off on your own.'

'Are you and Adam still at odds with one another?'

He shot her an impenetrable look, but answered clearly enough, 'He will bury the hatchet if I escort you to England.'

'Oh?'

'Aye.' He affected a shudder. 'It is so fearful a task. Who else would put up with you? All the way to England?'

She stuck him lightly on the arm. 'Beast. Are you ever serious?'

'Not if I can help it.'

'Ben?'

'Mmm?'

'Tell me, what was it you and Adam quarrelled

about? He never would say.' Ben stared out over the roofs of the houses and made no answer— sometimes he was such a dreamer. 'Ben?'

'Hmm?'

'The quarrel? What was it about?'

His broad shoulders lifted. 'Something was said about a visit to Genevieve's bathhouse.'

'Oh.' Rose wrinkled her brow. Genevieve's bath-house was also the town brothel. It was no surprise to learn that Ben had visited it, but it was surprising that it had caused such a rift between Adam and Ben.

Men. Would she ever understand them? A pair of long-lashed dark eyes were watching her, so she shook her head at him as he no doubt expected and let him escort her to the inn to discover what Mikaela had cooked up for supper.

The next morning, Rozenn met Ivona in the cool and quiet of the castle chapel, one of the few places where a private conversation could take place.

'What?' Ivona stared at her, mouth working. 'Have you gone mad?'

Rozenn swallowed. She and Ivona were sitting on a bench on the south side of the chapel, and she had just told Ivona about Adam's summons and her intention to settle in England. The news was not being well received, leaving Rozenn in no doubt that there was little hope of Ivona travelling with her to Fulford and so far she had made no mention of her intentions regarding Sir Richard.

'Let me get this straight…' Ivona put her hand to her brow. 'You are considering journeying to a foreign land with *Benedict Silvester* as your sole protector? Granted, the man plays the lute like an angel, but what use will that be if you run into thieves or cutthroats?'

'*Maman,* I am going. As I have just explained, Adam has invited us both—in fact, it is more than a request *and*—'

Ivona made an impatient sound. 'Adam should know better. For one thing, I am far too old to consider accompanying you on such a foolhardy enterprise. And as for you—who knows what may happen to you on such a journey?'

This was proving to be every bit as difficult as Rozenn had expected. '*Maman…*' gently, she touched Ivona's arm '…Ben's whole life has been a journey. I think he will know how to protect me.'

'Benedict Silvester, protect you? If he doesn't seduce you, he'll neglect you while he's seducing someone else!'

Rozenn sighed. 'I trust Ben.'

Ivona frowned. 'And I do not.'

'*Maman,* why do you dislike him?'

'Dislike him?' Ivona looked startled and shifted so that the bench they were sitting on creaked. 'I don't dislike him. He was a sweet child—indeed, I felt very sorry for him losing his mother and having to live the life of a nomad. And he and Adam…' her gaze drifted towards the altar '…they were such close friends. Of course, Ben was the one who found you under the rosebush by the tavern, and when you were children the three of you were so good together. I never had a moment's worry when you were with Adam or Ben.'

'What made you change your mind about him? Was it something about Genevieve's?'

Ivona shot her a sharp look. 'You know about that?'

Rose nodded. 'Ben mentioned it yesterday. Ivona, Ben is sorry for the rift between him and Adam. It is my belief he sees this journey as a way of mending things.'

Ivona's face was lost behind the fall of her veil. Hearing a muffled sob, Rozenn pushed it aside. *'Maman?'*

Another sob. 'Rozenn, I am sorry, but I do not want you to leave. I do not want to lose you.' A tear ran down Ivona's cheek. She wiped it away with the èdge of her veil, before straightening her shoulders and giving a watery smile. 'Forgive me.

It is just that I always knew that Adam would leave. Mothers know their sons will leave. I am being selfish.' Taking her hand, Ivona drew in a shuddering breath. 'I always wanted a daughter, and though you are not of my flesh and blood, in my mind and heart you have been a true daughter. Yann knew I ached for a girl. Every woman wants a child who will stay at her side and the boys usually leave. That was why when Ben found you, Yann was so swift to bring you to me.'

'I am so glad that he did,' Rozenn said. 'For you have been the best of mothers. I shall be sorry to leave you, but…'

'You are intent on joining Adam.'

'Yes.' Rozenn drew in a breath. 'And Ben is to be my escort. Naturally I am sorry if that displeases you, *maman*. Give me your blessing for my journey?'

Ivona squeezed her hand. 'You have it. I cannot go with you, but, my dear girl, of course you have my blessing.'

'Oh, thank you!'

Ivona tipped her head to one side and her veil shifted. 'What will you do in England?'

Rozenn smiled and felt some of the tension inside her begin to ease. 'Who knows? Pray for me, *maman*. I may marry.'

'You would consider Benedict?' Rozenn gave

her a sharp look. 'Oh, I wouldn't dream of inter-fering, dear. But I still maintain that the trouba-dour's life is not for you.'

Still maintain? What did Ivona mean? And then Rose thought of Per and bit her lip. 'The life of a merchant's wife was not for me, either.'

'No.' Ivona shuddered. 'Per was not a good man. Would that we had known that before you married him.'

'Forget him, *maman.* I am trying to. I want to look forward, which is the main reason I wish to travel to England. The past is to be left behind.'

'Seriously, Rozenn, might you marry again?'

'It is possible.'

'But not Benedict? You will not marry Benedict?'

Rozenn thrust the memory of Ben's kiss on the jetty to the back of her mind. 'No, *maman,* my friendship with Ben is not of that nature.'

Ivona frowned. 'You have someone in mind, I think.'

Rozenn fingered her gold cross, but said nothing—the words would not come. It had been so long since she had seen Sir Richard, and while Adam's message had suggested marriage, she would rather say nothing until a formal betrothal had been arranged. Her dream of marrying Sir Richard of Asculf was only a dream until she had looked into Sir Richard's eyes and he had made a formal offer. Rising from the bench, she shook out her skirts. '*Maman,* I must go. the Countess awaits me in the solar.'

Ivona stood. 'Have you told her yet?'

Rozenn grimaced. 'No.'

'She won't be pleased.'

'I don't suppose she will. I shall tell her next.' Impulsively, Rozenn gave Ivona a hug. 'Come with me, I would be glad of your support.'

Ivona's smile was sad, but she put her hand in Rozenn's and as one they turned for the door. 'When will you be ready to leave?'

'Within the week.'

'So soon?' Her adopted mother bit her lip, and Rozenn caught the shimmer of tears, swiftly blinked away. 'Still, there's time enough for me to prepare a package for you to take to Adam. He will be missing my quince paste and—'

'I am sure he would like that.' Rozenn made her tone light. 'But try not to send him half of Brittany, *maman.* Ben said he would hire a horse for me, but I doubt I will take it to England. I may have to walk once we land, so I'll only be taking the essentials.'

Chapter Seven

The following dawn, Ben woke before Rose and lay on his pallet, watching her. He was conscious of an uncomfortable feeling in his stomach, as though he had drunk sour wine. He hoped it was not guilt; he had no reason to feel guilt. He had used old friendships before in the Duke's name, and had always found it easy to justify. Brittany was a better place with Duke Hoël at its head; guilt was entirely misplaced.

Rose was curled on her side, facing him across the ashes of last night's fire. During the night her hair had loosened and it lay like a soft brown cloud about her face. Her lips were relaxed, almost smiling; her cheeks were lightly flushed, her breathing soft and even.

The Duke needed Ben to establish reliable links with his men in Brittany. It had been Ben who had given Duke Hoël the idea of involving Adam

Wymark; it had been Ben who had persuaded Adam to contact Rose. Rose's journey gave him just the cover that he needed to get to England.

Ben had not felt guilty when he had set the wheels in motion, so why on earth should he feel guilty now, just when everything was moving along so nicely?

Rose was serious about leaving Quimperlé, nay, about leaving Brittany.

Good.

She had discussed it with Ivona, who was not choosing to go with her; she had told the Countess.

Good.

All was falling out exactly as he had planned. His stomach churned. Frowning, Ben quashed an urge to cross the room to Rose, to brush aside that dark tendril of hair that was falling across one eye. Was he doing the right thing?

Grimacing, not used to questioning himself like this, Ben rolled on to his back, pillowed his head on his hands and fixed his gaze on a smoke-blackened roof beam. He must make certain she did not change her mind. The Duke's business apart, Rose was a widow, and Ben felt uneasy about letting her remain alone in Quimperlé, especially with Mark Quémeneur so hot to marry her. Rose had married a merchant before in search of a comfortable life and it had been disastrous. It was true that at the moment she didn't show the slightest desire to marry Quémeneur—the opposite, in fact. But she had stunned him once before when she had married Per and he wasn't about to risk that happening again.

Rose's ambition might yet be her downfall. Ben understood why she so hungered for respectability, for comfort—it was clearly in some way connected with her being a foundling. And Rose's ambition had been useful to him. Understanding her need to better herself had helped him create this double cover, travelling to England as her escort and as a carefree minstrel trying his luck in pastures new. Understanding Rose's ambitions had enabled him to sweeten Adam's summons with that lure about Sir Richard.

At this moment, all seemed to be going well. He must ensure it continued to do so. As far as everyone in Quimperlé was to know, he was simply Rose's escort. He was to take her to… What was the name of Adam's new holding? Fulford, yes, that was it, Fulford in Wessex… Yes, he was to take her there and then…and then…

It occurred to Ben that while they would encounter other people on their journey, he would at times have Rose to himself. The thought was a good one. He could show Rose something of his life and, while it was often a hard life, there were comforts too. Why, she might even like it. His mouth edged up at the corners.

Noblemen and knights alike were generally pleased to see him: they paid him well, they fed him well, they housed him well. Not always, of course. But he did not think that the wandering life was quite as bad as Rose imagined. It would be good to prove this to her, in deeds for once, instead of merely telling her so.

A cockerel crowed out in the street. Rozenn stirred, sighed, and was still, that glossy twist of hair still over one eye.

Quietly, Ben pushed back his bedclothes and sat up. Gathering up his clothes and lute, he slipped into the shop where he dressed quickly and let himself out of the house. There was a slight chill in the air, but the clear sky was already filled with the screech and chatter of swifts and martins. It would soon be warm; he had no need of a cloak. He started downhill.

First, to the castle stables to check on his horse, Piper. A fine-boned brown gelding, a gift from the Duke himself, Piper was Ben's pride and joy. But Piper was not the sole reason Ben was heading for the stables. It was time he spoke to Count Remond's head groom. Quickly, he would act quickly. He had plenty of money and would call in a favour or two. The sooner he got Rose away from Quémeneur, the better; the sooner he got Rose far, far away from Quimperlé, the better. The Duke had need of her, *he* had need of her; Quémeneur could go hang.

Once they had put a few miles between them and this place, she would not find it easy to change her mind and return.

It was odd to think of Rose travelling with him day after day, night after night…

His spirits lifted. Only a couple of months ago he would have sworn that nothing would prise her from her place here, that she was stuck in Hauteville, like a limpet on its rock, but everything was changing. The only danger that he could see was that, once on the road, Rose might change her mind. Well, he would urge her on as swiftly as he might and see that she did no such thing. It should be easy.

The streets were almost empty, save for a few hens and Anton and his cart. This morning he was hauling a wine butt uphill. They nodded as they passed each other.

'Good morning.'

'*Holà,* Ben.'

Yes, by the time the sun had lifted above the walls of Castle Hellon, Ben intended to have a horse for Rose. Quickly, that was the key word.

Quickly. Get her away from Ivona before she was persuaded to stay.

Whistling under his breath, smiling as he approached the Pont du Port, Ben wondered if Morgan, the head groom, had a decent horse to spare.

'This one,' Ben said, running a knowing hand down the leg of a black mare with eyes soft as a fawn's. He was closeted in the end stall with Morgan. 'I like the look of her, though she's almost too pretty. You are certain she can go all day carrying a grown woman and her baggage?'

'Provided you don't go at a gallop from dawn till dusk,' Morgan said. 'She's sturdy. Good sire.'

'And shod, I take it?' Straw rustled as Ben lifted a hoof to examine it.

'Yes, she'll do you. Count Remond couldn't resist buying her for the Countess, but she wasn't enough of a challenge. Countess Muriel likes a mount with a stronger head on her.' With a grin, Morgan made a suggestive gesture. 'This one's far too docile.'

'What's her name?'

'Jet.'

'Jet?' Ben released the mare's foot and folded his arms. 'Jet's a hard name for a soft horse, if indeed that is her true temperament.'

Morgan shook his head on a laugh. 'No, Ben, you

have her nature pinned. Jet took her name from her colour, nothing more. She has good teeth, is sound of wind and limb, and is certainly biddable enough for Mistress Kerber to learn to ride on. You are looking at a mare with no hidden faults…'

Stepping forwards to stroke Jet's glossy neck, Ben nodded. 'Good. So, as I recall, Count Remond would be happy for you to sell her…'

Morgan grinned. 'Provided the price is right.'

'Naturally. So…what is your price?'

The two men haggled amiably over the amount and shook hands to seal the bargain. Money clinked as it passed from one to the other.

'You had better be right about her temperament,' Ben said. 'I wouldn't want her taking chunks out of my Piper.'

A gleam entered Morgan's eyes. 'Are you sure it isn't Mistress Kerber you are concerned about, not that mangy gelding?'

'Mangy? You dare call my Piper mangy?'

Morgan shook his head. 'You don't fool me. When do you leave?'

'Tomorrow, the next day?' Ben shrugged.

'As soon as you can get away, eh?' Raising a brow, Morgan made another suggestive gesture.

Ben ignored it. A little ribbing was inescapable when someone had known you on and off for years, as Morgan had known him. And in any case, the man was right. He did want to bustle Rose out of here, though not for the reasons that Morgan supposed. He would cajole her on to Jet's back as soon as he might, and they would have Quimperlé behind them before Rose could so much as blink. But Ben's cheeks were warm as he jerked his head in the direction of the tackroom. 'I don't suppose you have any saddles going begging?'

It was two days before Ben succeeded in getting Rose mounted and then that was only when they were about to leave. She sat astride Jet, fingers white on the saddle Ben had cajoled out of Morgan, biting her lips and staring anxiously at the cobbles. Her skirts were hiked up almost to her thighs, but, seeing the tension in her face, Ben thought it best not to draw her attention to this.

He stood at her knee by the mounting block in the castle courtyard, holding Jet's reins, positioning Rose's legs. 'Like this, little flower.' His fingers seemed to develop a disconcerting tendency to linger. Hastily, he stepped back, trying to radiate confidence.

'B-Ben?'

'Mmm?'

'The ground seems awfully far away, and…and it looks very hard. I… I don't think I like this.'

'You'll be fine,' Ben said, praying he was right.

Nodding his thanks at Morgan, he relieved him of Piper's reins and swung into the saddle himself. He took a moment to adjust the shortsword belted at his waist. As a minstrel, Ben had not earned the right to bear full knightly arms, but when on the Duke's business he never travelled without his shortsword.

'You… You were in the right. I should have made time for riding lessons,' Rose acknowledged, in a small voice.

'Perhaps, but you've hardly slept these last few days.'

And that was no less than the truth. Rozenn had flung herself into such a frenzy of activity that Ben had hardly seen her. Countess Muriel had insisted that her daylight hours should be spent bent over the wall-hanging, and the rest of the time Rose had been taking her leave of every last acquaintance in both town and castle. There had not been a second in these past two days for her to even look at Jet, never mind have riding lessons.

Ben had a suspicion that Rose had kept herself busy deliberately, so that she would not have to think too much about the life that she was leaving behind.

'You're a quick learner,' he added. 'You will pick it up as we go.'

A farewell party had gathered on the steps of the keep. Ivona, Countess Muriel, Lady Alis…

Not long now, but this was the moment Ben had been dreading. Were there going to be tears? Probably. Would she change her mind, when actually faced with saying goodbye to everyone and everything she had ever known? *No, Ben.* He could hear her voice in his head, as though she were actually speaking. *How could you possibly think I would really leave? I never meant a word of it...*

Anton appeared under the market arch with Mikaela at his side and a couple of girls whose names escaped him. Denez was there too, Stefan, Jafrez... All her friends had come to wave her off. Not Mark Quémeneur, thank God. The wretched merchant had had the gall to turn up at her house at dawn with a posy of mallows and marigolds and a length of the finest silk. Light as a cobweb, the fabric had an iridescent sheen to it and was fit for the Duchess. Rose's eyes had lit up when she had seen it, and she had kissed the man—but only on the cheek, Ben had noted—before tucking the silk into her saddlebag, alongside a bundle Ivona had insisted she carried to Adam. One of Quémeneur's mallows was even now tucked into Rose's girdle, a discordant splotch of purple against the blue of her gown, and one of the marigolds was nestling in the opening at her neckline. Ben was looking at the flowers, when he realised she was watching him.

'Ben? Is something the matter?'

'Not at all, but we will have to get you some gloves as soon as we may.'

'But I told you, it's too hot to wear gloves, just as it's too hot to wear a cloak.'

The merchant's blasted marigold was drawing his attention to the bosom of her gown, to the tantalising curve of her breasts. With difficulty, he dragged his gaze away. 'As I explained, you would be wearing them to *protect* your hands, not keep you warm.'

Jet champed on her bit and sidled. Rose squeaked.

'Loosen the reins a little, *chérie.*' Ben sent her a comforting smile. Rose was definitely not a natural horsewoman. The reins were wrapped tight as tourniquets round her fists and she was clinging to that saddle as though her life depended on it… Still, they had time.

Intercepting his glance, she grimaced. 'Placid, you swore Jet was placid?'

Ben nodded and gave Morgan a pleading look. 'So I am told, but your reins are far too short. Hold them like this.'

Morgan adjusted the length of her reins and her grip. 'Jet's as calm as they come. Like this, Mistress Kerber, you don't want to damage her mouth.'

'Oh. Sorry.'

'Ben, you might need this,' Morgan murmured, holding out a neat coil of leather. His lips quirked upwards. 'No charge, call it a parting gift.'

'My thanks.' A leading rein. Grinning, Ben showed it to Rose. 'I think Morgan is in the right, until you become accustomed.'

'Y-yes, please, just for today.'

Leaning towards her, Ben clipped one end of the leading rein to the ring by Jet's bit and kept a firm hold of the other. 'Ready?'

'Lead on.'

Thus it was that they clopped out of the castle courtyard, towards the group of friends in the market gate.

'Farewell, Rose!'

'Farewell!'

'Bon chance!'

There was no sign of Mark Quémeneur. One of the mallows fell from her girdle to be crushed under one of Jet's hind hoofs. 'Relax your hands on the reins,' Ben said, biting back a smile. 'Try and let go of that saddle.'

'I'll fall!'

'No, you won't, you have stirrups. And use your thighs. That's better.' Perhaps it was no bad thing that there had been no time for riding lessons. Rose was so busy concentrating on staying seated and on the unaccustomed motion of the horse, she would have no energy to spare for tears. At least so he hoped.

Ivona and the Countess remained on the steps of the keep. A veil fluttered, Countess Muriel gave a cursory wave and whisked back inside. Ivona lifted one hand and wiped her eyes with the other. Her voice carried across the yard. 'Keep her safe, Benedict.'

Raising a hand himself in acknowledgement, Ben dug his heels into Piper's brown flanks and led Rose out of the castle precincts. Her face was set, she was staring at the back of Jet's head, and her mouth was a thin line. The hands holding fast to both reins and saddle were now bone-white. There were no actual tears, though—just a pale, set face as everything Rose had even known fell back behind them.

The horses walked—a trot was probably too much of a distraction—through Market Square and past Ste Croix. Several workmen were winding a hoist to position one of the great blocks of stone that had been unloaded on the docks a few days earlier. A dove fluttered past, heading for the dovecote in the castle garth.

Rose spared the dove a nervous glance and resumed her study of Jet's ears. In this way they reached the easternmost bridge and the road to Vannes. Ahead of them was the forest, several days of it, if they kept on at this pace.

She twisted carefully in the saddle and peered over her shoulder as the walled island of Basseville and the castle and her old life shrank to nothing.

'Ben?'

'Little flower?'

'Which way did you say we were going?'

Good, she was distracting herself, there would be no flood of tears. At this realisation, a knot of tension in Ben's stomach that he had been unaware he was carrying untied itself and fell away. 'We follow the road to Vannes as far as the Hennebont crossroads. From there we go to Josselin and thence to Rennes.'

The track was wide enough for them to ride side by side. Ben shortened the leading rein and drew close. Their knees nudged.

'Ben, is Rennes *en route* to the sea?'

'Not directly, but from there a road runs to the north coast which will mean a shorter voyage.'

'Oh.'

'Duke Hoël has made Rennes his headquarters,' Ben went on. 'It has a mint and is counted the capital of Brittany. I thought you would like to see it.' He could not, of course, give Rose the whole truth. Abbot Benoît had given Ben a letter, and had asked him to forward it to the Duke in Rennes. He could say nothing of this. It was true, however, that

Rennes was larger and more cosmopolitan than Quimperlé, and Rose would be interested in seeing it.

'How long will it take us to get there?' she asked, her voice light.

Ben wasn't fooled; her tone was brittle, she was teetering on the edge of tears. 'We...ell, considering you do insist on riding at a snail's pace, I should think it will take us at least a month.'

'A month!' White teeth worried at her lower lip. 'Surely not?'

'It is over a hundred miles. If I were on my own, I could make it in two or three days at an easy pace, but with extra baggage...' Grinning, he let his voice trail off.

Her chin lifted. 'This *extra baggage* will try not to slow you down too much. By the end of the day I should be able to go much faster.'

By the end of the day, Ben thought to himself, you will be as stiff as a board. Aloud he said, 'Glad to hear it.'

'Ben?'

'Mmm?'

She was looking at the forest that was encroaching the town boundaries. 'Is it wooded all the way to Rennes?'

'Pretty much.' He lowered his voice dramatically, as if he were coming to the heart of one of his epics in some lord's great hall. 'It is the haunt of great wizards like Merlin.'

Her lips curved, and Ben found himself staring. Rose did have a fascinating mouth. Lord, he should never have kissed her, he was fast becoming obsessed with the thought of kissing her again.

'And witches?' She raised a brow.

'Indeed. One of the greatest witches of all time lives in one of these forests. Her name is Vivienne and she—'

'Ben, I'm all right. I *want* to go to England. I don't need a fairy tale to distract me.' A dark brown curl had escaped her veil. Briefly, she released her grip on Jet's reins long enough to tuck it behind her ear.

'No?'

'No.'

This was the point when the road to Vannes narrowed and became more of a trackway—its surface was no longer cobbled, but simply beaten earth covered in beech mast. The sound of Piper and Jet's hoofbeats changed from a sharp clopping to a muffled drumming. Ben began to relax, to really relax. Finally, they were underway. He would have the pleasure of Rose's company until they reached Adam in Wessex. And she—he did not pause to examine why this thought pleased him so much—she, having never travelled out of

Quimperlé in her life, would be dependent on him for the whole journey.

The trees loomed closer, shading them with luxuriant green canopies. Beech, oak, hornbeam…

'I am sad to leave, of course,' she murmured.

'You are not afraid?'

She shook her head. 'Not when I am with you.'

And there it was again. Guilt. How would Rose react when she learned that she had been manipulated into making this journey? Heaven help him.

'These roads are strange to me,' she went on, oblivious of the effect her words had on him. 'But you have travelled roads like this very often.'

'So I have.' Ben stared into the shadows under the trees. He had not travelled these roads simply in his capacity as a minstrel, but Rose knew nothing of that. In the past he had often carried letters from the old Duke to the Abbot at Ste Croix. The letter he was now carrying to the new Duke was tucked away in his tunic, for Abbot Benoît had in the end proved to be of more use than Lady Alis. His lips twitched. A case of the confessional winning out over the gentle art of dalliance? But since Abbot Benoît was a blood relation to Duke Hoël, and Lady Alis was young and untried, he had not been truly surprised that the Abbot had been better informed.

Ben could not tell Rose about the letter he was

carrying, just as he had never been able to tell her about any of his work as personal private envoy to the Duke and his predecessor, Duke Conan. In the early days, the messages he carried were trivial, but lately, with the threat of local unrest and Normandy's ambition, the letters that he carried were more weighty. The Duke's enemies would kill to get their hands on them. Ben judged the letter he carried today to be important, if Abbot Benoît's expression had been anything to go by. No, it was safer for Rose if she continued in ignorance of the missive he was carrying.

'As I mentioned,' he went on, 'Rennes is not the most direct route to the coast.' Since Rozenn had never left Quimperlé, her sense of geography would be poor to non-existent. She was not unusual in this regard, for most people never travelled more than half-a-dozen miles from their homes in their lives. 'I am thinking that with your hatred of water, Rose, we shall definitely cross the Narrow Sea, rather than risk the Great Sea. The less time you spend in a ship, the better.'

'I will manage, but I bow to your knowledge,' she said, shooting him a brief smile, before grimacing and transferring her gaze to Jet's ears. 'Even though I expect that will mean more riding.'

'Yes.'

Rose groaned.

She needed confidence in her ability to learn to ride. Surreptitiously, Ben lengthened the leading rein until there was a sword's length between them. The pace he would maintain for the time being, a steady walk. Mentally crossing his fingers, he gazed across the gap and said, 'Soon you'll feel as though you were born in the saddle.'

She gave a short laugh, but did not break her perusal of Jet's ears. 'I doubt it.'

'That bad, huh?'

Another grimace. 'I do feel rather awkward.' She plucked at the hem of her gown and tried to pull it down. 'I don't like showing my legs. I must look like one of the girls at Genevieve's.'

Deliberately, Ben let his gaze linger on her calves and ankles, smiling at her feet in their sturdy, practical boots. 'Rather better, I'd say.'

She flushed. 'Don't, Ben. It… It's all right when it's just you and me but…' she glanced up and down the track '…but what when we meet other travellers? It is most unseemly. Shouldn't I be riding side-saddle?'

'Side-saddle? You'd find that even more awkward. Most ordinary women learn to ride astride.'

'Most ordinary women—' her tone was tart '—never leave their home town.'

'You are very brave,' he said finally. 'Especially given your nature.'

'And what might that mean?'

He opened his eyes wide. 'You are and always have been a girl for hearth and home.'

'And how you hate that,' she muttered.

Ben opened his mouth to gainsay her, but she turned her head away from him and dug her heels into Jet's flanks. Jet's pace did not alter. Jet was, as Morgan had promised, slow and placid, thank the Lord. Ben didn't want Jet haring off over the next hill; the last thing he wanted was to have to pick Rose out of a ditch.

Biting back a smile, he allowed himself the pleasure, and it was a pleasure, of looking at her profile. Oddly, it was as though part of him needed to memorise her on this ride through sun-dappled woods, as if he had been waiting for years to see her like this. Something within him softened as he looked at her smooth, high brow, at the long dark lashes, the straight nose. That slight flare of her upper lip—it was so subtle a curve, yet it was all Rose, inescapably Rose, and merely to gaze at it had a curl of awareness—no, it was more powerful than that. It was an ache of pure longing that caught him unawares, so strong it actually *hurt*.

Rozenn tossed her head so that her veil danced, and their eyes met. Her expression lightened and she stuck her tongue out.

He found a laugh and blew her a kiss. Lord, she was going to be livid when she learned what he had done. He hoped to hell she did not really care for Sir Richard, but, in order to discover the answer to that question, he first had to get her to admit to her real reasons for joining Adam. He plunged in.

'Tell me, Rose, why did Adam send for you?'

She shifted in the saddle, avoiding his eyes. 'I am in hopes that he might offer me a place at Fulford.'

Ben nodded. Yes, Duke Hoël had suggested as much. Not that Adam had been hard to persuade; he was generous to a fault and he loved his adopted sister. 'I only hope that it is safe for you in England. Not long since, the Saxons were hell-bent on ridding the place of Franks.'

'Yes.' Her voice was low, her expression concerned. 'That is one of the reasons I wish to go. I would like to see for myself that Adam, and Sir Richard, are both well.'

'Sir Richard?'

'Yes. Adam…' Rose cleared her throat, a spot of high colour on each cheek. 'Adam said that should anything befall him, I could apply to Sir Richard for assistance.'

'Sir Richard.' Cold fingers gripped Ben's heart. It had been his plan, but he did not like the look in her eyes when she mentioned the knight's name.

'Mmm.' There it was again, that dreamy expression. 'Adam told his messenger to say that I could put my trust in Richard, if anything should happen to him.'

This was what he had aimed for and yet Ben frowned as the fingers tightened their grip on his heart. 'Richard.' *She thinks of the knight in familiar terms, and not by his title.*

'The messenger also said,' Rose continued as the horses wound their way through a copse of hazels, 'that Richard had my best interests at heart.'

Ben's fingers clenched on the leading rein. Out of the corner of his eye, he saw a flash of red as a squirrel scampered down a tree trunk and scrabbled through the leaf litter, searching for cobnuts. Lifting a brow, he kept his voice level. 'What do you suppose he meant by that?'

She didn't answer at once. 'Rose?' *Lord, we are not halfway to England, and in her mind she is already wearing his ring.*

His persistence had her averting her head, giving all her attention to her mare's ears. Pulling gently on the leading rein, Ben brought their horses abreast and his knee bumped hers. The squirrel, a nut triumphantly in its mouth, vanished beneath some undergrowth. A moment later, a branch rustled above them, there was another flash of red, and then silence, save for the plod, plod, plod of their horses' hoofs and the thud of his heart.

'Rose?' He wanted to be sure, he wanted her to say the words. Rose was a hearth-and-home girl. But he knew her better than anyone, he knew that she had one characteristic that might be strong enough to override her need for a simple, orderly life—ambition.

She and Sir Richard had enjoyed each other's company. Ben had seen them laughing together many a time, most notably when the man was practising his lute. He shook his head. Sir Richard might be a champion with his sword, but he certainly needed practice with his music-making. Not that Rose had found Richard of Asculf's ham-fistedness with a lute off-putting—far from it. His mind produced a clear image of the pair of them, happily ensconced in a corner of the White Bird, heads close together while the man struggled to get even the most basic of chords right.

He drew in a breath and kept his voice level. 'Adam's message came at the right time, then?'

She shot him a swift glance. 'Yes, it was very timely.'

'Would you ever consider marrying Sir Richard?' He was pleased with the casual way the question emerged. As though he didn't care, one way or the other. Except that he was beginning to realise that he did care, far more than he ought.

Her veil quivered as she gave him another darting, sideways glance. 'I think that I may,' she acknowledged, flushing.

'He has not yet asked you?'

'Not in person.'

'And Adam said you could put your trust in him.'

'Mmm.' That dreamy tone was back in her voice. 'Apparently Richard has my best interests at heart.'

There were those words again, at heart, *at heart...* Ben swallowed down a groan, though he only had himself to blame for this. 'Do you love him, Rose?' Hell, where had *that* come from?

'Love him?' She wrinkled her nose. The marigold at the neck of her gown was moving up and down with her every breath. 'He's very handsome. And strong.'

'And a gallant knight,' Ben muttered. Becoming aware that Rose was regarding him with a puzzled expression in her eyes, he pulled himself together. It would not do for her to become suspicious of his questioning, not when they had only just set out. 'So…' he shrugged, and gave her a flirtatious look '…it seems I have a rival.'

'A rival?' She rolled her eyes. 'Ben, be serious!'

He gave a dramatic sigh. 'I am, but it is not easy. How may a lute-player compete with a knight, particularly one like Sir Richard who outranks me on all fronts? It is enough to drive me into a monastery…'

Her eyes began to dance, her lips twitched, the marigold quivered at her breast. 'A monastery— *you?* Oh, Ben, you idiot,' she said, lips curving so compellingly that he wanted to kiss her. Briefly, she released her death grip on Jet's pommel and touched his sleeve.

Her eyes were glowing with warmth and affection, beautiful brown eyes. Ben was smiling into them when out of nowhere a fierce anger shook him to his core.

Damn Sir Richard and his knighthood with his acres in Normandy. Damn him to hell!

Chapter Eight

The road was rising on a gentle incline. Rozenn's legs were going numb—no, if truth were told, they had gone numb some miles back.

They had been on horseback for ever, or so it felt, and though the highway was beginning to open out a little, for the most part they were hemmed in by clumps of oak and beech and hazel.

'Won't the horses be tired?' she asked. 'Shouldn't they rest?'

Ben's mouth twitched as he leaned forwards to pat Piper's neck—his warm, gentle, mobile mouth, the mouth that had kissed her so beautifully... Oh, heavens, this would *not* do!

'Don't worry about them, we're only walking. Horses can walk day and night if need be.'

Oh, good. Rose gave him a steady look. 'Day *and* night? You are teasing, I hope?'

'Why, *chérie,* are *you* tired? You only have to say.'
He reined in and the horses came to a standstill.

Rose gave him another, more covert glance from
under her eyelashes. Ever since they had set out,
she had been wary of speaking to him because a
disturbing thought had entered her mind, one that
should perhaps have entered it somewhat earlier.
Her only excuse was that she had been so busy pre-
paring to leave Quimperlé, she had not had time
to think. But this afternoon, although trying not to
fall off Jet, she had had plenty of time. And her
thoughts made her blush.

Where would they sleep? Separately? Of course.
But what if the inns were full, what if they had to
sleep out in the open? She should have discussed
this earlier. It was embarrassing to bring the
subject up at this late stage. Ben might think that
she wanted… Her cheeks flamed.

At the docks, when Ben had volunteered to escort
her to Adam, she had been both pleased and relieved.
She had managed to relegate that kiss in the marshes
to the back of her mind. She had told herself that,
delightful though she had found it, it had only been
a momentary aberration on Ben's part. That kiss—
together with the one he had given to Mikaela—had
been but a part of his performance for Denez and the
guards on the bridge. It had been no more than that.

But on this journey, she and Ben would be constantly in each other's company. In the whole of Brittany there was no one with whom she would rather travel, yet the question remained. *What would happen tonight?*

Unlooping his wine-skin from his pommel, Ben held it out to her. 'Here, it is watered, but it will give you a little strength.' He jerked his head down the road. 'There's a tavern ahead, a good one, it is worth reaching it. Three miles, Rose—can you survive another three miles?'

The wine was a red, rich and sweet even though watered, and it flowed smoothly down her throat. Ben was right, it *was* reviving. Rose flexed her feet and shifted in the saddle, but the sensation did not return to her thighs or buttocks. 'Three miles? I reckon so, but only if there's a feather bed at the end of it.' An image of her and Ben, entwined on one such bed, flashed into her mind. Her cheeks burned again. *Feather bed? With Ben?*

Taking back the wine-skin—why were her fingers trembling?—Ben tipped back his head and raised it to his lips.

Thoroughly discomfited, but glad he could not read her mind, Rose studied him as he refreshed himself, as she had never studied him before. She seemed to notice his every last feature, even the track of a drop of wine as it ran down his mouth and chin. He needed a shave, his chin was dark with stubble, but it was that mouth with its finely chiselled lips that was the most distracting. A small, tickling sensation, not unpleasant, made itself felt in her belly. She looked at his musician's hand, holding the flask. It was browned by the summer sun. She looked at his fingers, shapely and strong, and wondered how many women they had caressed. She frowned. The sleeve of his tunic flopped back. Ben's forearm was shapely and sprinkled with dark hairs. Ben was more than just a musician though; that shortsword was not mere show. He was as athletic as any knight, more athletic in many cases… The unfamiliar sensation in her belly increased.

And yet, sometimes Rose could wish Ben were not quite so frivolous, not quite so light-hearted. Sometimes she had the feeling there could be more to Ben if only he set his mind to it and sometimes she wished…

A feather bed, and a man that I care for…

Shaking her head, Rose tore her gaze away. The wine—it was much too rich on an empty stomach. Tipping her head back, she stared into the endless blue of the sky. Thank God my thoughts are hidden from him, she thought, shocked and surprised at herself. It was not as though she was a particularly sensual person, so why was she having such thoughts?

Rose had never enjoyed the so-called delights of the marriage-bed.

She had heard the women chatter at the Quimperlé wash-house down by the river; she had listened, mystified, while they had giggled and boasted of their husbands' prowess and endurance between the sheets. And while Rose had listened and had smiled and had tried to join in, she had had to hold part of herself aloof because she had nothing to contribute to that particular topic. The fault must be in her, she had concluded, for, while Per's touch had not revolted her exactly, she had hardly enjoyed it. And as for endurance, as far as she was concerned, the quicker the whole business was over and done with, the better. Luckily, Per had never taken long; it had always hurt.

So why, Rose wondered, her frown deepening, should the thought of her and Ben lying together in a deep feather bed make her cheeks fire up and her hands tremble on the reins?

'Rose?' Ben broke into her thoughts. 'If you are exhausted we could camp here for the night.'

'No, no.' Rousing herself, Rose dug her heels into Jet's flanks and urged the mare back to that slow, steady pace. 'The idea of an inn is infinitely more appealing. We'll go on.'

Lifting a corner of his mouth, he inclined his head. 'As *madame* commands.'

'Ben? I've just remembered, you have not told me how much I owe you for the hire of this horse.'

'For Jet?' He looked away. Somewhere deep in the forest a woodpecker drummed. 'Nothing. You don't owe me a penny.'

'That can't be right.'

He shrugged. 'Rose, you owe me nothing. I called in a few favours, that's all.'

'But, Ben—'

Abruptly, he turned in the saddle to face her, and for a moment his face was infused with such anger that she drew back. 'You are my friend, my *best* friend.' His voice was harsh. 'There are no debts between friends like us.' And then the fierce expression was gone as though it had never been. His eyes gleamed with something of the old familiar devilry. 'You may thank me later, though…in a manner of my choosing.'

She arched a brow at him. 'In a manner of your choosing? That sounds dangerous.'

He nudged Piper closer so there was no gap between them. 'It is, Rose, it most certainly is.' Pointedly, he looked at her mouth and raised an eyebrow at her, the flirt. Leaning forward, he dropped a swift kiss on her lips, a kiss that was over before Rose had time to do more than close her eyes in anticipation and…

He laughed and her eyes flew open, but he had

kicked Piper back into a walk and his eyes were back on the road. 'I shall claim my thanks properly later.'

She could not be certain, because Piper and Jet had just ridden under the shade of a large oak and he was slightly ahead of her, but she thought that his cheeks were tinged with colour. It was probably a trick of the light.

The sun was sinking by the time they rode into Hennebont. Aching in every muscle, Rozenn at first thought she had no energy left to take in her surroundings. Lifting her head, what she did see was reassuring in its similarity to Quimperlé. Like Quimperlé, Hennebont was built on the steep banks of a river, in this case the Blavet. And reassuringly, as at Quimperlé, the sky above it was alive with swifts and martins. The river basin at the bottom was so big that William of Normandy's entire fleet could have moored there, though of course Rose hoped it never would. However, Normandy had England fast in his grip—who could say where he might look next?

On leaving the highway—it had broadened out as it led up to the town gates and passed through the outer walls—their horses' hoofs struck cobbles and they entered a market square that, despite the late hour, was filled with activity. Rozenn blinked away her fatigue. There were people, lots of them, talking and shouting as they finished their business in the last of the light. Geese cackled, dogs barked, children laughed and shrieked in turn.

This was more like it. People. The loneliness of the road had made her nervous. Naturally, none of the faces of these townsfolk were familiar as they would have been at home, but it was easy to guess most of their trades by their clothes and their manner. That thickset man, with the face tattooed by flying stone-chips, he could only be a mason or mill-stone dresser. In a church doorway a robed priest was deep in conversation with a black-garbed Benedictine. A knight in chain-mail with a couple of links missing was riding ahead of them. The battered shield slung over his shoulder was covered in black chevrons on a white ground, and his grey stallion looked as exhausted as she was. The knight was accompanied by his squire, a gangly dark-haired youth on a brown mare he had outgrown several years earlier, for his feet almost reached the ground. Idly, Rozenn wondered if the knight might have met Adam or Sir Richard.

And there—a man on foot with a blue cloak and a shock of red hair like… Red hair? Arrested by a sense of familiarity, Rozenn watched the man slip into an alley between two houses.

That man—surely she had seen him before? His blue cloak was cut in an unusual manner. It was semi-circular and, though she had only seen him from the back, she knew it fastened under the chin with a silver brooch. As a seamstress, Rose was sensitive to cut and quality, and she had seen that cloak, not to mention that shock of red hair before. That man, she would swear, had a nose as sharp as a blade….

Brow furrowing, for to her knowledge no one she knew lived in Hennebont, Rose peered up the alley when they rode past. It was empty; there was not even the swirl of a blue cloak.

'Ben, did you see…?' But Ben's mind was elsewhere. Naturally. His attention had been snared by a pretty woman selling eggs by the roadside. The woman clearly knew him. Her face was split by a delighted smile, her cheeks and eyes were bright and she looked happy—no, she looked ecstatic, Rose amended, with an odd cramping sensation about her heart.

Ben grinned and gave the woman a casual wave.

'Benedict! Benedict!' The woman's voice cut through the general hubbub. You would think, by her expression, she had stumbled across a crock of pennies that were hers for the keeping.

'*Chérie?*'

'You are singing tonight at the Bridge?'

'So I hope.'

The woman's smile broadened. And, unpick that previous thought, the woman had found a crock containing pure gold, not pennies. ''Til tonight then,' she said, beaming. 'I'll bring the girls.'

'I look forward to it, Paola.'

Heaven blast him, he knew her name. Ben probably knew the name of every last woman in the Duchy. Gritting her teeth, Rose glanced back at the alley. Ben had been too busy being his usual heartbreaking self to notice the red-haired man, but surely that man had been the twin of the fellow she had seen in Castle Hellon's stable yard and again by the docks at Quimperlé?

'Look, Rose—' Ben had shortened the leading rein so there was not an inch between them '—see how these houses are built on the edge of the precipice? No need for city walls in this quarter.'

Rose looked. It was true. 'Just like Hauteville by the White Bird,' she murmured.

'I thought you would find it familiar.' Reaching across, he stroked her cheek with the back of his fingers. Her heart stuttered, her cheeks burned and she had to drop her gaze as the vision of a wide feather bed swam into her mind. 'Not far now, you've done very well. See, over there…'

Outside one of the wooden buildings, a painted signboard was swinging in the evening breeze. It showed an improbable-looking bridge spanning an enormous gorge. The bridge was crudely drawn, in clear bold lines. This must be the inn. From the roof of the inn itself, smoke was curling in soft plumes. Inside, several lanterns had been lit, Rozenn could see their quiet glow through the windows and door.

Reaching the forecourt, the horses came to a standstill. Ben dismounted with his usual lithe grace. How did he *do* that after a full day in the saddle? Even knights like Adam and Sir Richard would grunt and flex muscles grown stiff after a day riding. He tossed Piper's reins to a boy sitting with his back against a water trough, cutting a reed. '*Holà,* Tom. Making another whistle?'

The boy flashed him a gap-toothed grin, and nodded.

'We can test it later, if you like,' Ben said, absently resting a hand on Rose's thigh. His thumb caressed her, once, twice, thrice; she could feel it through the linen of her skirt, sending tiny darts of sensation all the way to her belly, which was something of a miracle, given that she was so numb she had thought she must be dead to all feeling.

The boy, Tom, grinned. 'Yes, please, Benedict!'

Ben held his hand up to help Rose dismount. She blinked blankly at it. She was swaying in the saddle, quite certain that none of her muscles had any movement left in them.

'Rose?'

'Ben, I don't think I can…'

Ben shook his head and reached up both his hands. 'It's all right, *ma belle,* lean towards me. I have you.'

She practically fell into his arms and when her feet met the ground they buckled. She clung to him and, flirt that he was, he made the most of the moment, grinning down at her, and taking her firmly by the waist. 'My apologies,' she muttered, 'my legs have gone to sleep.'

'They will waken in a moment.' Dropping a light kiss on her nose, Ben went down on his haunches with his back to the inn. Before she realised what he was about, he had slid his hands, both of them, under her skirts and was massaging her calves. It was heaven. 'Sorry to push you so hard today,' she dimly heard him saying as she looked down at his dark head and the ball of his thumbs pressed deep into her muscles. 'But I thought, on our first night of our journey, you would appreciate being safely ensconced in a decent inn.'

Almost groaning aloud with a mixture of both pleasure and pain as the blood returned to her legs, it was a struggle to recall they were in the very public yard of a strange inn in an unfamiliar town. What would people think?

Rose looked up to see that a young woman had appeared in the inn doorway and was wiping her hands on her apron. Her sleeves were folded back and she was watching them, head tilted on one side. A curious, knowing smile played about her lips as she looked at Ben's back.

Rose felt herself blushing and tried to extricate herself from Ben's massaging hands. They were rubbing the life back into her limbs, but she was still hobbled by weakness. Grabbing one of his broad shoulders for balance, she tugged at his hair. 'Ben! *Ben!*'

The woman raised a plucked eyebrow, amusement in her eyes. 'Good evening, mistress. Is that Benedict Silvester you have on his knees before you?'

'I… Yes.' It was a long time since Rozenn had spoken to someone who was a complete stranger, but out of the blue it came to her that this was a good woman, and she could trust her, might even like her. She laughed. 'And a rare sight, I am sure, Ben on his knees.'

The woman inclined her head. 'Indeed,' she said, eyes lighting up. 'It is a moment I shall treasure.'

Ben stopped whatever magic he had been

working on her calves and rose. 'Irene!' Unhooking his lute from Piper's back, he shouldered it and strode across.

Rozenn did not crumple at his abrupt departure, which was astonishing given how wobbly she had felt moments earlier. Ben took Irene by the hands and kissed her on both cheeks and finally, with a swift glance over his shoulder at Rozenn, on her lips.

'You are a provocative rogue, Benedict Silvester,' Irene murmured. 'Are you staying?'

Ben stepped back. 'If I may. Is the best bedchamber free?'

The plucked eyebrow arched and Irene sent Rose a considering look. 'The private one?'

'Aye, the one the Duke uses.'

'It might be, for a price.'

Returning to Rozenn, Ben's arm went back about her waist.

'All right, Rose? Legs holding up?'

'Yes.'

He led her to Irene. 'Rose, this is Irene, a friend. Irene, meet Mistress Rozenn Kerber.'

Irene murmured Rose's name softly under her breath and held out her hand. 'I am delighted to meet you. Please, do come in.'

While the boy took charge of the horses and their baggage, Rozenn entered the inn with Ben's arm about her waist. It seemed perfectly natural that she should wrap her arm around his waist too.

The room Ben and Irene had referred to as 'the private bedchamber' was, as Rozenn soon discovered, a curtained recess set a little to one side in the loft above the inn's main room. The space was almost completely taken up by the grandest bed she had ever seen; it had a bedhead and bedposts, richly carved with fruit and flowers.

How Rozenn had managed to force her overworked limbs up the wooden stairway from the hall below, she never knew, but somehow she did manage. Once in the bedchamber, she gave the room a cursory glance and crawled on to the bed. Feather mattress. Soft. Rolling on to her back, she groaned with relief, closed her eyes, and let her limbs relax. It was some minutes before she stirred.

The bedchamber had a sloping ceiling and what light there was entered via a couple of narrow slits at the gable end. On the right stood a brazier, empty of coals. Rose smiled; it was so warm that it would certainly not be needed tonight. And she would *not* permit herself to think about her and Ben lying entwined in this bed.

Two thick tapestry curtains did duty for walls, and while they did not insulate the room from sounds coming up the inn below or from the public sleeping chamber next door, in winter they would keep the worst of the draughts at bay. Now, in July, the bedchamber was stuffy and airless. Still, if this bed was good enough for Duke Hoël, it was good enough for her; indeed, it was better by far than any she had ever slept in. Candles stood ready on shelves on either side of the bed. Peeling back a corner of the embroidered coverlet, Rose found that the bed linens were white as snow and scented with lavender.

The loft overlooked the main room of the inn. With its central hearth and fire, and the grey smoke wafting up to a roof-vent, it reminded Rozenn of the Great Hall at Hellon Castle, except that here, of course, everything was built of wood and was on a much smaller scale. Below, Irene's customers sat on stools grouped around the fire; they sprawled on various benches beside an assortment of trestles.

Experimentally, Rozenn moved her legs—yes, they still worked—and grimaced. She should not be lying in her boots on such a beautifully embroidered bedcover. Forcing herself to her feet, she stooped to examine it. It was a lightweight wool and every inch had been covered in a loose, looping design of curling vines and flowers, which echoed the carving on the bedhead and bedposts. Why, this bed rivals the one at Castle

Hellon, she thought, awed. Finding a loose thread, she deftly tucked it back into place. Not wanting to be the unwitting cause of any more such damage, she carefully folded the cover out of the way and sat down on the edge of the mattress. Her legs were still shaky. She dragged off her boots.

Was Ben intending to sleep in this room with her? And if so, where? Of course, she wanted him to be close at hand, but the uncertainty of their sleeping arrangements was very unsettling. She had left him below, happily haggling with Irene over the cost of their night's lodgings. Almost, Rose wished she had insisted on going by sea with Ketill and his son, but, no…it had to be better to travel with Ben. Ben knew how to find places like this, places with beds fit for Dukes, and—if the mouthwatering smells floating up through the floorboards were anything to go by—food fit for them too.

She liked the look of Irene. How long had Irene known Ben? Many years by the easy way they began bartering with each other. She ran her gaze over the room, the bed. How many times had Ben slept here? How many women had he…

No, she must not think such thoughts! But before she could stop herself, she seemed to hear Ben's voice, laughing, as he said, 'I have to maintain my reputation as a flirt… I need to be notorious…'

'*No!*' Startled, Rose realised she had spoken

aloud. She sighed. She must be realistic. Ben was a showman, flirting was his stock in trade. Why, even while he was bargaining with Irene, he would be romancing her a little as he persuaded her to let them use this chamber if he entertained her customers. Ben, the minstrel. Ben, the entertainer. Ben, who was *never* serious. Her dearest friend. But why, oh, why could she not shake off the thought that he did have a serious side to him that he never revealed it? She bit her lip. Lately, there was something about him, something that did not quite ring true… He was like…he was like…a sleeping lion, she thought. Ben might have such power, but he never uses it.

What if one day the lion wakes and discovers he is hungry? What then?

Staring blindly at the rush matting, Rose dug a stockinged toe into a gap in the plaitwork. Ben did little to disprove his reputation, though. Indeed, judging by the women who flung themselves at him, one might say he worked most assiduously to keep it.

'Notoriety guarantees a crowd for every performance.'

Ben himself had told her as much.

'People come to hear me because they think me a devil.'

'Not a lion, but a devil,' Rose muttered, pulling

off her stockings and wriggling her toes. 'A handsome, heartbreaking butterfly of a devil who would not be pinned down for all the gold in the Duke's treasury.' And that should not matter to her. But it did. It made her sad.

Light footsteps sounded on the landing outside; the curtain rings rattled and in strode that very devil. As devils are, he was achingly handsome— straight of limb, with shining dark hair and soulful eyes fringed with black lashes. A heartbreaker. Where was he intending to sleep?

'Madam, your belongings,' the devil said, depositing Rose's pack next to the brazier. Incongruously, she noticed he was standing on the last of Mark Quémeneur's mallow flowers, which had fallen to the floor unnoticed.

'My thanks, kind sir.' Holding herself very straight, Rose unpinned her veil and began to loosen her braid.

Ben remained motionless for a moment with a lopsided smile on his lips, before slowly approaching the bed. Irene's best bedchamber seemed to shrink to one tenth of its size. 'You are welcome, little flower.'

He was looking at her mouth and she wished he wouldn't. It made her want… Wrenching her gaze away, Rozenn smoothed her hair and swiftly began to re-plait it.

'Rose, are your legs very sore?'

She nodded.

'I have a cure for that…' Taking the half-finished braid from her, he gave it a gentle tug, urging her to meet his eyes. They were very dark; his pupils looked enormous.

'A c-cure?' Oh, Lord, he was staring at her mouth again, and he was still smiling that lopsided smile that never failed to melt her insides. Out of nowhere the urge to run her fingers over his chin came over her. She wanted to test the roughness of his beard. Dear heaven, a devil indeed.

'Mmm, a cure,' he said, on a small sigh. Giving her plait one final tug, he released it. 'There's a bathhouse at the back of the inn—would you care to go?'

Rose blinked. A bathhouse? His cure was that she should take a bath? For a moment she had thought…

'Rose?'

'A b-bath?'

'Yes, Rose, a bath.'

'In the town bathhouse?'

He shrugged. 'Where else?'

Her mind reeled. Only Ben would have the gall to make such a suggestion. Rose was a respectable girl and respectable girls did *not* frequent public bathhouses, tempted though she was by the thought of a bath. Of course, the bathhouse in

Hennebont might not have quite the reputation of Genevieve's in Quimperlé…

Ben frowned, but his voice when he spoke was amused. 'You'd be quite safe, Rose, I'd see to that.'

Ivona would be furious! But Rose was hot and sticky and uncomfortable and the idea of a long soak in a tub of water was tempting. Besides, Ivona was a day's ride away, and who in Hennebont did Rose know who would care whether she went to the bathhouse or not?

No one. The only person hereabouts whose good opinion she cared about was the unshaven devil standing in this room with her.

A feeling of liberation such as she had never felt came over her. *No one would know.* It was a heady feeling. Lifting her eyes to Ben's, she smiled. 'A bath sounds heavenly. Provided that you will be nearby,' she added hastily, for the thought of disrobing amongst strangers *was* alarming. 'I shouldn't care to go alone.'

Stepping back from the bed, Ben bowed. 'My lady, I am yours to command. I can be your body servant, if you wish.'

'My body servant!' she exclaimed, shocked, before she saw the wicked laughter gleam in his eyes. She got up and hobbled over to her baggage with as much dignity as she could muster. 'Do they provide linens in bathhouses, Ben?'

'Towels, soap, oils…' he lowered his voice suggestively '…massages, whatever you wish, little flower. I will command whatever your heart desires.'

She gave him a quelling look. 'Privacy, Ben, that is all I shall need.'

Unabashed, he lifted a brow. 'Are you certain?'

She folded her lips together. 'Privacy. Will you grant it?'

Folding his arms across his chest, he nodded. 'Of course, my lady. As I said, I am yours to command.'

Chapter Nine

Rozenn let Ben take her hand and lead her through the warm evening to the entrance of the Hennebont bathhouse. The moon was high and bats were flitting about above them, scraps of sooty blackness that made the stars flicker. Ben halted before a one-storey wooden building where a double door yawned wide. Behind the fire, a row of stalls had been set against the back wall.

'It looks a bit like a stable,' Rozenn murmured, lingering doubtfully in the doorway.

'Not once you get inside,' Ben said, smiling.

Indeed, closer inspection proved him right. Great swathes of cream cheesecloth were draped over hooks in the ceiling. Rose eyed them with some misgivings. Here and there lights shone through the cloth and it was a moment before she realised what she was looking at. In each stall a light was burning—the white cloth ensured privacy from its neighbour. Behind one of the screens came a giggle that was unmistakably lascivious and the sounds of splashing water. Someone—a male someone—groaned with undisguised pleasure.

'Oh, n-no, Ben,' Rozenn stammered, hastily backing away from the threshold. 'I… I think I'll wait for you back in the Bridge.'

Shaking his head at her, Ben gave her hand a tug.

Stumbling over the threshold, Rose realised that inside it was far from the scene of great debauchery that she had imagined. Lights glowed from behind the flimsy white curtains and shadowy figures moved about in the stalls. Lanterns hung on hooks on the walls. There was plenty of light to chase the night away and not a speck of dirt in sight. Orderly. Rose began to relax.

One half of the central fire had some form of brick oven built over it and a gleaming copper vat had been let into the bricks. It was full of steaming water. Hanging over the other half of the fire from a chain attached to the roof ridge was a blackened cauldron. That too steamed gently. Ladles of varying sizes dangled from hooks on a wooden post, at the foot of which several wooden pails were stacked. Linen was airing on racks suspended from the ceiling. Exotic scents—jasmine, musk and sandalwood—

mingled with more homely ones of rosemary, soapwort and sage.

A young girl approached. Her gaze was open and friendly and as innocent as a newborn lamb's. 'Benedict? Benedict Silvester?' she asked. She looked to be about twelve years old. More of Rose's tension ebbed away.

'Soaz, it is good to see you.' Ben bent to kiss the girl's cheek.

The girl's gaze moved to Rose and back to Ben. 'You want a bath?'

'Please.'

Rose jabbed Ben in the ribs. '*Two* baths, Ben. Remember we're having *separate* baths.'

Ben's dark eyes danced. 'Oh, I was hoping to persuade you to scrub my back…'

'Ben…' With a scowl, Rose tried to free her hand, but he had it fast. 'I'm warning you…'

'Relax, *mignonne*. If two baths are what you want, two baths are what we shall have.' He grinned at the little girl and shrugged. 'Two, if you please. I have to let Rose have her way, else she loses her dimples.'

'Sir?'

'Yes, it is very sad, Soaz. I'm in love with her dimples, but whenever she is angered they go into hiding and I have the devil's own job to coax them out again.'

The girl Soaz seemed to be used to Ben and his ways, for she bit back a smile and gave him a little curtsy that Rose could see was deeply ironic. 'Yes, sir.' She turned to lead them towards the stalls. 'You'd like bath linens?'

'Please. Oh, and, Soaz?'

'Sir?'

'Since Rose won't attend me, could Barbe do the honours?'

Barbe? In an instant, a tight band of tension made itself felt about Rose's head. She had been wearing her veil far too long this day. *Barbe?* Yet another of his women, she supposed. But what had she expected from the notorious Benedict Silvester?

'Of course, sir.'

'And we would like neighbouring stalls if possible, and could you attend to Rose personally? She has been riding and she would enjoy a massage after her bath. Use some of your jasmine oil, that special blend.'

'As you wish.'

Thus it was that Rose found herself in the stall next to Ben's. There was room for a wooden bathtub and a bench strewn with so many cushions it resembled a couch. A couch. She chewed her lip. Where these massages must take place. She recalled that groan of pure pleasure when they had first entered the bathhouse. Did anything else, she wondered, take place on those benches? The presence of the girl Soaz would suggest not, but…

The curtain opened and closed behind Soaz, who dropped some white linens next to a silk cushion. The cushion was gold and edged with shiny red tassels that Countess Muriel would have coveted.

Soaz smiled. '*Madame* would like me to help her disrobe?'

'Oh. Yes, if you please,' Rose said, though she felt awkward. She had never had help undressing in her life.

'Better let her.' Ben's voice, with a distinct smile in its tone, came clearly through the cheesecloth curtain. Afraid he was watching her, Rose glanced suspiciously in his direction, but all she could see was the light from his bath stall filtering through the fabric. Two figures were silhouetted against it and it was no challenge to work out which was Ben as one of the figures was tall and had a distinct masculine shape, wide shoulders tapering to a narrow waist. Barbe seemed to be very curvy with a generous bosom. Hmm.

The two silhouettes became one and Rose swallowed. 'Oh, yes? Is Barbe undressing you?' An unnecessary question, since from the silhouettes she could already see that Barbe had her hands at Ben's waist and must be unbuckling his belt, but somehow the words were out before she could stop them.

'Of course.' His voice floated over the partition, relaxed and conversational. 'You may not know this, Rose, but it is customary in noble houses that when honoured guests bathe they are attended by the women of the house.'

'This is not a noble house!'

'No, but the same service is available. What can we poorer folk do but mimic our betters?'

'Oh.' There had been that teasing edge to his last comment, but Rose was frozen, fixated on the silhouettes in the next stall. Swallowing down bile, moved by an unpleasant emotion that she could not begin to name, she took a step towards him.

Soaz touched her arm just as she was about to tear aside the curtain. '*Madame?* You would attend him after all?'

Recalling herself, Rozenn shook her head and sank on to the cushion while Soaz unpinned her veil.

'We will wash your hair, *madame?*'

'Please.' When Soaz had loosened her hair, Rozenn stood and lifted her arms and had her gown unlaced for her as though she were a great lady. She felt utterly miserable.

'Little flower?'

'Mmm?' She kept her back firmly to that silhouette. Barbe must be removing his tunic… No…maybe she would be unwinding his leg bindings… No, *no*. She would not think about which piece of his clothing Barbe was removing, she would *not*.

'Best observe everything Soaz does,' Ben continued, 'if you truly wish to be the mistress of a knight's household. Sir Richard will expect you to be familiar with the customs.'

Deftly, Soaz drew Rozenn's gown over her head, and helped her out of her undergown. Rose blushed, for Per was the only person to have seen her naked and she had found even that profoundly embarrassing. However, Soaz had an easy smile, a gentle smile, which made everything seem quite natural. Calmly, the girl reached for a water jug.

'Your hair first, I think, *madame*.'

Nodding, Rozenn climbed into the bathtub. The water was warm and scented with jasmine. Ben remembered, he remembered how I love it, she caught herself thinking as she sank into the water and felt it lapping her breasts. She had to admit, the bath was heavenly for stiff limbs and aching muscles.

The drapery between her stall and Ben's billowed in a sudden draught. A door slammed, the lights on the other side flickered. She heard splashing—Ben climbing into his bathtub? She heard his groan of pleasure; she heard snatches of a conversation taking place in another part of the bathhouse.

She would not imagine Barbe pouring water

over Ben's hair in the same delightful way that Soaz was doing for her. She would not imagine Barbe massaging Ben's shoulders in the same way that Soaz was massaging hers. In any case, it was perfectly innocent.

Wasn't it?

Closing her eyes, Rozenn leaned back and surrendered to the sensation of Soaz rinsing her hair. She willed herself not to think about whatever was happening in the next stall. It was nothing to do with her. And then, by stages, she discovered it was possible to relax, particularly when she succeeded in focusing solely on the clever hands of the young girl in the Hennebont bathhouse.

Rozenn went to bed early. She had enjoyed the roast chicken and glazed onions that Irene had offered, she had enjoyed them very much. She had also enjoyed hearing Ben treat Irene's guests to his version of the epic of Roland and would have liked to linger, but when her head almost fell into her trencher for the third time, she realised it was time to retire. The riding had worn her out.

Pausing at the bottom of the stairs to compliment Irene on her cooking, she made her way to the bedchambers in the loft. Candles flickered in polished metal wallsconces, bouncing the light back at her. Ben's voice followed her up the stairs, comforting in its familiarity. She passed through the public bedchamber. Several bundles were laid out on the floor: a child's doll lay on one; a pair of shoes sat next to another—proof that other travellers had booked into the Bridge that night.

Rozenn closed the curtain that screened off the private chamber from the public area and opened her pack to pull out her nightshirt.

Ben's belongings were strewn over the boards. She stared, puzzled. It was not like Ben to be so untidy, but then he had probably been in a hurry. When they had returned from the bathhouse he had not had long to tune his lute ready for the performance. The instrument always took longer to tune when he was travelling; something about the motion of the horse, he had once told her, or perhaps changes in temperature or humidity.

Bearing in mind that Ben's singing was providing them with their board and lodging, Rose took a moment to reorder his things. The seam of one of his shirts was coming apart so she put it at her bedside to mend in the morning when the light was better. She folded his tunics and other shirts and stowed them in his pack; she rolled his spare leg bindings into a neat coil; she replaced his short-sword on the hook where she would swear he had hung it earlier…

A few minutes later, leaving a candle burning for

him, she was sinking into the great bed, sighing with delight at the softness of the mattress and the cool fragrance of clean, lavender-scented linen.

She must have dozed, for she awakened to the thought that the night sounds in Hennebont were different from the night sounds in Quimperlé. But then, she was no longer in the merchants' quarter of Hauteville. This was the first night that she could remember that she had not slept in Quimperlé.

Her eyes snapped open. Something was being dragged across the floor in the public chamber. Just another traveller, she told herself. A child called out, *'Maman!'*

A woman answered in low, soothing tones. There was another fretful murmur from the child and more motherly soothing. Rozenn tried willing herself back to sleep. It was just more travellers like herself, she repeated in her mind, but that little disturbance had upset her equilibrium. Earlier, she had been lulled into relaxation by the bath, and by Irene's roast chicken and the familiar cadence of Ben's voice. But none of those things could alter the fact that here she was, sleeping in a place that was alien to her.

Ivona was miles away; Mikaela was miles away; Adam was miles away.

Screwing her eyes shut, Rose tried to recapture

that pleasant feeling of sleepiness. But though the sound of the leopard's-head lute continued to filter up through the floorboards, her sleepiness had vanished as surely as morning mist burned away by the sun.

In the public bedchamber on the other side of the curtain, a man gave a soft laugh. A woman— the mother who had been soothing the child?— whispered back. The man laughed again, the woman giggled and there followed a rustling of clothing, of crisp linen sheets.

A grunt. A sigh. Heated breathing. Rozenn put her hand to her cheeks. She did not have to be in the next room to know what was about to happen.

She heard a bump. An, 'Oh, love, *yes!*' A gentle but regular thudding. The woman moaned, as though she were enjoying it.

No? Surely not in the public bedchamber?

Thank God that Ben is nearby, she thought. Imagine if I were alone on Ketill's ship in the shelter set aside for passengers and other travellers started to do…to do…*that* right next to her. Thank God for Ben. His presence in this inn makes this easier. He looks out for me. He *always* looks out for me, whenever he is with me, that is. Which is not often. She gnawed on her thumbnail. But when he *is* with me he always makes things easy for me; in fact, at times Ben takes great pains to please me—the costly jasmine in the bat-house…

Would Sir Richard do the same? She fiddled with the cross at her neck, but no answer sprang to mind. Sir Richard remained, for all they had talked together over meals at the inn, for all that he was one of her brother's greatest friends, a stranger. However, Rose did think that if she were to marry Sir Richard, he would be more reliable than Ben could ever be. Sir Richard would be able to spend more time with her, for a start. Certainly, knights had to give service to their overlords, but they also had manors to which they must return. A knight was bound to the land in ways that a minstrel never would be. Land represented security.

At that moment, the man on the other side of the curtain gave a shout of completion. The gentle, repetitive thudding stopped. The woman murmured and it was a loving sound, a sound that told Rozenn that the woman's husband had not hurt her. Which was very much to the good, for if every woman hated performing her marital duties the way Rozenn had hated it with Per…

Would she hate it with Sir Richard?

She started chewing on another nail. Sir Richard might expect her to enjoy it, but what if she was one of those women who could *never* enjoy it? There were such women—according to the girls doing their laundry by the river in Quimperlé. There were women who could never get an ounce of enjoyment out of a man, frigid women. Perhaps she was one.

Quick footsteps were approaching. Ben? Rozenn heard the drone of conversation; the clunk of spoons and knives on wooden plates; the clattering of pans. But the singing had ceased.

The curtain parted and Ben stepped into the room, leopard's-head lute in hand.

Rose lay motionless, her eyes half-closed as though she were drowsing, but she could see him clearly in the candlelight, tall and dark and heartbreakingly handsome. Where would he sleep?

Putting his lute into its bag and sliding it carefully under the bed, Ben glanced towards her and unbuckled his belt. Thus had Rose watched her husband Per as he had readied himself for bed. But then there had been dread in her watching, and a determination to be thought fast asleep in the vain hope that Per would leave her alone and not press his attentions on her.

It was different today. Rozenn could lie here in this bed that Duke Hoël used, she could watch Ben bedding himself down, even though she did not know where he would choose to lie, and she felt calm. There was no dread. Ben, wherever he might sleep, would never hurt her.

She opened her eyes and sat up. The question that had been nagging away in the back of her mind ever since they had arrived at the inn tumbled off her lips. 'Ben, where will you sleep? On the floor or in this bed?'

His eyes gleamed in the candlelight before those luxuriant dark lashes came down, shuttering his expression. 'Wherever you want me, *ma belle.*' He sent her an easy grin. 'Floor, bed—I have slept on far worse floors than this.'

She smiled. There, she should have known there would be no problem with Ben. Unlike Per, Ben considered her feelings.

He dragged off his tunic and shirt in one and she let herself watch the way the muscles of his shoulders moved. He is so well formed and he carries not an ounce of spare flesh, she thought, taking in the broad chest, sprinkled with dark hairs, hairs that arrowed down to the waist of his trousers. Ben wore fine clothes to impress his audience, but truly, he was impressive without them. With a lurch, it came to her that perhaps even the act of love itself might not be bad, with Ben. His person was attractive and she had enjoyed that kiss.

Would she enjoy Sir Richard's kiss? Would she enjoy the act of love with Sir Richard? Would it be love? Ben had asked her if she loved Sir

Richard; in her heart, Rose knew she did not. But perhaps she might learn…

Scowling, she thumped her pillow into shape and lay back while Ben finished undressing. He tossed his boots to one side, but when his gaze fell on his little heap of belongings, a sudden stillness in his body warned her that something was amiss. He padded over to her, a question in his eyes.

'Ben?'

He jerked his head in the direction of his pack. 'Rose, have you been through my belongings?' His voice was cold and hard.

'Only to tidy it, you left everything every which way.'

'I did?'

'Yes.'

His gaze became thoughtful. 'So you tidied it for me?'

'Yes. Ben, what's wrong?'

'Rose, if you please, I'd prefer it if you didn't root through my things.'

For a moment she could only stare, wounded that he should feel the need to say such a thing, and in such a tone, when all of their lives they had happily shared everything. She shrugged. 'My apologies.' Leaning over the side of the bed, she grabbed his torn shirt and tossed it at him. 'No doubt you will not wish me to mend this for you either.'

Catching the shirt, he spared it no more than a glance, but his expression gentled. 'You don't need to sew for me.'

Crossly, she dragged the sheet over her shoulders. 'Mend it yourself, then. Wanted to thank you for bringing me here, that's all.' To her horror her voice was thick with tears, and she knew, she just knew, that Ben's sharp ears would pick up on the intonation.

His gaze burned into her back. She heard him sigh and a sound that could only be a pallet being dragged out from under the bed.

'There's plenty of room in here,' she said gruffly, reaching behind her to pat the mattress. 'You may as well share with me, if you can bear the thought of it, that is.'

Another sigh. The pallet scraped as it was pushed back under the bed. The mattress shifted and dipped as he dropped down next to her. 'Thanks, *chérie*.' He stifled a yawn. 'I would appreciate a good night's sleep. We will be roughing it before we reach Adam's holding in Wessex.'

And then he must have pinched out the candle for the room went dark. It was a dark that was soft and warm and filled with murmurs and bumps and mutterings from people in the common sleeping chamber; with the stray burst of laughter from below; with the homely smell of woodsmoke.

'Irene let me come up early,' he said, easily, and she knew then that he would talk a while. Ben would not want to fall asleep with anger between them. In that they were alike.

'I wondered. I thought you had to sing for her guests until midnight, but it doesn't feel like midnight.'

'No. Irene is generous to let us have this room for the price of one epic.'

'She likes you.'

'Aye.'

At her back, Ben sighed and stirred. She caught the faint fragrance of sandalwood, which he must have used in the bathhouse when he had shaved.

'Rose?' He touched her shoulder.

Half-heartedly, she tried to shrug him off, but her heart leapt at his touch and his hand remained where it was, gentle, soothing. 'Mmm?'

'Don't sulk. Remember those dimples.'

'Idiot.' She rolled on to her back. 'It's black as pitch in here. You can't see my dimples.'

'But I know, Rose. I don't have to see you to know when they've gone into hiding. And I like it best when they're visible. Even in the dark.'

'Fool.' She rolled fully towards him, briefly touching her fingers to his.

'Am I forgiven?' he murmured.

'Aye.'

'That's good, because it's time for me to claim my reward…'

Her heartbeat speeded up. 'Reward?'

His thumb was caressing her shoulder through the thin fabric of her nightgown. It slid up to her ear and back down her neck, and left a trail of sensation in its wake.

'Mmm? Had you forgotten?'

'Y-yes.'

'Liar. Now, what was it we agreed? You would thank me for finding Jet in a manner of my own choosing. Was that not so?'

'Y-ye-yes.'

'Come here then, Rose.' The gentle pressure on her shoulder increased, drawing her towards the warmth of his body. 'I don't want you sewing for me, but I claim a kiss. As a good woman who always pays her debts, *you* must give *me* a kiss.'

Rose held back. 'Just a kiss?'

'Why, Rose, you think that the finding of Jet is worth more than that? No, I couldn't possibly accept more, that really would be dangerous.'

Her stomach gave a lurch. Didn't Ben want her? Not that she was offering herself to him, of course she was not, but he seemed to want every other woman on God's earth. Why not her? 'Dangerous?'

'Oh, yes.' His fingers were in her hair now,

loosening it, spreading it out down her back, following its length, stroking, stroking. He was so close his breath fanned her cheeks and she could smell the spices in the wine that he had been drinking. 'Far too dangerous. We shall stop at kissing.'

Chapter Ten

'We will?' Her heart ached. Ben was drawn to every woman on earth with a pulse, yet when it came to her…

'Certainly. Come here, little flower, give me my kiss.'

She moved her head. It was a small movement, an almost imperceptible movement, but it was enough to bring her lips into contact with his. She felt a distinct tingle. His hand continued its gentle stroking of her hair, but he made no attempt to draw her closer.

She put her lips more firmly against his, and waited. She felt him smile.

'*You* must kiss *me*, Rose.'

She gave him a small kiss, a chaste kiss, a kiss that was more of a peck than a kiss.

'Mmm,' he said. 'But not enough. Again. Properly.'

Face hot, and with a tightness in her stomach, Rose was thankful for the dark that shielded her from his eyes. She pressed closer and gave him another tiny peck of a kiss, another. And still Ben had not pulled her to him, there was just his hand on her hair, gently stroking, stroking, and his familiar scent filling her nostrils.

'Ben, please…' Giving an exasperated sigh, she reached for his head, pressing her lips firmly against his, boldly outlining his mouth with her tongue, painfully aware that he was not responding.

With a groan, he gathered her to his naked chest, holding her as tightly as she could wish. Her breasts were squashed against him and his mouth was moving softly in response to hers and he was kissing her, kissing her with lips *and* tongue. His hands were whispering over her body—up and down her back, her sides, her buttocks, and she was kissing him equally enthusiastically, and his breath was coming fast, as fast as hers, faster…

Her limbs were turning to water and, oh, the delight. The kiss on the marshes paled into insignificance. This was…this was… One could die of joy…and this was Ben… *Ben!*

Nothing like this had *ever* happened with Per.

Shaken, Rose pulled back, but now that Ben had joined in with the kissing, he didn't seem able to stop. He was nuzzling her neck, and she did not seem to be able to take her hands out of his hair either. It was soft, soft as silk and she could touch it for ever. And when she stroked the back of his neck where it was shortest, he moaned and gave a little shiver and she felt the shock of that slight shiver in her core.

Kissing Ben was a pleasure that was almost too painful to bear. And it was not over yet, for he was impatiently pushing her cross aside, pressing rows of kisses along her collar-bones, rolling over her, half-covering her with his body.

Rose tensed, waiting for the inevitable feeling of dread that must accompany the moment when she put herself so completely at the mercy of a man as to lie beneath him, but it simply was not there. On the contrary, Ben's weight was a burden she could happily bear. Her insides were melting as though he had entranced her and she had to steel herself not to caress and stroke his back and buttocks as he had been caressing hers. The feel of him, pressed hard and hot into her belly, did not repel her either. Rather, she had to grit her teeth to stop herself reaching for the ties of his trousers and…

'Ben!'

'More,' he murmured, nibbling at her earlobe. 'Don't stop.'

'Ben!' She tugged at his hair.

He lifted his head, pressing a last kiss to the opening at the neck of her nightgown. 'Mmm?'

'Dangerous, I think you said.'

His weight shifted to one side, but his leg still lay between hers and his hand was on her hip, caressing her. He drew in a shuddering breath. 'Did I say that?' His voice was husky.

'Yes.'

A sigh. 'Momentary burst of insanity.' He leaned his forehead against hers. 'Beautiful, more like.'

'Flatterer. But, Ben, we should sleep,' she said firmly, before he destroyed what was left of her will. 'We have a long ride tomorrow.'

'Sensible Rose.' He shifted away.

Her breathing was slowing, approaching normal, when he groaned and reached for her. 'Rose, at the least, I would hold you this night.'

At the least, I would hold you this night. She swallowed and it was hard to get the words out. 'Dangerous, but I trust you not to pounce.'

He gave a shaky laugh, but settled her head against his naked shoulder amenably enough. 'Pounce?'

'Per would pounce on me unexpectedly.'

'You did not like him pouncing?' he asked, toying with her hair, as she slid her hand around his waist.

'No.'

'I promise not to pounce.'

They fell quiet, but there were sounds in the bedchamber: the quietening of their breathing, the drone of a mosquito, the rustle of clothing and bedlinens in the public room. The public room— Rose almost gasped aloud when she realised that while she and Ben had been kissing she had been so enthralled that she had completely forgotten about listening ears on the other side of that curtain. Her behaviour was shameful.

Ben cleared his throat. 'It is hard though, Rose, because I want to pounce.'

'But you will not.'

'No.'

And it was odd, because although Rose knew that Ben was yet aroused, and although he had that notorious reputation, she believed him.

After that, though, sleep was elusive. Being in Ben's company must be affecting her, Rose decided, for she could not stop thinking about the act of love.

She was going to England to realise her ambitions to marry a knight, to marry Sir Richard. Adam's good friend and sponsor, she knew and liked him. Yet the more Rose thought about it, the less she could imagine the act of love with Sir Richard. In her present state of mind, she was far from ready even to contemplate it with him, never mind to actually do it.

Lifting her head from Ben's shoulder, wanting to read his expression, she peered through the dark, but it was absolute and she could see nothing, not even his profile.

Ben. She breathed in his scent. Spices, wine, the sandalwood from the bathhouse, Ben. How fortunate to have him as her travelling companion. She didn't mind kissing *him*. That kiss on the jetty in the marshes might have only been for show, but it had been the first real kiss that had not repulsed her. She sighed. To be honest, she *adored* kissing Ben. Tonight, the slightest, most subtle response from him had had her melting, practically melting, into the mattress. And when she had caressed his neck and he had groaned and shivered…she had been lost, *lost*.

Her head fell back. It must be part of his charm. Women of all ages and of all classes flocked to him—witness Irene here, little Soaz in the bathhouse, Barbe, Paola and her friends, Lady Alis, even the dour Countess Muriel… They all loved him. Ben had something that drew women to him like moths to a flame. Ben could bring out the wanton in a stone.

Perhaps with Ben the act of love would be a joy.
Her breath caught.
Perhaps Ben could teach you how to enjoy it. He would not mind. Ben cares for you—

As a brother, Ben cares for me as a *brother—*
How brotherly was that kiss you have just shared?
Rose chewed the inside of her mouth.

Think about it. You know how Ben enjoys women—he can never have enough of them. Sexual savoir-faire oozes from his every pore. Why not put that ill-gotten knowledge to some use? Let him teach you to enjoy the act of love. Sir Richard would not want a frigid wife. Ben can teach you to be the kind of woman that Sir Richard would want, and he would enjoy teaching you. You could give him the carnal love that all men hanker for and he would have no worries about being constrained to marry you afterwards.

She could ask Ben for help. She could get him to teach her. In this, Ben would be a good teacher.

Ask him.

But…

'Rose, are you all right?'

'Mmm, just thinking.'

A warm hand ruffled her hair; it slid down her neck and her arm, down to her hand. He linked his fingers with hers.

'If you want anything, I'm here,' he said, on a yawn.

Rose opened her mouth, but the words stuck in her throat. It was so confusing. She settled against the satin warmth of his shoulder and listened as the rhythm of his breathing gradually softened. She knew the moment when sleep took him, because the hold on her fingers slackened.

Ben could help you be a good lover. Ben could help you...

Tomorrow. She would ask him tomorrow, if her thoughts had untangled by then. Her affection for Ben had always been sisterly, but she was not actually his sister in blood. But still, doubts remained.

Coward.

Lying in bed listening to a peel of church bells, Ben winced at the unmelodious blurring of the top note and opened his eyes. That bell definitely needed to be re-cast, it was cracked. The strength in the spears of light slanting through the window slit told him that dawn had passed some time ago—they had overslept.

They. Rose was in the bed next to him. He could feel her warmth, he could hear her breathing. Inhaling her scent, he was startled to find himself wishing that he could inhabit this moment for ever. She was sleeping in her habitual pose, curled on her side a mere handspan away. Her hair, which he vaguely remembered loosening in the night, trailed across the white linens like brown silk, and one strand curled across his chest as though it were embracing him. The tie at the neck of her nightgown was loose—had he done that too?— and the fabric had slipped, baring a shoulder that seemed to him to be begging for a kiss. He could see the tempting shadow of her cleavage and had to fight the urge to gather her into his arms.

Dangerous indeed.

Shifting his head, he pressed a delicate kiss to her shoulder and inhaled deeply for the second time. Hell, he was hard as a rock. He only had to look at the girl and he was rigid with desire. Lust for Rose was a complication he had not planned on and one this journey could do without. This latest commission for the Duke was the most important of his life and he wasn't about to foul it up. In any case, he had long since buried any deep longings for Rose. Hadn't he?

Merde. If he wasn't careful, this journey was going to be more pain than pleasure.

Fortunately Ben had other things to think about. Shaking his head, he disentangled himself from Rozenn's hair and rolled away. He groped under the bed to ensure that his lute was lying where he had put it. It was. He lay back against his pillow— not prolonging the moment for more than a second or two—put his hands behind his head, and gazed blindly at the rafters.

'Rose,' he muttered under his breath, vaguely irritated that his mind insisted on giving her so much attention, when in all honour he should be concentrating on working out the safest route to his *rendezvous*. 'Rose who does not like to be pounced on, Rose who has her heart set on Sir Richard.' He drew his brows together.

She had fallen in with his plan so eagerly. He should not complain at that, it had been his idea. Nevertheless, his brow darkened. Naturally, Rose would not in truth marry Sir Richard, particularly since the man did not have the first idea that his name was being used to provide Ben with cover for the journey.

Hell. Ben would feel happier if Rose had *not* embraced the thought of marriage to Sir Richard quite so easily. Not on his own account, of course not. Marriage was not for him. He had realised that years ago, when he had put thoughts of settling down with her to one side. The Duke's special envoy could not put down roots and therefore he could not marry. And, in any case, Rose had chosen Per. Her choice had been a clear indication of her need for a settled life. As for himself, he had been mad even to consider marriage, especially with Rose.

And now she wants Sir Richard and, you, Benedict Silvester, have yourself to blame for that.

And when she discovers that Sir Richard has no intention of marrying her?

And when she discovers that *you* are to blame for misleading her and dragging her to England? *Merde.*

Carefully pushing back the sheet, Ben got out of bed, but it was not so easy to get Rose out of his mind. Last night, she had enjoyed his touch. It might have driven him mad to have held back as he had, but it had been worth it.

Lord, this would *not* do. Last night, someone had been through his belongings. It might just have been thieves, thinking to steal his nightly takings, but he could not be certain. He must think. It would not do to put Rose in danger….

Hurriedly washing in the ewer on the stand, Ben dressed and slung his lute over his shoulder. Then he slipped through the curtain, leaving Rose to her dreams.

Coming swiftly down the stairs into the tavern proper, Ben scanned the room. Last night, a down-at-heel knight with a scarred face had come in, accompanied by his squire. Judging from the state of the knight's arms, he was landless and as such might be glad of the chance to earn a penny or two….

Yes, they were at that trestle by the window. Irene was sharing a bench with the squire, a lad with some pretensions to fashion for his dark hair, like Ben's, was cut in the Norman style. Before them stood a jug of wine, half a loaf of bread, a pat of butter and some cheese. A battered white shield with black chevrons lay on its side against the wall, along with a couple of saddlebags and the knight's chain-mail and helm.

Casually, Ben wandered over, but one glance at Irene made the hairs on his neck stand up.

Something was wrong. Irene was not, as he had first assumed, breaking her fast with the knight and his squire. The bowl at her elbow was a washbowl, and she had twisted her veil back over her shoulders to keep it out of the way. Face filled with concern, she was dipping a bloodstained cloth into the water. She wrung out the cloth and dabbed gingerly at the squire's face. It came away covered in more blood.

The squire—a gangly youth of about thirteen— had an ugly cut on his cheekbone and a bloodied nose which fortunately did not appear to be broken. His knuckles were raw and his green tunic—the colour was almost an exact match for one of Ben's—had been ripped from shoulder to waist. His undershirt was torn.

The knight—who was watching Irene like a hawk—was wearing a thunderous scowl, which only made the livid scar across his cheekbone more prominent. For a moment, Ben wondered if the knight had given his squire one buffeting too many, but a more searching glance revealed that his anger was not directed at the boy.

Catching his eye, Ben gave him a sympathetic nod and joined them. Too many knights were careless with their squires, and under the guise of discipline beat them mercilessly for the smallest transgression. Not this one apparently.

'What's going on?' Ben asked, hoping that the fact that these two had listened to his singing for a couple of hours last evening would gain him admittance into their circle. He reached for some bread.

The knight clenched his fists. 'Bastards,' he muttered. 'Bastards lay in wait for Gien at the stables.'

Wincing, the squire jerked away from Irene. His skin was milk-white and against it his hair stood out, a dark crest above pale eyes, eyes that were so light as to be almost translucent. They were watching Irene warily. 'My thanks, mistress, but it is not that bad. I do not think I need stitching.'

Shaking her head, Irene persisted. 'Let me be the judge of that, Gien. You may be right, but I cannot tell until I have cleaned away the blood. Hold still.' She smiled. 'You have survived being set upon by three men—surely you are not afraid of my little washcloth? Lift your head.'

With a shrug, the squire did as he was told.

Under his chin was a thin red line—a knife had been held to his throat.

'You are lucky to be alive by the look of it,' Ben said. 'Thieves, was it?'

'Bastards,' the knight muttered.

'It is me who is the bastard, Eudo,' the squire said, in a bitter voice.

It was not lost on Ben that Gien had not used the knight's title when addressing him. This could mean one of two things: either the boy was deliberately trying to anger his master, or the affection between them was deep. Ben leaned towards the latter explanation.

Gien was indicating the purse strings at his belt. They had been cut. 'As you say, thieves.'

That slash in the boy's green tunic was long. Ben narrowed his eyes. 'Did you lose much?'

'Didn't have much to lose,' Gien mumbled, flushing. 'An old dagger given to me by my father, a silver ring of my mother's….' for an instant his voice wavered, then he had himself in hand again '…and a couple of deniers. Hardly worth their while, I should have thought.'

'They lay in wait, you say?' Ben was conscious of a distinct prickle of unease. Last night someone had gone through his pack. It might be a gang of thieves, it might be something more sinister. 'They were after you personally?'

'No, no,' the squire said. 'It was my ill fortune to be in the wrong place at the wrong time. I would wager they hoped for bigger fish than me.'

'Would that I had gone,' the knight said, fiercely. 'I would have filleted them top to tail.' Clumsily, he reached across the trestle and patted Gien's arm. 'We'll replace your things at the market, lad.' He glared around the room, daring anyone present to mock him because he, a knight, had been seen expressing sympathy to his squire. He removed his hand from Gien's arm.

Irene resumed her gentle bathing of Gien's face. 'This is not too bad. You will have bruises, but the scars will fade.'

'No need for stitching?' Gien asked.

Irene smiled. 'No, lad, no need. You won't frighten the crows yet a while, though—' she lifted a thin, teasing eyebrow at the knight's scarred countenance '—that time may soon come if you insist in remaining on Sir Eudo's company.'

The knight grunted and helped himself to a generous portion of cheese. 'Boy chose to serve me. Told him I'd done without a squire for so long, I wouldn't know what to do with one. Told him I couldn't afford to mount him properly. Boy's like a burr, though, can't shake him off.'

'Where are you bound, sir?' Ben asked, reluctant to voice the question he really wanted answering in case it should offend—namely, was the knight currently bound in service to an overlord, or was he, as Ben had surmised, a landless knight in search of employment?

'Ben!' Rose was weaving her way through the tables towards them. Green gown, black silk girdle, cream veil, and pretty as a princess. As she drew near everything else seemed to fade into the background. Bobbing a swift curtsy at Sir Eudo, she slid on to the end of the bench next to Ben. He could feel the warmth of her thigh next to his. 'Good morning, mistress,' she said, smiling at Irene.

'Good morning.'

Rose nudged Ben with her elbow and whispered, 'You should have woken me. I thought we intended setting out at dawn.' Leaning forwards, she gave the knight a direct look and reached past Ben to offer him her hand. 'How do you do, sir? My name is Rozenn Kerber.'

'Eudo Bélon.' The knight briefly touched his fingers to hers. 'And this is my squire, Gien.'

'*Holà,* Gien.' Her eyes flickered unobtrusively from the hurts on Gien's face, to Irene, to the washcloth in Irene's hand, absorbing everything in her quick way.

'*Holà,* Mistress Kerber.'

'While we are at it,' Ben said. 'My name is—'

'Benedict Silvester, yes, we know. Irene

reminded us last eve,' Eudo said. 'But we have heard you play before.'

'Oh? Where was that?'

'Rennes, last Michaelmas. We go there now.'

'Rennes,' Ben said, hiding his delight at this discovery. 'What a lucky chance, we go there too, via Josselin. Do you leave this morning?'

'Aye.' Sir Eudo glanced doubtfully at Gien. 'If you are right to ride, boy?'

'I'm well enough, just a little bruised.'

Ben smiled. 'Let us go together.' Normally, news that thieves were at large would not trouble him overmuch; he had also dealt with the Duke's enemies perfectly satisfactorily on his own. But Rose's presence changed matters. Ben would breathe more easily if they travelled with an escort.

'Yes, let's,' Rose said as Ben slid the bread platter towards her. 'It will be good to have company. But you will have to be very patient with me, I'm afraid.'

Eudo frowned. 'How so?'

'My legs have seized up.' Grimacing, she smiled at Gien. 'I am learning to ride, you see, and as yet I am not very good at it. This morning I can hardly walk. So I am very sorry, but you will have to go at my pace.'

At her words, some of the worry seemed to leave Sir Eudo's expression, and Ben knew that he and Rose had their escort to Rennes.

* * *

The road to Josselin was densely wooded and the leaf canopy thick. The sun highlighted a patch of beech mast here, a tangle of briars there. They rode the entire day in pairs, with Ben and the knight riding out in front and Gien and Rose bringing up the rear. Sir Eudo had removed his helmet and it swung by a strap from the pommel of his saddle, bouncing slightly with the motion of his grey. His elongated shield hung on his left.

Squinting over his shoulder, Ben was relieved to see Rose managing very well without the leading rein. He had been keeping a discreet eye on her, and throughout the day she and Gien had been chatting like old friends. The words 'Fulford in Wessex' and 'Adam' and 'Cecily' had come to him over the soft thud of the horses' hoofs and the jingle of bits.

Gien was a pleasant boy with an easy manner about him, and Ben found himself grimacing as he wondered if Rose would be encouraged to reveal her marriage ambitions. He sighed—was it possible Rose might have considered this journey without the lure of marriage to Sir Richard? Perhaps the lure of life with Adam at his new holding in Wessex would have been lure enough? He had made a grave lapse of judgement when he had raised her hopes of marrying Sir Richard, and he could only pray that he could set it right.

'Pretty girl, your Rozenn,' Eudo said.

Ben stared. 'Rose? She's not mine.'

Sir Eudo's eyes were sympathetic. 'But you want her to be?'

Firmly, Ben shook his head. 'I've no ambitions for settling down.'

Eudo regarded him thoughtfully. 'She knows this?'

'Rose knows me better than anyone. We have been friends since childhood. No, sir, you've read us wrong. I am a lute-player, it is in my blood. Rose, on the other hand, has ambitions for hearth and home.' He shrugged. 'A minstrel is not in a position to offer her such. She wants a knight.'

Eudo gave a self-deprecating grimace. 'Not all knights have land, lad.'

'The one she has in mind has vast acres.' The story of how Rose had been abandoned as a baby was on the tip of Ben's tongue, but it occurred to him that Rose was starting a new life, and was anxious to leave her past behind, so he bit back the words. He could only hope that she would not discard him along with the rest of her past when she discovered how he had misled her.

'Eudo?' Gien's voice had both Eudo and Ben reining in.

'Aye?'

'Do we reach Josselin tonight?'

'No, tonight we sleep under the stars.'

Rose tucked a strand of hair beneath her veil and looked about them with wide, anxious eyes. She was leaning forwards, clinging to the pommel of her saddle as she had done on the previous day. In fact, she had such a poor seat that Ben knew that she must be saddle-sore and was nearing the end of her limits.

'No, no,' she said. 'Ben will know of a reputable inn nearby. You do, don't you?'

'Sorry, *chérie,* not unless you can keep going for another two hours or so.'

She groaned and, waving Gien past him, Ben reached for her reins. 'But there is a good spot for a camp a short way ahead.'

'Wh-what about wolves? Aren't there wolves in these woods?'

Wolves *had* been sighted hereabouts, as well as wild boar. There had even been tales about bears; of the three, Ben would far rather face wolves, but he was not about to mention the other wild animals. In any case, he was far more concerned that they might be being followed.

Another party had been riding out of Hennebont that morning but, having lost sight of them in the market square, Ben was not certain which road they had taken. They could not have taken the Josselin road, though, for, if they had, surely they would have overtaken them?

Aloud, he said, 'Rose, we will build a fire—wolves fear fire.'

'They do?'

'Yes, really. There's water ahead to wash in, and we can make you a shelter. You will be as snug as you were last night.'

Rose's look named him a liar, but she made no further protest and after a moment Ben kicked Piper back into a walk and they trailed after Eudo and Gien.

A jay broke cover and flew across their path. Piper danced sideways. 'Steady, boy,' he said, while he searched in his mind for a story that would lift the tiredness from around those beautiful eyes.

Chapter Eleven

'Expensive horse you have there, Benedict,' Eudo said. With a grunt, the knight heaved the high-backed saddle from his big-boned grey and dropped it to the ground.

They had chosen a small clearing in a hazel copse just off the road and were about to make camp. As Ben had promised, there was a stream, plenty of dry kindling with which to start a fire, and the hazel bushes could be used for a makeshift shelter. Ben always carried a couple of stitched hides with him and could fashion a tent of sorts in no time.

'Worth a king's ransom, I should say,' Eudo went on. 'Gift, was he?'

Ben gave him a sharp look. 'Piper is exceptional,' he agreed, wondering if Eudo imagined he had stolen him. 'Duke Hoël chose him for me when my previous horse became too old for the road.'

Eudo let out a low whistle. 'You must have played a damn fine tune, to earn such a reward.'

Under the pretence of loosening Piper's girth, Ben turned his back on his companion—partly to conceal his expression and partly to eye the road along which they had come. 'Several, actually,' he said, careful to keep his voice conversational. 'At the turn of last year Duke Hoël put me in charge of the entertainments at his Christmas court. Got in tumblers, dancers, jugglers…you name it, the Duke had to have it. Kept me run off my feet from Christmas Eve until well after the Epiphany.'

The empty highway made Ben uneasy. Instinct was telling him that the other travellers had been bound for Josselin too. So where the devil were they? Their own party had been going at such a slow pace they should have been overtaken. Unless the others were deliberately concealing themselves—and why should they do that? Of course, they might have been taking another route, but Ben did not think so….

Twilight found the four of them sitting in the clearing around the embers of their fire. Ben was strumming softly, dark head bent over his lute; Eudo and Gien sat on the other side, picking over the bones of a couple of trout that Gien had caught. It promised to be a warm night.

With her belly full of fish—Rozenn had baked them in leaves—and the bread and apricots and fresh white cheese she had bought at the market in Hennebont, Rozenn's mood had lifted and she felt more relaxed than she could have imagined. A week ago she would not have believed it possible, but here she was, miles away from civilisation, about to spend the night in a wood with Ben and two strangers, and she really did feel perfectly content.

Wrapping her arms about her knees, she tipped back her head and looked up at the sky. The branches and leaves made a dark pattern through which she could see the stars. It would make a good design for an embroidered coverlet, she thought, dark stems of branches criss-crossing a mid-blue fabric with white stars peeping through like flowers…

'It doesn't look as though it will rain,' she said.

The firelight flashed on the varnished surface of the leopard's-head lute. 'No, no rain tonight,' Ben said.

Rising, Rose went to inspect the tent. It stood a little to one side of the clearing and Ben had made it, for her apparently, by bending several young hazel branches together and tying them fast. Then he had slung a couple of hides over the frame and secured them with rope and pegs.

Crawling inside, Rose pushed experimentally at the sides. Given that Ben had put it up so swiftly, it seemed sound and it would keep any rain off. But whether it would keep out wolves, she had no idea. No, she would *not* think about wolves or she would never sleep.

When she crawled out again, Eudo and Gien had vanished. Ben lifted his head, fingers moving lightly over the lute strings. 'It meets with *madame*'s approval?'

'Yes, thank you.' Did Ben intend to share the tent with her, or was he planning to sleep under the stars with their companions? Hoping he would sleep with her, but too shy to ask, Rose dragged her pack to the tent entrance. 'Where are Eudo and Gien?'

'Washing.'

Fumbling in her pack, Rose found her comb and settled herself cross-legged on her cloak. Under cover of the gathering night she watched as Ben filled the glade with music—a gentle floaty folk tune she had heard many times. His high cheekbones were highlighted by the fire, and his eyes, always dark, seemed full of mystery.

Absently, she ran the pad of her thumb along the tines of her comb. As was his habit, Ben had pushed the sleeves of his tunic up so they did not tangle with the lute strings, and the fingers of his right hand moved deftly over the soundboard, plucking, strumming, while the fingers of his left slid up and down the frets on the neck. Music streamed out of him, like an endless river. It had always been so. Ben and his music, he simply could not stop. Tonight Ben was not being paid, yet he played on. He would be a minstrel to his dying day.

As Rose regarded his downbent head and the naked skin at the nape of his neck, his fringe flopped forwards and something within her twisted. It felt like yearning, but surely it was too painful for that? It felt like…

If only Ben were a knight, she thought, I would far rather marry Ben than Sir Richard who, pleasant thought he is, remains an acquaintance. What would it be like to be Ben's wife, to be on the receiving end of all that charm day after day…?

It would be bliss.

Even though he is such a flirt, even though he would never *settle?*

Yes, perhaps with Ben, even the so-called act of love might not be unpleasant. Rozenn could hear echoes of the Quimperlé washerwomen as they beat their laundry against the rocks in the river and boasted of their husbands' prowess; she could hear the soft murmuring of the woman at the Bridge last night….and…her cheeks burned as she recalled the way that she had responded to Ben's caresses.

No! Be practical. Think about the discomforts of a life with Ben, remember the uncertainties. She would never know where she was going to lay her head from one day to the next. No, the minstrel's life was *not* for her.

She wanted a house she could call her own, one with a small orchard perhaps, and maybe even a herb garden… She wanted neighbours who would grow old alongside her, she wanted friends…

You had many of those things in Quimperlé, a little voice said, *yet you left them behind.*

Yes, but Sir Richard… Rose shivered. She did not want to think about Sir Richard.

At that moment the last chord of the folk tune faded. 'You are ready for sleep?' Ben asked.

'I… Yes.'

Sliding the lute into its bag Ben came over with it, as Gien and Eudo were returning from the river. Squatting on his haunches, Ben relieved her of her comb. 'Allow me.'

Eudo glanced across the fire at them, cleared his throat and shifted farther away. Motioning Gien to do the same, he shook out his blanket and settled himself for sleep.

Biting her lip, Rose glanced at Ben, who said nothing, but tugged at her so she ended up sitting with her back to the warmth of his body. His fingers moved gently in her hair, fanning it out, spreading it over her shoulders. Delicately, he began to comb and for a couple of minutes there was silence in the clearing but for the crackling of the fire and the rustling of the breeze in the hazels. Rose relaxed and leaned into him, enjoying the feeling of his fingers as they lightly touched her neck, her shoulders, her arms.

He smoothed her hair out to its full length, carefully, as though it were the costliest of silks. His breath caressed her neck. She felt a soft touch—a kiss?—at the neck of her gown, and abruptly her comb was tossed aside and his arms slid round her, hugging her tight against him.

Another kiss. Yes, it was indeed kisses Ben was pressing to the nape of her neck. A realisation that had something, an indefinable emotion that twisted her insides, tightening into a dull ache. Want. She wanted him.

'Rose…' Ben's whisper was a husky reminder of the previous night '…is something amiss?'

As she leaned back against him, her hands were covering his before she had even thought. 'Ben, I… I…'

'Hmm?'

'Th-there is something I would ask of you, but…'

'Ask away.'

Throat dry, she hesitated. Across the clearing, on

the other side of the fire, Eudo and Gien seemed to be fast asleep; at least they were lying with their backs to them. Ben must have sensed her looking in their direction, for he came to his knees and, with his hands on her hips, guided her into the privacy of the tent.

'Ask away.'

'I… I…' Sitting back on her heels, Rose covered her face in her hands and shook her head. She could not ask, not even with Ben, it was simply too wanton. Even he would think badly of her. 'Nothing.'

'Rose…'

'Nothing, Ben, except…'

'Yes?'

She reached for his hand. 'You will stay close?'

'Within arm's reach,' he said, a distinct smile in his voice. He pressed a kiss to her nose. 'Or closer, as you command.'

He made to turn away, but she clung to his wrist. 'Oh, Ben, how I wish *you* were a knight.'

For the space of a heartbeat, he did not reply. Then, lightly, 'I am what I am, little flower. But if you wish, I can pretend.'

'Pretend? How so?'

His arms slid round her waist, pulling her up and drawing her close, so they were kneeling breast to breast. 'Tonight, this tent will become my pavilion, I am a knight at tourney and you are my lady fair.'

She had to laugh. 'Ben, are you never serious?'

'Serious? Me?' As he laughed alongside her, Rose realised that she could ask him and not be ashamed, and this knowledge was so large there was no room for any thought but one. This was Ben, she could ask him anything. Ben would *never* turn his back on her, Ben would *never* be cruel.

'Ben, there is a fault in me…'

His hand came up and stroked her cheek. 'A fault? In Rozenn Kerber? In the most beautiful, most talented seamstress in the Duchy? In the most organised woman in Christendom, who not only pays off every last penny of her husband's debts, but also takes in reprobate minstrels and gives them houseroom whenever they need it? You have a fault? I am so devastated to hear this that I wonder if I should permit our acquaintance to continue.'

She held his hand to her cheek and burst into speech before she had time to change her mind. 'Ben, stop fooling for a moment and *listen*. Of course I have faults, many of them, but the one I refer to concerns… It concerns the marriage bed.'

His fingers were busily weaving with hers, but at her words they froze. In the dim light their eyes met. 'Go on.'

Rose swallowed. 'It… I… I cannot like what happens in the marriage bed, and I wondered if you could…if you would…help me.'

'Help you?'

A swift sidelong glance told her that he was startled, perhaps even stunned by what she had said. She hauled in a breath. 'Yes, yes. You can help me. I know it would work with you.'

His face had softened, his eyes had darkened, but the light was almost gone from the tent and his next words proved he had not understood what she was asking.

'It would work…?'

'Yes, Ben, it would.' She hauled in another breath. 'I like your kisses, I like your touch.'

His mouth edged up at the corner and, pulling her closer so their bellies were pressed one to another, he looked at her mouth. 'Much thanks, little flower.'

'Yes, yes, I do.' This was deeply embarrassing. Her cheeks were on fire, her heart was pounding, but she ploughed on. 'So you see, Ben, I was hoping you would help me overcome my aversion to…to the carnal acts required by marriage.'

His eyes narrowed. 'The carnal acts required by marriage? If by that you mean making love, Rose, why don't you say?'

'Because my experience has not been good,' she admitted, staring fixedly at the neck of his tunic. 'I… I cannot think of it as making love.'

Silence.

He tipped her head up and peered into her eyes. 'Per? It was *never* good?'

She shook her head. 'No.'

'Not even once?'

'No. But the fault is in me, Ben.'

Ben swore. 'In you? I doubt it, *chérie*. Did the man even try to please you?'

'Please me? How would doing…*that* with him please me? In any case I am too small. He told me so, and each time it hurt, so I know he was right.'

'Dear God! Rose, when a man and a woman lo…desire each other in the right way, it should *not* hurt!'

'Even when the woman is small?'

'Even then.' His voice was warm and affectionate. 'Rose, there is no fault in you. If fault there was, it was in your husband, who did not take care with you.' He slid a hand round her neck and, bringing his lips to hers, gave her a sweet, almost chaste, kiss. 'I *knew* you had secrets you were keeping from me, and am glad that you have confessed them.'

'You are the only person I could tell. You will help me?'

His dark lashes lowered, briefly shielding his expression. 'Help you? Of course, *mignonne*. I am, as always, your devoted servant. But first I must understand one thing…'

'Yes?'

'Remind me why, exactly, you want us to do this, lest I am in danger of forgetting.'

'Because you are the only person who can help me overcome my aversion? So that when Sir Richard and I—'

'Sir Richard,' he repeated, slowly. She thought he bit his lip. He looked down at her for a long moment, his head and his broad shoulders no more than a shadowy shape against a darkening back-cloth. 'I see. Very well, I will do my utmost to help.'

Reaching up, Rose drew his head down and pressed a shy kiss to his mouth. Her fingers lingered at the nape of his neck. 'Thank you, best of friends.'

'There is, however, a caveat…'

'Yes?'

'I will do my best to…overcome your aversion, as you put it, Rose, but we must take care that we do not create a child.'

Rose blinked.

'Think. There can be no issue, little flower. No knight would want a wife who is carrying another's child, and Sir Richard will be no exception.' His voice softened and he stroked her cheek lightly with one finger. 'I think it would be best if we avoided *complete* union.'

Rose felt her jaw drop. Could this be Benedict

Silvester urging *her* to caution? The minstrel who openly admitted that he worked hard to maintain his notoriety? Ben must have tumbled more girls than there were stars in the sky above this clearing, but *he* was urging *her* to caution? 'You? You tell me this?'

'Indeed.' His voice was laced with laughter. 'I fear in this one small matter, I must disappoint you.'

Small matter? And he was right, may the devil blast him, she *was* disappointed. She had the feeling that he might be the only man in the world who she would permit…but, no, for her pride's sake she could never admit as much. In any case, she ought not, in all conscience, let Ben love her fully if she really intended to marry Sir Richard.

She huffed out a breath.

'You are in agreement, *ma belle?*'

'Y-yes, I am in agreement. It is just that your principles startled me.'

He bowed his head. 'As ever, I thank you for your good opinion. I see it has not changed.' His tone was dry, and it shamed her.

Wincing, she pressed an apologetic kiss to his cheek. 'I am sorry, Ben, it was just I found your…delicacy in this area…unexpected.'

He pulled back; and if Ben had had dimples, she knew that they would have vanished, for she sensed him scowling down at her. 'Rose, I'll have you know I would never bring an unwanted child into this world, *never.*'

He sounded so definite, as passionate as a preacher. The darkness was almost complete, but Rose could just make out his silhouette. With a jolt, she realised that Ben felt this way because of *her,* because he misliked the thought of any child of his being abandoned by a roadside tavern as she had been abandoned in Hauteville.

Her heart turned over. 'I am right glad to hear it. And I… I agree to your terms, sir. Everything but…but *that.*' She forced a laugh, to cover the fact that she had actually been moved to her marrow to learn that Ben took care with his women. 'In any case, it is probably just as well. I doubt I could like the *full* act with anyone, even with you.'

He caught her by the waist. 'Be careful, Lady Rozenn, that sounds like a challenge, and if I am to pretend to be your loving knight, you must know that knights can never resist a challenge.'

'No?'

'No.'

Ben lowered his head and nuzzled her cheek, her temple. Smoothing her hair down her back, he held her to him while his teeth nipped gently at her earlobe.

She could feel that he was aroused, but that

knowledge did not alarm her as it had with Per. With a slow warmth curling in her belly, she leaned into him, offering him her neck. Another gentle nip. Another. His breath was warm in her ear, on her cheek. Their lips met and her mind emptied of everything but him.

'Ben,' she murmured. 'Ben.'

He drew back. 'My lady?'

'Hmm?' Blindly she wound her arms round his neck and offered him her lips again, and again they kissed, and again the world was Ben and only Ben. She was running her fingertips up and down over the nape of his neck, ruffling that short hair, and he made that small sound, part pleasure, part pain, that had her legs turning to water, so that she tumbled on to a blanket spread out on the groundsheet.

He lay half over her, kissing her collar-bones through the opening at the front of her gown and then he lifted his head and cleared his throat. 'Ready for more, Lady Fair?'

'Yes, oh, yes.' She was hanging on to his neck, chasing his lips with hers, but he did not let her catch them.

'Good. But listen, *chérie*. If I really were a knight and you were my lady, I would not permit you to wear so many clothes in our bed.'

'No?'

'Certainly not. So first…'

And then his hands were at her girdle, fumbling with the knot, as he finally allowed her to capture his mouth.

'Ben.' She sighed on a note of pure pleasure. 'Ben.'

He was taking his time over the girdle, perhaps she should help him…but, no, he had it free, was dragging it away, tossing it aside.

'And now, my lady…' his voice was low in her ear, seductive '…if I were your knight, at this point I would tell you how much I love you.'

Her heart twisted, as if it believed him, as if it loved him back. 'You would?'

A hand slid on to her breast, and instinctively she arched towards him, wanting to know his touch without the restrictions imposed by her gown and shift. Wanting to caress his naked chest.

'I would tell you that the rose is always more beautiful than the lily,' he said, pressing tiny kisses on to her lips, kisses that made her drag his head to hers to keep him close.

'Roses have thorns,' she managed, between kisses.

'So they do, Rose, so they do.' His thumb moved once, twice over her breast and her nipples felt heavy, aching for more contact. 'I would tell you that you are the sun to me, you are my life.'

She gave a little laugh. 'Ben, you betray your true calling. No knight ever used such flowery phrases.'

'This one does,' he said with a sigh, as experimentally, he moved his hand over her breast, head close as though trying to see her reaction.

Rose groaned.

'You like that?'

'Yes.'

'That is good, Rose. Because if I were your knight, I would think it was time to remove your gown.' Sliding his hand down over her hips, he found the hem and tugged. 'Come on, little flower,' he said, a new breathless note in his voice. 'Sit up, your knight would have this off.'

Obediently, Rose sat.

'And your shift,' he said, 'that may as well come off too.'

'M-must it?' she said, overcome with sudden shyness.

'Your knight commands it.' He touched the tip of her nose. 'Don't worry, *ma belle,* it is pitch-dark in here. Your knight cannot see a thing.'

Chapter Twelve

'Think of Sir Richard if it helps,' Ben said.

'Very well.' Rose's throat was dry. How on earth was she to conjure Sir Richard when it was Ben's voice that was murmuring so seductively in her ears, and Ben's musician's fingers that were melting her bones to wax?

Meekly she submitted while he dragged her gown and shift over her head and laid her gently on the blanket. So very different to Per, she thought. Ben touches me as if I were the most precious thing in his world. But then, he has had much practice at this. He has made it his life's work to learn how to pleasure a woman.

Sir Richard? It was Ben who was causing the ache to build inside her, it was Ben whose skin she burned to touch. There was tension in her, but its cause was desire, not fear.

'Ben,' she murmured, and was hard put to recognise her own voice, it was hoarse with need.

'Little flower.' He lay beside her, stroking her cheek and drawing her hair over her shoulder in one long, caressing movement that took in her breast. He pressed a brief, oh so brief, kiss to her lips that had her about to object, but then his head was at her breast, pushing her hair aside, and the touch of his lips and tongue had her gasp out loud.

He lifted his head. 'All right, Rose?'

Swallowing, beyond speech, she nodded and urged his head back.

His hand was running up and down her side, leaving fire in its wake. Hot, so hot. It was as though he were branding her, making her his for eternity. And now he had her legs apart, was gently touching here—there—in a way that Per had never… It was too much, it was…

'Oh, Ben…' As sensation ripped through her, and she found herself pulsing and throbbing all over, she caught his wrist. 'Stop, please!'

'Stop? Are you certain?'

'Y-yes. N-no. More. Do it again, please.'

He gave a shaky laugh and then he gave her more. Despite all she had heard by the river at Quimperlé, she had never imagined feeling anything like this—longing, need, sensuality, a driving desire to give as much pleasure as she was being given….

Her hands were cradling his head, they were lingering in his hair, they were running over those beautifully muscled shoulders, but it was not enough. He, her make-believe knight, was intent on pleasing her, but he was fully clothed and that had to be wrong. Her hands ached to be gliding over naked skin—his naked skin. Desperately she moulded him to her, but the feel of that strong male body through the fabric of his tunic was vaguely dissatisfying. She wanted actual skin contact, no, she wanted more than that. She wanted to brand him in the same way that he was branding her.

His leg slid between hers at the precise moment that she slid her fingers into his hair and gave it a gentle tug.

'Ben?'

'Hmm?' His head lifted, his breath was ragged.

Placing a hand in the centre of his chest, she pushed. He made no resistance and in a moment was lying on his back while she leaned over him, hair trailing everywhere. If it were not too dark for him to see, he would think her a wild woman. And yet, under her palm, his heart was thudding as fast as hers.

'Ben—' her voice was croaky as a frog's '—I

am glad I asked you to help me. You are very good at this…'

He caught her hand and kissed it. 'I thank you.'

'So far.'

'So far? *So far?*' His grip shifted and he pulled her down on top of him. 'I'll show you so far…' Possessively, his hands slid to her buttocks and he caught her to him, rocking his pelvis against her as he did so. Both of them groaned. Dragging her head down, he gave her a hot, hard, proprietary kiss.

'Wait, Ben. I have something to say.'

His grip eased and though she was ravaged by desire—a desire that, given their agreement, could have no satisfactory conclusion—she put a smile in her voice. 'If you were a knight, and I were your lady, I would not permit you to remain thus in our bed.'

'Hmm?'

'No, sir knight. I would carry on where your squire had left off.' Purposefully, she reached for his belt and undid the buckle. 'And now, your tunic. Sir, that must come off.' She tussled with the fabric.

He shifted and sat up. Clothing rustled. She heard him swallow. 'And my shirt, Rose? Does that come off too?'

She lifted the hem. 'Of course.'

Another rustling. Then silence.

Rose's throat was dry. She wished she could see

him. She could hardly believe it, but she was sitting naked on the blanket in Ben's tent, *naked,* and Ben was sitting next to her, his breathing as uneven as hers, and she felt neither fear nor dread.

'Your boots, sir knight,' she said, finding her way by feel as she slid her hand down the hard length of his thigh and over the leg bindings on his calf. 'Your squire didn't do a very good job, did he? He left you with your boots and they are certainly not needed here.'

Ben grunted and moved and his hands brushed hers aside.

'There. No boots, lady fair,' he said, taking her by the shoulders and drawing her close. A slow kiss had her toes curling and her belly aching and her body straining towards his. His tongue outlined her lips and parted them; his hands covered her breasts, weighing them; his thumb gently circled her nipples, circling, circling. She was about to collapse back on to the blanket, melting with need when, groaning, he drew back.

'My leg bindings,' he said, on a shaky laugh. 'What about my leg bindings?'

Rose bit her lip. They had to be careful. They had agreed not to consummate their love— *love?*—their desire, she amended hastily. 'D-do you sleep with leg bindings on?'

'Too restricting, I don't usually.'

Since it was Ben and in this she trusted him, she felt bold enough to reach for his calves in the dark. Helpfully, he bent his knees and she was able to untuck the ends of the braid by feel and carefully begin unwinding the bindings. It was hard, though, because her fingers were trembling and all the while Ben's hands were in her hair, stroking it distractingly and using his fingers to comb it out to its full length.

She liked undressing him like this, touching him in this familiar way, as though it were her right, but she fumbled at rolling up the leg bindings and dropped them. 'Sorry.'

'Never mind,' he muttered, leaning towards her to plant a necklace of hot kisses on her neck. He was apparently as eager to touch her as she was to touch him. He was exploring her shoulders, tracing tiny patterns on her skin, leaving fire and yearning in their wake.

Tentatively she reached for his chest. If only she could see him. But she could feel his warmth and the satiny texture of his skin; she could feel those toned tumbler's muscles and the dark hairs that she knew arrowed down to the top of his chausses; she could hear the swift indrawn breath as she too stroked and caressed. When her hands glided around his waist and over his buttocks, they bunched under her hands.

Leaning towards him, she bent and planted a series of kisses on his chest. One hand followed the course of the hairs on his chest and slid lower.

He groaned and took her upper arms to ease her back. 'Enough, Rose. This is far too dangerous.'

'Surely not?'

'There are limits. Saints! I think it might be best if you put your shift back on. Otherwise…'

Otherwise what? They would make love? She would not mind. Benedict Silvester could do anything to her, *anything,* and she was sure she would enjoy it.

And that, she reminded herself, was the whole purpose of this.

Ben is doing this with me because I asked him. He is doing this with me because he is Ben and he loves women, *all* women. He has no special feelings for me, other than the bonds of affection he might feel for a girl he knows as well as his sister.

A sobering thought, that, one that brought her up short. Apparently in accord, Ben edged away, but he took her by the hand as though to lessen the distance that he had just put between them and his thumb moved up and down in her palm.

'That is very…chaste,' she said, returning the pressure slightly resentfully because he had not let her lie against him with her naked breasts against his chest, and she burned for him, she burned…despite the agreement they had made. This is Benedict Silvester, she repeated to herself, Benedict the minstrel who loves everyone.

'It is meant to be chaste,' he said, softly. 'Rose, we *must* be chaste.'

They sat side by side in the tent while their breathing slowed, and Rose wondered frantically what Ben's definition of chastity might be since she was sitting naked in the dark with him, and his scent filled her nostrils and he only wore his chausses and they had touched each other everywhere. Well, almost everywhere. She had still not touched…

'It is not what I want, little flower,' he added. 'But it is dangerous.'

'I know. There might be…issue.' Children. A brief vision of a laughing boy with brown eyes that had green and yellow flecks in them flashed unbidden into her mind. Her heart twisted and, ruthlessly, she snuffed the vision out; Ben and she would never have children.

'Yes.' Puzzlingly, Ben's voice was bleak, as though he had his regrets. But Ben would not be regretting that they would never have children. He would be regretting that they had not lain together fully. He was a man and that, the women at the Quimperlé washing place had told her, was all a man ever wanted. To lie with a woman carnally, they had said, was the sum of a man's desire.

Rose held down a sigh and fumbled for her shift in the dark. She could not complain, Ben was Ben and he had done exactly as she had asked. So swiftly too. A few caresses and she'd been panting for him. And Sir Richard?

Her skin chilled and she frowned. The thought of permitting Sir Richard to touch her in like manner... No. *No!* It gave her goose bumps to think about it. An unpleasant suspicion was forming in her mind—what if the only kisses she could tolerate were the ones that Ben...

She could not and would not let herself fall in love with Ben. For he was not simply Ben, her good friend, he was also Benedict Silvester, the most celebrated lute-player in the Duchy. Yes, he was welcome in every hall and castle in the land, but he was a minstrel, for pity's sake, a rootless wanderer, and *music* was his life. The woman had not been born who could compete with that.

Squaring her shoulders, she pushed past the most crippling feeling of melancholy. 'I am glad I asked you to help me, Ben,' she said, brightly.

The grip on her hand increased. 'You no longer feel...an aversion?'

'Not at the moment.' *Not with you, at least.* 'You are very good at this, I knew you would be.'

'What?' His voice was dry. 'A man of my reputation, you mean?'

'What else?' she said lightly. 'My thanks, Ben.'

'You are welcome, little flower.'

Ben was not the only one with acute hearing; there was definitely a slight edge to his voice. Rose could not think what it meant.

Ben woke with a start. Snatching up his short-sword, he peered into the dark. A short distance away, the screech of an owl sliced through the pre-dawn gloom. Then came a second screech, farther off. The owl was moving away.

At his side, Rose's breathing was soft and even, like the gentle ebb and flow of the sea on a calm August night. Putting out a hand, Ben slid it over the warmth of her back. She murmured and turned towards him, nestling close. His mouth twisted. Rose slept as trustfully as a babe and he envied her that luxury. Last night, shortly after she had fallen asleep, he had heard wolves howling to one another. Rose hadn't so much as stirred. Ben hadn't slept in that way—ever—as far as he could recall. A life on the road and the necessity of staying alert did not lead to deep and dream-less sleep.

Absently running his fingers down the silken length of her hair, he lifted it to his nose and inhaled. Jasmine, soapwort, and beneath them, Rose. Sleeping like a baby with not the faintest notion that her companion had lain awake half the night yearning for something that he would never have. The force of his desire had shocked him, but he would never act on it. When Ben was younger he might have dragged Rose away from Quimperlé and forced her to share his life. But she had chosen Per and in time the yearning had left him.

But now…but now… Ben shook his head. This journey seemed to have reawakened those longings, longings he could not pursue, especially as Rose thought Sir Richard had offered for her.

Wearily he rubbed his face. And when they got to England, and she learned that Sir Richard had *not* asked for her? Lord, what a tangle. By then Rose wouldn't even be speaking to him.

She might forgive you, in time.

Right. And I might pretend I have the right to court her, but the only life I can offer her is at best a ramshackle one. A special envoy, a secret nego- tiator, a 'behind the scenes' figure who spends most of his time masquerading as a minstrel…

Rose would be far better off with a knight, a *real* knight. Lord, what am I doing? I can't be thinking about offering for her myself. What would I do with a wife?

The owl screeched again and Ben caught the faint sound of an animal—or a man, perhaps?—

rustling through the undergrowth. Every muscle snapped to attention.

Another rustle. The cracking of a twig. Ben's heartbeat quickened. It could be a badger, or even one of the wolves he had heard earlier, but he didn't think so. Easing himself away from Rose, he dragged on his boots—no time for cross-gartering—and gripped his shortsword. Crawling to the tent flap, he peered out.

Damn, no light. The stars must have clouded over. There was nothing to be seen but the embers of their fire, glowing like an amber eye in the grey of the clearing. If someone *was* creeping about, they could not be up to any good, and Ben had no intention of making a target of himself. Crouching almost double, he headed—he hoped—for where Eudo and Gien were lying. Reaching out, he found a tousled head. Gien, by the cut of the hair. The space next to Gien was empty.

Clapping his hand over Gien's mouth, he shook the boy awake. Under his hand, Gien bucked and kicked. 'It is me, Ben,' he whispered, and felt Gien relax. 'I heard something. Hold your tongue, eh?'

Gien nodded and Ben removed his hand from the boy's mouth. 'Where's Eudo?'

'Don't know.' Ben felt, rather than saw, the boy's shrug.

'Hell.' He sat back on his heels.

A faint glow in the east told him that the dawn chorus was but a few minutes away. If they were to be ambushed, this would be the time when it was most likely to happen.

Dimly aware that it was cold outside the tent without his shirt, Ben held fast to his sword and rose, muttering, 'I'm going to beat the bounds.' Gien moved as though to accompany him, but Ben put a hand on his chest. 'No, lad. Keep watch here. Rozenn is in your care, understand?'

'Aye, but, Bened—'

'No arguments.' Pressing a finger to the boy's lips, he stole out of the clearing.

Methodically, he quartered the area. Guilt had his mind racing—he ought to have warned Eudo of his suspicions that they were being trailed. He'd not known the knight above a day, but his instincts told him he was trustworthy. Reliable enough to be told that Ben was carrying a private missive for the Duke? *Merde.* He gritted his teeth. He had been too long on his own in this business and had learned not to trust or rely on anyone. Light on his feet, he moved quietly as his father had trained him to do.

His father, Albin, had run similar errands for the Duke's predecessor, Duke Conan. But Albin had trusted once too often and had ended up dying in a ditch. So much for trust. After his father's death Ben had resolved to trust no one. He worked alone; it was safer for everyone that way.

Which was why last eve, he had not expressed his concerns to Eudo. Which was why Rose, who knew more about him than anyone, knew nothing of his secret life. *Then why in God's name did you deliberately involve Rose in this, your most important mission?*

Ben's foot caught in a tree root. Why indeed? His heart banged. The light was strengthening to pearly grey and trees loomed towards him, tall, dark shadows. Overhead, a blackbird tried out a note or two, hesitated, and then launched into a full trill.

Where the *hell* was Eudo? Ben's stomach tightened. Not, he hoped, lying in a ditch like his father; not bleeding his life away because he, Ben, had failed to warn him that unscrupulous men could be following them.

The same men, he suspected, who had lain in wait for him in the stables and had nearly done for poor Gien instead. Ben was almost certain that the attack on Gien had been a case of mistaken identity, but he had said nothing. And now, if something had happened to Eudo…

Guilt was piling on guilt, it seemed, enough to drag a man down if he thought about it too long.

Ben dived through the thick scrub, working his

way round to the river. Briars scored his skin. Cold
sweat trickled down his back.

Guilt. He should have let Eudo know that the
attack on Gien had probably been meant for him.

Guilt. He would not be in this mess if he had
been travelling on his own as was his custom. But
one thing led to another and since Rose was with
him, Ben had found that the thought of her getting
hurt was unbearable. Which was why he had
asked for Eudo and Gien's company on the road
to Josselin. Distractedly, Ben ran his hand through
his hair. It had been a mistake to involve them, but
since he had, he didn't want them to come to any
harm either.

Abruptly he came to a dead halt, cold to his
marrow. Rose. He should have forseen this. If
Rose came to any harm because of his commission, he would *never* forgive himself.

No man can serve two masters. He could not
care for Rose *and* accept dangerous missions for
the Duke. Witness the way simply being in Rose's
company had lowered his guard. He had not
thought through the implications of the attack on
Gien any more than he had realised that by solic-
iting for the company of the knight and his squire,
he was placing them in danger.

'You are a fool, Benedict Silvester,' he muttered
under his breath. A rush of wind teased the hair at

the nape of his neck and raised goosebumps on his arm. 'A damned fool.'

'Amen to that!' Behind him, someone laughed.

Sword tight in his fist, Ben made to turn, but the waking wood exploded in a blinding flash of pain, and night returned.

'Ben? Ben? *Please* wake up.'

Rose was calling, but she had fled the Duchy and Ben could not reach her. He was running, running to get to her, but by the time he got to where he thought she was, she had gone. Always receding ahead of him, always over the next hill.

'Ben? *Ben?*'

His head, which ached and throbbed like the devil, was pillowed on something soft and a damp cloth feathered across his temples. He groaned.

'Eudo, I think he's waking.'

Her voice was laden with concern. He should stir himself to reassure her that he was all right, except it was so damned hard to move…

Eudo muttered a response, but Ben couldn't catch the gist of it. Again the cloth whispered over his temples. The pillow beneath his head shifted, gentle fingers parted his hair.

'The bleeding has stopped,' Rose said.

Ben wished the thudding in his head would stop. Experimentally, he tried to open his eyes.

'Ben?'

She was bending over him, tears of anxiety tumbling out of those huge brown eyes. Her thighs were his pillow and someone had flung a blanket over him. He forced a smile, was aware it probably emerged more like a grimace. 'No dimples, *chérie?*'

She did not smother him with kisses, for which, with his head pounding as it was, he was grateful, but she gave him a watery smile and one of her dimples did briefly appear. Her hand rested lightly on the blanket on his chest and, catching it, he wound his fingers with hers and let his head fall back.

'Eudo?'

'Aye, lad, right here.'

'You found me, I take it?'

'Aye.'

'Did they…' lifting a leaden arm, Ben rubbed his forehead '…did they get my shortsword?'

'No, I have it. Lucky for you I came along just as he'd felled you. He took one look at me and was off sharpish.'

'What did he look like?'

'Couldn't say. Beggar had his hood up.'

'Alone, was he?'

Eudo raised a brow. 'As far as I saw. Were you expecting trouble?'

Ben grimaced, undecided how to play it from

here. Rose could not know about any of this, for her safety's sake. But Ben needed Eudo and Gien's help if they were to reach Josselin in one piece; and the more the knight knew, the better prepared he would be. Eudo could not be told the whole, of course. He could not be told of the Duke's plans concerning England, but he could be told about the Abbot's letter….

Ben glanced at Rose, who was gently massaging his temples, and struggled to a sitting position. Her hands fell away. The back of his head throbbed, and when he touched it he found a lump the size of a pigeon's egg.

'Rose, be a sweetheart and fetch my shirt and tunic, would you? I'm cold and loathe to move for the minute.'

Rose looked searchingly at him and for a moment Ben was afraid she would object, but she gave him a curt nod and, rising, disappeared into the tent.

'Listen, Eudo.' Ben spoke softly and swiftly. 'Rose does not know, but I am on a mission, carrying messages for Duke Hoël from his cousin at Quimperlé.'

Eudo frowned. 'The Abbot?'

'Aye. I had thought to carry them to the Duke at Rennes myself, but he has a man stationed at Josselin and I now think it best to surrender it to him to take the rest of the way. I dare not carry them farther, lest harm come to Rose.'

Eudo glanced towards the tent, and his sudden smile in that direction warned Ben that Rose was already returning with his clothes. 'Never fret, lad,' he said. A battled-scarred hand patted Ben's forearm. 'You will feel yourself in no time.'

Chapter Thirteen

Josselin. Thank the Lord, Rose thought. She glowered at Ben's back as he led them at a bone-shaking trot up the ride towards the castle gates. So what if Ben had a thundering headache? That was no reason for him to have put Jet back on the embarrassing leading rein, and neither was there any reason for him to keep secrets from her. Rozenn had seen the look that he had exchanged with Eudo when he had sent her to fetch his tunic from the tent—and she had also noted Eudo's somewhat less-than-subtle attempt at reassurance as she had emerged. The two of them were up to something and they were excluding her. She did not like it, not one bit.

Gripping Jet's reins as they clattered along the cobbled way, Rozenn straightened her shoulders.

The ride was bordered on the one side by the River Oust, and on the other by a line of merchants' houses. They were wooden for the most part, as in both Quimperlé and Hennebont. Though Rozenn ached in every limb, she was determined to hide her fatigue as they overtook other travellers headed towards the castle. Adjusting her seat, she held herself straight as a poker as they jounced along, but when Ben *finally* slowed to a walk she couldn't prevent a sigh of relief escaping.

Ben glanced back, and she thought that he might have sent her a smile, but she could not be sure because she pointedly avoided his gaze, staring up instead at the high walls of Josselin Castle, which reared up on their left, like a cliff. Men, Rozenn thought bitterly, they were all the same with their silly secrets. Per had hidden his debts from her and she did not care to wonder what Ben was hiding.

And what a time to learn that Ben was keeping secrets from her! Just when she had begun to think that Sir Richard might *not* be the ideal man for her… Just when she was beginning to think she might prefer a certain minstrel. If only he could prove himself reliable.

Rose might not remember her mother, but it took two to make a child. Where had her father been when Rose had been abandoned? Men. Were they ever trustworthy?

Out of the corner of her eye, she noticed Ben waving at a pretty young woman with yellow hair.

The woman was wearing a garish gown with a deep slashed neckline and tight lacings that emphasised an enviable bosom and proclaimed her profession to all but the most naïve. Eudo also exchanged greetings with her. Hmph! No secrets as to what they were planning *there.* How typical.

As they rode under the shadow of the gate, Ben unclipped Jet and held Piper back till Jet drew level with him. 'You can rest here, *mignonne,*' he said. His face seemed to have relaxed a little as if the pain of his headache was leaving him. 'I think you will like Josselin, but a word of warning—it is the annual horse fair. The bailey will be bustling.'

Briefly he leaned across and squeezed her hand. It was an affectionate gesture, which had Rose regretting her mental diatribe of a few moments ago. She had been unfair. Ben might smile at the girl with the yellow hair, but that did not mean that he and she were anything more than fellow entertainers acknowledging each other, and when Rose was not hurt and angry, she knew that. She bit her lip.

Bustling? Ben did not exaggerate. The castle yard resembled the mêlée in Count Remond's practice field with carts and horses and men jostling for position. The din was deafening: harassed grooms were bellowing at one another, battling for the few remaining stalls in the stables;

horses whinnied, great hoofs struck sparks on the cobbles; a wolfhound snarled at a gaggle of honking geese....

The air was heavy with the mingled smells of horse dung, human sweat, baking bread and cooking meat. Across the bailey, several youths were eyeing a buxom kitchen wench who was giggling and preening herself in the doorway of the cookhouse.

How Ben did it, Rose never knew, but sooner than she would have believed it possible, he had secured the last of the stabling for the horses, and they were elbowing their way through the insane crush, climbing the keep steps.

With the hubbub in the bailey at their backs, they entered the relative cool of the Great Hall.

The Josselin keep was grander than the one at Castle Hellon and the Great Hall just as frantic as the yard outside. In the centre a large fire blazed. The walls were hung with pennants belonging to the knights who owed fealty to the lord of Josselin. There were gold pennants striped with silver; there were red diamonds set on a green background; there were blue and yellow pennants sporting devices Rose did not recognise—the colours of half the nobility of Brittany seemed to be on display in this hall.

Servants were setting up trestles, they were

spreading acres of white linen. Dogs darted underfoot, yapping and yelping and scuffling up the rushes. Children were playing tag with the dogs....

Ben shouldered his lute and pack and cleared a path through servants, dogs and children. Taking up her things, Rose followed, stomping stiffly along; she had no wish to lose him, not in this great cavern of a castle.

'*Holà,* William! *Ça va bien?* Is all well?' Ben switched to Norman French to address a ruddy-complexioned man of about fifty years of age who was directing the placing of a barrel at one of the serving trestles. A portly fellow, Rose guessed he must be the castle steward.

'Benedict!' The man's face lit up. 'Indeed it is, and all the better for seeing you! You are in good health, I trust?'

'Never better.'

As Rose continued her survey of the hall, she gave half an ear to the conversation between Ben and this William Steward, glad that her years among Countess Muriel's ladies meant that it was no hardship for her to follow Norman French. She eyed the wall-hanging at the end of the hall with something approaching awe and wondered who were lord and lady here. Rose had thought the wall-hanging she had designed for the Great Hall at Quimperlé was large, but this one dwarfed it by several yards. Silver and gold thread gleamed as it wafted in the draught. She was busy calculating the cost in terms of material and women's time, when Ben caught her hand and pulled her to him.

'William, this is Rozenn Kerber. Rose, meet William Steward.' He lowered his voice to a conspiratorial whisper. 'William, Rose is…that is, we… Can you offer us anything other than the common hall tonight?'

William nodded pleasantly at Rozenn before shaking his head. 'Sorry, Benedict, but you could not have come at a worse time. What with the horse fair tomorrow, I would be hard put to find space for a mouse this night, let alone give you a private chamber.'

Pointedly, Ben indicated his lute. 'Not even for an unscheduled performance?'

William shook his head. 'I am desolated, but no. If only you had given me warning of your arrival, but Alfonse le Brun and his troop have long been booked for tonight.' He grinned. 'They are almost as popular as you.'

'I'll wager they do not have Turold's new "Song of Roland" in their repertoire,' Ben said, casually.

William's gaze sharpened. 'You tempt me. You really know it?'

'Assuredly. Heard the great man perform when I was in Normandy last.'

'And you have every last stanza?'

'To the last note,' Ben said, raising a brow, 'provided, of course, you find us a chamber. I find my memory works best on a good night's sleep.'

The steward turned knowing eyes on Rose. 'Sleep, eh?'

Hot-cheeked, Rose couldn't meet the steward's gaze. Ben grinned. She would kill him when he was on his own, she would kill him…

William Steward rubbed his chin. 'There is a storeroom in the north tower,' he said, thoughtfully. 'For someone who is able to give us Turold's "Song", a small space might be cleared…'

'William, you are a prince!' Ben said. Hand warm at Rose's waist, he turned for the door.

'Mind, there are no fireplaces in the north tower,' William said.

'No matter, it's summer. Come on, Rose.'

Rose hung back. 'What about Eudo and Gien?'

Eudo gave a little bow and took Rose's hand in a courtly manner. 'It is the Great Hall for us, little lady.'

'Will I find you again?' Rose asked, suddenly afraid she would lose her new friends in the maelstrom that was Castle Josselin.

'Assuredly, I shall seek you out at dinner.'

Ben led her from the Great Hall.

* * *

Dinner at Château Josselin on the eve of the annual horse fair was a crowded, brilliant and somewhat disorderly affair. The trestles had been dragged together to form three sides of a rectangle. White drapery dazzled. Wax dripped down from candelabra hanging from the rafters, and reflected candlelight shimmered in brass pots and exotic imported glassware. The logs in the fire roared; knives clattered on wooden plates; the voices of the diners rose and fell; children shrieked.

Eudo had claimed Rozenn for his dinner partner and they—as befitted their relatively humble status in this glittering array of lords and ladies and knights and retainers—were seated towards the lower end of one of the trestles, near the door and farther from the fire.

The smells were strong—burnt fat, wine, dogs, sweat. Even horse. Rozenn wrinkled her nose. Ewers of water were available on the side-tables, but apparently not all of this company had made use of them; many still had the stink of their journey on them.

'Eudo, where's Ben?' Ben would not be eating, *that* Rozenn knew, but she would feel better if she could place him.

'Last I saw, he was exchanging heated words

with Alfonse le Brun over the re-ordering of the evening programme.'

Rose nodded, smiling her thanks as Eudo speared a chunk of lamb and dropped it on her trencher. 'He will eat later, I expect. Turold's "Song" is long and he will prefer to eat when it's over.'

'He gets nervous? I would never have thought it,' Eudo said, catching the eye of a serving girl and indicating that she should refill their wine-cups.

'He's always ill at ease before a performance, but he strives to hide it. As a child, when his father was training him, he would get most vilely ill.'

'It is why he is so talented.'

Rose brought her brows together. 'Because he gets nervous?'

'Because he cares—it is one and the same.' The knight sent her an easy grin. 'It is like that in my line of work also; a little nervousness sharpens the ear and eye, it steadies the hand.'

Reaching for the stem of her wine-cup, Rose turned it thoughtfully. 'How strange, it is the exact opposite with me. When Countess Muriel was in one of her rages, I could scarcely hold a needle, let alone set a stitch.'

'Aye, we are none of us made the same.' He gave Rozenn a straight look. 'And what a blessing that is, to my way of thinking.'

Absently, Rozenn murmured her agreement. Where *was* Ben? A brace of servants stood behind the top table, in front of the wall-hanging. Not there. The great tapestry was magnificent though, the way that silver and gold threadwork glistened, catching all eyes. And the *mille-fleurs*—yellow, red, blue—cluster after cluster. It must have taken months and months to finish.

Someone was standing in the north tower stairwell, half-hidden by the shadows. It wasn't Ben, but—Rose sucked in a breath—that man. That red hair was unmistakable, particularly when the torchlight turned it to fire. She frowned. Not again! She had first noticed him at Quimperlé, apparently watching Ben. Next she had seen him at the quayside, and again at Hennebont, dashing into that alleyway. And now, behind the red-haired man, in the dim recess of the north turret stairwell, *another* shadow stirred. Rose narrowed her eyes. She knew that profile anywhere. Ben. Her skin chilled. Why should Ben be acting so furtively?

Slack-jawed, she watched the red-haired man's head turn, apparently in response to something Ben was saying to him. Throwing a glance over his shoulder, the red-haired man stepped into the stairwell with Ben. The door closed behind them.

'More lamb, Rozenn?' Eudo said.

'I… I beg your pardon? Oh. My thanks.' While Eudo helped her to more meat from the platter, Rose frowned at the closed stairwell door. What was Ben up to?

Rozenn was dimly aware that Eudo and the knight on his other hand were airing their views on Duke William of Normandy's accession to the English throne. Duke William's campaign of the previous autumn came up, and they discussed the ruthless methods the Normans were employing to suppress revolt in England. Rozenn toyed with her food, vaguely wondering if Adam was having to be ruthless at Fulford, but her mind kept straying back to Ben.

What was he doing? Rose thought that she knew him, had hoped that there were no secrets between them. But this furtiveness suggested otherwise. What business could Ben have with that man? Her every instinct was shrieking that the red-haired man was danger personified, that he was a man who would slit your throat as soon as look at you. Surely this was a man ruthless enough to be working for Duke William….

And what was it that Ben had been discussing with Eudo just before they had broken camp in the wood? Scowling at her meat, Rose poked it with the tip of her eating knife before pushing it to one side.

Just as she was beginning to hope that Ben

might be more dependable, more reliable; just as she was beginning to think that she might trust him… She was even beginning to realise that she had made a grave mistake pinning her hopes on Sir Richard because it was Ben whom she loved.

She *loved* him? *Ben?*

For a moment Rose was blind to the shimmer and shine of Josselin's Great Hall; she was deaf to the clatter and babble. She loved him. Throat dry, she groped for her wine and brought the cup to her lips. She loved Benedict Silvester. And she did not love him as a sister loves a brother, or even as a girl loves a favourite childhood friend, she—she drained her cup without tasting the wine and stared blankly at the lees—she loved him as a woman loves a man, the man she would marry.

No, *no,* she must not! She would not permit herself to love Ben, not a minstrel who had little more than the clothes he stood up in. She could not marry him.

But she could not marry Sir Richard of Asculf either. And he had lands and… What an idiot she had been! It was Ben, and it had been all long. Mikaela had known. While she… What a blind, stupid…

The door to the north tower swung open and Ben stepped alone into the hall, leopard's-head lute fast in his hand. Across the smoky haze their eyes met. His expression lightened. And Rose's heart, her stupid, foolish, wayward heart, ached as though it would break. What *was* he up to?

As soon as Ben's song and the meal were over, Rozenn took a candle and made her escape from the Great Hall. It would be a while before Ben could leave the revellers. His performance had been received with shouts of applause and he was at present lost in a crowd of admirers crying for an encore.

Rozenn hesitated at the bottom of the spiral staircase that wound up to the storeroom that she and Ben had been given. The stairwell was black as night. Hooking up her skirts, she tucked them into her girdle and began to climb. Her feet rang hollow on the boards.

The boards? Glancing down, Rose scuffed one of the steps with the toe of her boot. Wood, yes, and it definitely sounded hollow. Frowning, she held up her candle to examine the walls. The rope banister was attached to a metal ring in the usual way, but something did not seem quite right.

Rose rapped at the curved wall with her knuckle. More wood. The north tower was not, as she had assumed, made of stone, it was made entirely of wood! Quicker and cheaper to build in wood, of course. Perhaps Josselin's lord was not as rich and powerful as he pretended, but he wanted his castle to appear unassailable. Like Countess Muriel's wall-hanging, this castle was as much a statement of its lord's ambition, as it was of his actual power. Bluff and bluster: a dog raising its hackles to drive off other dogs. In a word, trickery. But then, if Rozenn were lord of this place in these fractious times, perhaps she too would resort to trickery.

A draught from a window slit had her candle guttering and, as Rose shielded it, she realised that this was why the north tower was so ill-lit—torches in wall-sconces would be a considerable fire risk.

Gaining the landing outside the storeroom, she heard a scuffling and shuddered. There must be rats here; it was easy to imagine them gnawing through the panels to get at whatever William Steward had stored here.

Another draught threatened to snuff her candle out. Jealously guarding the flame, Rose hoped there were other candles in the storeroom. Plenty of light would scare off the rats. Making a point of stamping loudly on the landing to drive them away, she pushed open the door.

The storeroom was hung with shadows, save for a tiny glow in a corner where someone had left a lantern burning. Rozenn did not think it had been left for her. No, it must have been forgotten. Dangerous!

Just then, the darkness took on form and rushed at her from the corner where Ben had left his pack. A man! In a dark, hooded cloak.

Time seemed to slow. Rozenn heard herself gasp. Her candle wavered as the man came at her, growing ever larger till he—she was certain it was a man though the hood and the shadows hid his features—towered over her.

Hot wax spilled on her fingers. 'Wh-who are you?'

A pretty silver arc cut through the gloom even as a fist thudded into her chest.

Rose flung out a hand and staggered backwards. Her head cracked against limewash; her candle flew through the air and winked out.

The figure loomed over her. There was another silver flash and her right hand burned. The cloak swirled, the room went dark, and she was alone, breathless and shaking in every limb. The intruder pounded down the stairs.

The palm of Rose's right hand was stinging, but with both her candle and the lantern out it was impossible to see the damage. She lifted it to her lips. Wet. A metallic taste.

Blood!

The intruder, whoever he was, had been going

through Ben's pack. A shiver ran down her spine. This had happened before! At the inn at Hennebont, when she had found Ben's belongings in a tangle—Ben hadn't been in a hurry as she had assumed, someone had been going through his things. The same someone who had just run off?

She sucked the blood from her palm. Had Ben left the Great Hall? Where was he? She was sitting alone in the dark in a strange castle and someone had slashed her palm. No matter that there were secrets between them, no matter that he was unreliable, she needed Ben.

'Ben,' she muttered. 'Where *are* you?'

Ben was perched on a stool in a gallery above the Great Hall, waiting for Gurth to join him. He had had proof that Gurth, the red-haired man he had seen at Quimperlé, was another of Duke Hoël's envoys. Gurth would deliver the Abbot's messages to the Duke. Thank God. Ben trusted that once he had handed the messages over, he and Rose could continue to England, unmolested. To Ben's knowledge, only three people knew of his other commission: the Duke, Adam and himself. It was vital it stayed that way. As far as the world was concerned, he was simply a minstrel, escorting an old friend to her brother in England.

Lute in his lap, and with a new set of lute strings

to hand, Ben was turning the pegs to loosen the strings when the curtain rings rattled and Gurth ducked under the curtain and took a seat beside him. At this late hour, the Duke's envoys had the gallery to themselves, though voices could be heard murmuring in the Hall where people were dragging out bedding and arguing over spaces.

Glancing up from his lute, Ben nodded at Gurth. 'It might have helped if I had known you were Duke Hoël's man back in Quimperlé,' he said, softly, so his voice would not carry. He was remembering the abortive attack on Gien and later on himself at their camp outside the town. 'I had marked you down as Duke William's.'

'My apologies.' Gurth spoke equally quietly. 'But Duke Hoël charged me with watching your back. If you had known…'

Ben stiffened. Gurth did not need to expand. If Ben had known Gurth was in the pay of Duke Hoël, he might have inadvertently revealed it to those whose interests lay elsewhere. 'The Duke should know he may trust me not to make clumsy mistakes.'

'He does, man. Don't take it personally, this is politics. Duke Hoël was looking out for you. He's a cautious man.'

Unwinding the last of his lute strings from the soundboard, Ben nodded. It occurred to him that Gurth might have been told about Ben's other, more important commission, but he thought not. When the Duke had charged Ben with establishing regular contact with his supporters in England, he had stressed the need for discretion. King William would not take kindly to a furthering of Breton interests in his new kingdom.

'You have Abbot Benoît's letter?' Gurth asked.

'Of course.' Glancing over his shoulder to ensure they were not being overseen, Ben reached into the soundboard, feeling for the manuscript. His love of his lute and of music was not the only reason the instrument never left his side. This was not the first time he had hidden messages in the soundbox. 'Here.' The vellum was dry and, once he had it loose, it crackled as he drew it out.

'My thanks.' Gurth glanced at Abbot Benoît's seal, saw that it was unbroken, and the letter vanished into his tunic.

'I suspect Duke William's men are after it. You had best be wary.'

'Oh?' Gurth's voice was casual, but Ben was not fooled. The man was as tight with tension as the new lute strings would be when Ben had set them in place.

Briefly, while he wound on and tightened the new set of strings, Ben told Gurth that someone had been through his belongings; he also mentioned the attack on Gien in the stables and the fact that Gien's tunic was an exact colour match to one of his; and finally, he mentioned what had happened at dawn at their campsite in the woods outside Josselin. 'As I said, my suspicions were first aroused when we were staying in Hennebont.'

'*We?*'

'Rose and I.'

'So, that pretty wench is your mistress?'

'Rose is not my mistress. Rose is…' Ben was hit by an unexpected wave of longing. *If only Rose were my mistress.* 'My relationship with Mistress Kerber is not a matter for discussion.'

Gurth shrugged. 'Have it your own way. But, back to business—the lad who was attacked in Hennebont—are you sure he was mistaken for you?'

'Build and colouring similar, tunics same colour. In the poor light of the stables, it's easy to imagine how we might have been confused. And then I was clobbered at our campsite.' Ben lowered himself on to the stool and, rubbing the back of his head, gave Gurth a rueful smile. 'I could have done with your help then, my friend. A word of warning wouldn't have gone amiss—what if they had hurt Rose?'

Ben slid the final string through its peg and began tightening it. Gurth was fiercely loyal to Duke Hoël just as he was—he caught his breath—no, that was not strictly true, not any more. With Rose in his company he had to admit his loyalty to the Duke was being put to the test as it never had been.

Saints. He should *not* have involved her, he should have realised it would be like this.

He glanced across at Gurth. 'Do you go direct to Rennes from here?'

'Aye. Will you follow?'

Ben shook his head. 'Rose needs me to escort her to England, but after that…' He lifted his shoulders.

Opening his purse, Gurth counted out some gold coins and thrust them into Ben's hand. 'The Duke bade me give you these.'

'My thanks.'

'I wish you well.' Gurth made to rise, but checked. 'See you at the Christmas court.'

'And I you.' Ben gave the expected answer, though in truth he had no idea where he would be at Christmas. If the Duke's interests called for him to be at his Christmas court, he would be there, but he could just as easily be in England…

The curtain at the western end of the gallery wafted in the breeze. Ben tilted his head. 'Someone's coming, and they are in a hurry.'

Gurth rose and, silent as a cat, moved to the other side of the gallery. 'Farewell, then. Good luck.'

'Good luck to you too,' Ben murmured.

A quick bow, a rattle of curtain rings, and Gurth was gone.

'*Ben!*' Rose burst into the gallery and practically tripped over him in her haste. 'I've been searching for you everywhere!'

One look at her face and Ben was on his feet, tossing the lute aside. Rose's eyes were wide, her cheeks were chalk-white and her veil, instead of being on her head, was wrapped round her fist like a bandage. A bandage?

'*Rose!*' She stumbled into his arms, hugging him to her, trembling from top to toe. Ice in his guts, Ben drew back to look at her. 'What happened?'

'A man…someone…in our room! He… It was dark, but he… My hand…'

'It'll be fine. Let me see.' Quickly, Ben stroked her hair, then took her wrist and carefully unwound the veil. Someone had taken a slice out of her. His gut tightened. 'Bastard!' The cut was not deep, but it was bad enough. 'Christ, Rose, who was it?'

'It was too dark to see. He…he had been going through your things. It was horrible. I thought there were rats, but…'

While Rose babbled, Ben led her towards a pair of candles on a stand and held out her palm to examine it. 'It looks clean, but I want this looked at lest it becomes inflamed. Come on.'

He steered her towards the curtain, mind racing. Rose's assailant had to be one of Duke William's men. Hell and damnation. Ben had seen warriors hurt in combat, some of them seriously, but Rose was bleeding and *he* was to blame. He towed her to the curtain, cursing himself for dragging her into this. He should never have put her at risk. *Never.*

Rose halted, forcing him to stop. 'Ben?'

He turned and her eyes, those huge brown eyes, fixed on his. She reached up and drew his head down so their foreheads touched. She was still trembling.

'He did not kill me, Ben,' she said, softly stroking the back of his neck, as though she understood that he was racked with guilt and yet she forgave him. Her smile was gut-wrenchingly sweet.

Ben swallowed and he found himself having to quell the desire to tell her…everything. 'Rose…'

'It's only a scratch really.'

Reminding himself of the need to keep his head, Ben dragged on a smile. 'Nevertheless, you will not be sewing for some time.' He brought his body closer, appalled to realise that *he* needed the contact. Mirroring her, he caressed her head. She flinched and his blood chilled. 'Rose?'

'He…' she evaded his gaze '…pushed me and I hit my head. Fine pair we are—I too have a lump.'

Ben reached for the curtain. 'Rose, we are going to have this looked at. I know an apothecary…'

'Ben, I am fine. Yes, I was frightened for a moment, but that has passed, I just needed to find you. Anyway…' lips curving, she nodded her head in the direction of the abandoned lute '…haven't you forgotten something?'

Chapter Fourteen

Though the torchlight was falling directly on Ben's face, his eyes were shuttered and his expression unreadable. For a moment, when Rozenn had first stumbled into the gallery, Ben had seemed upset, deeply upset that she had been attacked. And for one blissful instant she had basked in that knowledge; she had felt loved.

But as Ben released her and turned to retrieve his lute, Rose also recalled seeing, and she would take an oath on this, a man with red hair whisk out of the gallery. A shiver ran down her back.

Lute in one hand, Ben caught her by the elbow with the other. 'Ready, *chérie?*' he asked, urging her back the way she had come.

'A moment.' Rose jerked her head towards the other curtain. 'Who was that man?'

'What man?' His face was a studied blank. Too studied.

She looked him square in the eye. 'You were talking to him when I came in. Who is he?'

Ben's lute tapped against his thigh, making a hollow sound. He'd been restringing it, she saw, noticing the curl of spare strings round his fist. She rubbed her forehead. It was very odd to have found Ben up here in the gallery. In truth, Ben *never* actually played from galleries—his music wasn't background music. When he played and sang, he was always centre stage with all eyes on him.

'Ben? I swear I have seen him before.'

With a shrug, Ben ran his thumbnail over the frets. Up and down, up and down. It made the tiniest of clicking sounds: click clack, click clack, click clack. 'There *was* someone here,' he agreed, vaguely, tugging her arm. 'Can't say I took much notice. Come on, Rose.'

She held her ground. Ben was lying, he was hiding something from her and that cut her to the quick. It was becoming clear that Ben did indeed have a hidden agenda, but what could it be? Rose gazed up at him, praying he would confess the whole, but his face remained shadowed. Her spirits plummeted.

When Ben had offered to accompany her to England, she had cherished the thought that he had done so because he cared for her as a dear friend. She had neither expected nor hoped for more from him, but since leaving Quimperlé, her feelings had undergone such a change. Her heart was no longer fixed on Sir Richard; in fact, she doubted she could countenance so much as a kiss from the man. This 'friend' of hers, this handsome devil standing before her with the torchlight gleaming on his coal-black hair and in his dark seductive eyes, had turned her dreams upside down. But he—this charming, *feckless,* devil of a lute-player—could *not* be the man for her.

Swallowing hard, Rozenn shook her head; she had been listening to too many of his romances. 'Ben, I have definitely seen that man before,' she said, giving him one last chance to come clean on whatever secret he was hiding from her. 'First in Quimperlé, then at Hennebont, and now in Josselin. Twice would be a coincidence, but so many times?'

He shrugged, not meeting her eyes. 'Most likely he was making his way here because of the horse fair. As you see, it attracts crowds from every village in the Duchy.'

The torchlight flickered. Ben shifted and his face fell deeper into the shadows. Not that she could have told anything if Ben stood in the full glare of the noonday sun, not with that blank expression on it. His thumbnail click, clicked against a fret. The lute strings trembled, slender curls that caught the light.

Several thoughts came to her, apparently at random, but they belonged together, if only Rose could find the pattern. She sucked in a breath. At Hennebont, Ben's belongings had been strewn about the bedchamber. Ben had been attacked at their campsite—and not only Ben. What about Gien in the Hennebont stables? And this evening in the tower room...

There had to be a connection between these incidents, but juggle them though she might, Rozenn could not find it. It was like working a patchwork, except that she had been given the wrong template and the pattern would not fit. Another patch floated into her mind—Gien's tunic, the fabric of which was almost an exact match for one of Ben's...

Stepping closer, so she could feel the warmth of Ben's body, she lifted her good hand and ran it over his head, up and over the longer hair of his fringe and down to the shorter hair at the nape of his neck. Her fingers lingered. She loved the texture of Ben's hair, smooth and silky. 'Hair cut in the Norman style,' she murmured. 'Like Gien's. And the colour is very alike too.'

He was pretending to be puzzled, she could read that much. He put his lute back on the stool and took her by the waist. 'Rose?' He smiled.

She smiled back, for his face had opened up.

Ben might be affecting puzzlement, he might have matters he wanted to keep from her, but he did want to kiss her. *That* was real. His eyes had dropped to her mouth and he was pulling her by the hips, pressing himself gently against her, causing a delicious swoony feeling in the region of her belly. No one else had ever had that effect on her. And his lips had not yet met hers…

With Ben's head lowering, until there was only an inch between them, it was becoming increasingly hard to recall why his evasiveness was so distressing. Rose had wanted Ben to be her escort and *only* her escort. Yes, that was it, she wanted Ben to have no other business in the world but her. In other words, she wanted what in her heart she had always wanted, but had refused to see because she could *never* have it. She wanted all of him.

As Ben's broad shoulders blocked out the torch-light, his scent filled her nostrils, seductive and dizzying. Her senses were greedy for him and only him, there was scant room for thought. She wanted Ben, all of him, as she had always done.

Perhaps she had better make the most of him while she might. Closing her eyes, lifting her lips to his, Rose sighed. It was utterly impossible in the long term, of course.

Ben's lips closed firmly over hers. With a moan,

Rose held his head tightly in place, opening her mouth the instant his tongue sought entrance.

It is not impossible, a little voice whispered, and somehow Rozenn found the strength to ignore the voice and draw her lips fractionally away from his. 'You must have seen him.'

'Mmm.' Warm lips found her ear and slid down to press a chain of meltingly sweet kisses round her neck. 'Who?'

'The…the red-haired man with the sharp nose. You must have seen him before.' Gripping a handful of dark hair, she tugged his lips from her collar-bones before her legs gave way.

He shook his head and smiled, his eyes—they genuinely looked glazed—moving straight back to her mouth. 'When I am with you, *ma belle,* I can see no other.'

Thumbs under her chin, he tipped up her face, and though Rose knew that Ben had to be lying and that he did remember the red-haired man, indeed, had probably intended to meet him all along, she let him have his way. She would give him her kisses while he wanted them, but she must keep in mind that even though Ben enjoyed kissing her, that did not mean she had his heart. If Ben had ever had the ability to love and remain faithful to one woman and one woman alone, his life on the road had probably destroyed it.

But, as his caresses heated her blood and weakened her knees, Rose realised she had little choice. She did love him, which was why she would take what little he offered. As Ben's lips moved over hers, she surrendered to the sensation. Hot. She pressed closer, breathing him in. Aching need. His hand ran up and down her back, leaving a trail of fire in its wake. Desire. He stroked her hips, drawing her closer, so that she could feel…

A slow hand clap…a whistle…

They had an audience!

Ben raised his head and grinned at someone over her shoulder. Rose turned, cheeks burning. William Steward stood there with his thumbs hooked over his belt and a knowing smile stretching from ear to ear.

Gritting her teeth in embarrassment, Rozenn wrenched herself out of Ben's arms. 'How long was he there, Ben?' she hissed, under her breath. 'How long?'

'Huh?'

Ben had the grace to look confused, but Rose was not mollified. Anger took her. 'Were you kissing me or performing for William Steward? Do you ever do *anything* with a whole heart?'

Glaring at the steward, Rose picked up her skirts and, head high, swept from the gallery.

William Steward stared after Rose, brows drawn

together as the door curtain swung to and fro in her wake. 'What's upsetting the girl?'

'She… She…' Ben could not give William the whole truth which was that he suspected Rose realised there was more to him than music and wanted him to confess it. He did not doubt William's loyalty, but the fewer people who knew about his work for Duke Hoël, the better. 'Rozenn has hurt her hand. Her knife slipped at supper. I would be grateful if you could send someone to look at it. I would hate it to become inflamed.'

'Of course, my boy, I would be pleased to help. Especially if you undertook to stay at Josselin a few days more.'

'What about Alfonse and his troupe?'

'They're leaving the day after tomorrow, once the horse fair is over, and we enter a positive desert with no booked entertainments.'

'My apologies, William, I cannot.' The longer they tarried here, the more danger there might be— the man who had attacked Rose might well strike again. The Abbot's messages had left Ben's hands, but Normandy's men did not know this. And Ben could only pray that England's new king had no inkling of his real reasons for travelling to Wessex.

'You will be well paid, I swear.'

'I am sorry, but it is out of the question. Rozenn and I…' may God forgive him for the lie, but after tonight Ben did not want Rose staying in Brittany a moment longer than she had to '…we have already booked our passage to England. We must make haste or we will miss the sailing.'

William's face fell. 'I am sorry for that, lad. I had a mind to hear my favourite songs again.'

'You are very kind,' Ben murmured. 'But we must make that sailing.' It was, Ben was learning, one thing to work for Duke Hoël when he only had himself to think about, but quite another when in Rose's company. He ran his hand round the back of his neck. Travelling with Rose was making him jumpy and he needed time to think. Jerking his head in the direction of the roof stairs, he said, 'Would anyone object if I took a turn about the ramparts?'

'Be my guest.' William grinned. 'Let the filly cool off, eh, while you do a spot of star-gazing?'

'Something like that.' He turned for the door, but swung back. 'William?'

'Aye?'

'You will send someone to see to Rozenn's hand?'

'Consider it done.'

'My thanks. And, William, ask them to stay with Rozenn until I get there, will you? I won't be long.'

'Of course, Benedict, if that's what you want.'

Ben grasped the steward by the hand. 'My thanks.'

'Think nothing of it. You just be sure to pass this way again. You would be wasted on those heathens in England.'

Smiling, committing himself to nothing, Ben bowed and left the gallery.

Star-gazing indeed, Ben thought with a sigh as he stepped out on to the castle ramparts. Resting his lute against the outer wall, he eased his hips into a crenellation and tipped back his head to gaze at the heavens. Jewels on black velvet, he thought, smile twisting. The image would probably appeal to Rose.

Rose. The woman was a mystery. One moment melting in his arms, as warm and loving as a man might wish, and the next snapping at him like a harpy. Had Per mistreated her so badly? Was that the problem? There was the matter of Per's debts, and clearly she had found no joy in the physical side of their marriage, but he did not think Per had beaten her. Was she mistrustful of all men, or was it just him? He gazed at the shimmering blackness. How he regretted having deceived her into making this journey.

Lord. Women. The trouble was, despite his so-called notoriety, Ben knew little about them. Oh, he knew the shallow short-term things: he knew how to entertain them; he knew how to seduce them. But he was woefully ignorant of what he was beginning to see were the deep things. He did not know how to conduct a long-term intimate relationship with one. Ben was shocked to discover that today Rose was as important to him as she had been when he had offered her marriage. He had thought all that was past. Apparently not.

A warm southerly breeze was lifting his hair. Shifting his position in the crenellation, for the stone beneath him was cold, Ben scoured the heavens for constellations he recognised. The Plough. Cassiopeia. Orion the Hunter. And there, brightest by far, Venus, Goddess of Love.

Goddess of confusion, he thought. No wonder the blindfolded Cupid with his arrows was entangled with the whole sorry business. Love.

Raking his hand though his hair, Ben grimaced into the night. Was that what he felt for Rose— love? It couldn't be, he couldn't afford to think of Rose in those terms. As a wandering minstrel who had lost both his father and his mother on the road, he had not the right. And as the Duke's special envoy? Too dangerous, far too dangerous. Ben could deal with danger himself, but as far as Rose was concerned—no. For her safety, their summer tryst must draw to an end.

And that, he realised with something of a jolt, saddened him more than it should. Ben had planned to take Rose to Rennes, to show her the capital of the Duchy—she would have enjoyed meeting Duke Hoël. But with Brittany crawling with Norman spies, and the need to keep the Duke's interests in England dark…

The sooner he got her out of Brittany, the better.

Ben's gaze rested on the dark line of the horizon as the image of his father Albin took shape in his mind. Albin's work for Duke Höel's predecessor had brought about his early death. He must have been mad to put Rose at risk.

And how would Rose react when she learned she had been manipulated into making this journey? Every instinct he had was screaming at him that this was the moment to confess, and yet he could not.

Merde.

Had his father felt torn like this while his mother had been alive? Ben shook his head. He would never know the answer to that one. Throwing a last look at the glittering sky, Ben eased himself out of the crenellation and picked up his lute. He only had the vaguest remembrance of his mother, a soft, shadowy female figure with a warm smile and gentle hands; he could not even recall the tone of her voice.

And Rose, he reminded himself, could have no memory of *her* mother. As Ben headed for the stairwell, his mind floated back nineteen years, to the day when he had found Rose outside the White Bird. He and Adam had been what—five years of age? They had been playing with wooden swords, pretending to be knights.

Moments before Ben had discovered Rose, he had noticed a shabbily dressed woman weeping in a longboat as it pulled away from its mooring in the docks. Why remember that woman tonight? He had not thought about her in years. Had she been Rose's mother? And as for Rose's father, there had never been any trace of him. Hence, Ben suspected, Rose's deep distrust of men. He grimaced. Rose's distrust would hardly lessen when she discovered how he had used her. And Adam too—he had dragged her beloved Adam into this and made him culpable as well. In a good cause, of course, for Brittany and its duke, but Ben suspected Rose would not see it that way….

Lord, what a coil. If only he might tell her. Another grimace. No, *no,* that he must not do, not when Duke Hoël needed those links with his supporters in England. Both he and Duke Hoël *needed* Rose to travel to Wessex.

Even if it put Ben's relationship with Rose in jeopardy?

Even then.

Shaking his head, conscious of a bitter taste in his mouth, Ben started down the winding stair.

* * *

The storeroom door creaked when he pushed it open. In the uncertain light of a candle, Rose and a young woman Ben did not know were seated side by side on a narrow pallet. The woman was tying the knot of a bandage wound round Rose's palm.

'My thanks, Jan.' Rose smiled.

Jan rolled up the unused bandages and put them in a willow basket. 'My pleasure.' Rising, she bobbed a swift curtsy at Ben and slipped out of the room.

'Does it hurt?' Ben put his lute on a wooden chest. There was not much space and it would be safer on the chest rather than rattling about on the floor.

'It throbs a little,' Rose admitted, shifting to one end of the mattress and pulling her pack towards her.

'Did she have to stitch it?'

'No.'

The candle's unsteady flame seemed to cast more shadows than it made light. As Rose turned to busy herself with her things, Ben missed her expression, but by her tone he knew that the anger that had gripped her on the minstrel's gallery was gone. Leaning against the door-frame, he pulled off his boots and began unwinding his cross-gartering.

'Ben?'

'Mmm?'

'Listen.' She rapped the wall behind her with her knuckles. 'This part of the castle is made of wood, yet it looks like stone from the outside.'

'Aye, many castles are made this way. The Count hopes to fool his enemies into thinking Josselin stronger than it is. There's less danger of attack.'

'So—' Rose brought her brows together '—the whole of Castle Josselin is one vast bluff.'

'The keep is stone, and the outer ramparts.' He shrugged. 'As to the rest, it probably is mostly wood.'

'Like a dog raising its hackles before a fight.' Rose gave the wall one last tap. 'I never would have guessed it, from the outside.'

'You are not meant to,' he said, watching as she drew her plait forward to loosen it. The bandage on her right hand glowed white in the candlelight and her movements looked awkward.

'Allow me.' He dropped to his knees before her and set to work. He was conscious of her examining his features; her gaze flickered to his eyes, his lips, his hair. Slowly, her unbandaged hand came to rest on his shoulder, as though it had every right to be there. As her glossy brown hair spilled free of its braid, the scent of jasmine filled the air, engulfing Ben in a wave of longing. Rose.

She was tearing him in two. He did not want to lose her at the end of this mission. The strength of his feeling disturbed him. It was overwhelming.

Her eyes looked black. Moisture gleamed on her lips, her unbound hair shone. Ben did not move, he did not breathe. He could gaze at her forever, Rose, sitting demurely on a crude straw mattress. He caressed the hand on his shoulder and reached for her waist. 'Rose, tomorrow…' he had to clear his throat '…tomorrow we should press on to the coast.'

'We are not going to Rennes?'

He shook his head.

'I see you are in a hurry to be rid of me,' she said lightly, in her teasing voice. Ben even saw a glimpse of one of her dimples, but her question did not deceive him—those huge brown eyes were sad.

He dropped a light kiss on her nose, and adopted a similar tone. 'Rid of you? Hand on heart, lady, I would stay with you till my life's end, if you would but have me.'

He must have imagined the swift sheen of tears in her eyes, for she shook her head with a little laugh and skimmed his cheek with her fingers. 'Careful, Ben. One day some girl will take your pretty words for truth and then you would have to flee the Duchy forever.'

Pain twisting in his belly, he looked deep into

her eyes and saw only shadows. He could read, precisely—nothing. On impulse, he guided her hand to his belt. 'Squire me, Rose, be my lady? Once more?' He was begging as he had never begged a woman in his life, but she did not seem to mind. Her cheeks darkened, she nodded, and then slender fingers were tugging at his buckle.

His mood lightened. Torture lay ahead, that agony and that ecstasy that being with Rose had become, but he could not help himself.

His chest constricted as she pulled off his belt and put it aside. Neatly. Carefully. Sensible Rose.

'What?' she said, noticing his change of expression. 'Why do you smile at me in that way?'

'You are always so neat and tidy, *mignonne.*'

She looped her arms about his neck and drew his head down. 'It is my way, Ben. I am not like you.'

That stung. He *was* neat, he *was* tidy. A man who was permanently on the move had to keep his belongings together if he was to keep them. He opened his mouth to object, to insist that she saw him as he was in reality as opposed to the image she had long been embroidering in her mind, but her lips were only a breath away and…

He groaned. They were warm and tasted of home. One touch and tension and confusion drained away. Home. Her tongue was seeking entry and willingly he gave it, losing himself in the kiss.

Home. His loins throbbed. It was almost unbearable.

Dizzy with yearning, burning with the desire to roll back with her on to the mattress, Ben lifted his head. Rose was wrestling with his tunic. An alarm bell rang in his mind. This time he might not be able to stop himself. And he would not ruin Rose's life for a few moments' ecstasy, tempting though that might be. 'No, Rose, wait!'

'Mmm?'

'Listen, little flower.' Gripping her by the shoulders, he gave her a gentle shake.

Her wide eyes lost some of their dreamy expression. 'Hmm?'

He put a smile in his voice. 'I am your knight, remember, and you must obey me.'

'Ben?'

'Rose, once again, we cannot make love fully, and this is where this is leading.' He gave her another shake. 'What if I give you a baby?'

Leaning towards him, she nuzzled shamelessly at the opening at the neck of his tunic, and he imagined, no, he was certain, that her tongue flickered over his skin.

'Rose, you're in a dream. Wake up. As we agreed before, Sir Richard—' the name and the lie behind it almost choked him '—will not want you if you are pregnant with another man's child.'

'Oh!' She blinked. Frowned. 'Of course not.'

'So…' he stroked her hair from her face and when she leaned into his touch, he knew his smile was crooked '…we must not get carried away.'

No dimples, and the disappointment in her eyes had him wishing he could consign the words he had uttered into oblivion. Instead, he pressed a chaste kiss against her cheek and turned away. 'We must stop, little flower. I am in danger of forgetting myself.'

Chapter Fifteen

Exactly a week later, a somewhat dazed Rozenn stood on the deck of a merchant vessel as it nosed its way into the narrow channel at the opening of Chichester harbour. The ship's prow was carved with the head of a sea snake in the Viking style, and above their heads a massive square sail bellied out with the wind.

England! Rozenn stared at the land that lay to the west and east, as if by looking at it, she could learn its secrets. This was England. So soon. A lump in her throat told her it was too soon. In a day, maybe two, they would reach Fulford. Sir Richard might be waiting for her there, lodging with her brother Adam.

Steadying herself against the slight swell, which was lessening even as their ship felt its way into the channel, Rozenn stepped carefully over the planked ribs of the hull and grabbed the handrail.

The sun was sinking behind the low-lying land. England! She swallowed and closed her eyes.

The water hissed as it stroked the side of the ship, the *English* water. The spume was chill on her face, it dampened her cloak. Rozenn's stomach churned. She had not thought about Sir Richard in days, not since she and Ben had left Château Josselin. The sense of nausea that had gripped her since sighting land had, Rose suspected, little to do with the almost imperceptible rise and fall of the waves, and everything to do with the fact that she no longer cared whether she set eyes on Sir Richard again. No, since leaving Josselin, she had not spared a thought for the Norman knight she had once dreamed of marrying.

Ben had hustled them out of the castle at such speed there had been little time for thought. There had been no horse fair for them, no visit to Rennes. If Rose had not insisted, he might even have ridden off without letting her bid farewell to Sir Eudo and Gien.

Today, Ben sat amidships on one of the roped wine kegs, dark hair ruffled by the breeze as he exchanged jokes with one of the sailors. It had been Ben who had drawn Rose's thoughts when she had not been occupied in keeping her seat on Jet; when she had been clambering down from the saddle stiff as a board after too many hours in the saddle; when she had fallen asleep, exhausted, in yet another strange inn.

He had been tireless, and the image that had come to her once before, that of a sleeping lion, had leapt back into her mind. Except that the lion was no longer sleeping. He had woken up and she wasn't sure what to make of him. He was indomitable, determined, and, towards her, cold. Tears pricked at the back of her eyes. So cold.

He had to have been working for Duke Hoël. His way of life fitted. Ben had entry into every noble house in Brittany—and in Normandy too, for that matter. And then there was the way he was constantly returning to the Duke's headquarters in Rennes. There had to be more to it than Ben organising the Christmas revels. As for that man he had met in the gallery at Josselin, he too must work for the Duke.

Was Ben on a mission at the moment? Was that why he had become so distant, because he was thinking about his work? If only Ben trusted her enough to tell her, if only…

Resolutely, Rose turned her attention back to the landscape, the alien, English landscape that was sliding past their ship. There was no point thinking longingly about Ben. She made herself notice the muddy shoreline; it was broken up by rocks. There were oystercatchers paddling in the shallows. A wide river estuary. Swans, reeds. A flock of gulls flying down the wind, came straight at the ship. They were screeching like the damned.

Blinking away a foolish tear, Rose drew in a lungful of salt-laden air and shivered. Soon she would see Sir Richard. Soon. The wind was cool on her cheeks. The ropes groaned. Behind her the sailors were lowering the sail, she could hear them shouting. Pulleys creaked, canvas flapped. In a very short time they would be making landfall—had she not seen the land for herself, she would have known it from the sailors' voices. Another voyage safely over, those voices said; tonight we will have a proper meal in front of a roaring fire.

If only the nausea would leave her.

'*Holà*, little flower,' Ben said, and she felt a gentle tug on her plait, as he came to stand beside her. 'Almost there.'

Rendered mute on hearing a hint of the old gentleness in his tone, Rose managed a smile. The seascape blurred.

Ben gave her a sharp look and rested his hand on the rail. He scanned the shoreline, keenly and thoroughly. The gentleness gone in a moment. A lion on the hunt.

Their elbows touched and Ben shifted, an imperceptible movement, but enough to put space between them. Since coming aboard, he had scarcely looked at her, never mind touched her. Which was why there was no point thinking about him—she was only making matters worse.

'Ben?' Deliberately, testingly, *foolishly,* Rose slid her hand along the rail and found his strong musician's fingers with hers. Again he edged away.

Her stomach clenched. He will not touch me. It is as though we are already apart. That, and the thought of bidding Ben farewell, she realised, was why she felt sick. She was not seasick, and her fear of water had vanished. Neither was she dreading meeting Sir Richard—the truth was she did not want to bid farewell to Ben. The sick feeling inside was warning her that Ben had already bid her farewell—he had done so when he had wrenched himself out of her arms, in that storeroom in Josselin Castle.

'Ben?'

'Mmm?' He turned towards her, hair pushed back by the wind, face lit by the setting sun. Not so far away—she was close enough to see those tiny green-and-grey flecks in his eyes.

'How long do you think, till we reach Fulford?'

'I am told it is not many miles from the coast.' He gestured at the sun. 'But, given the time of day, and the fact that I do not know the lie of the land, it might be best to find lodgings near the port. We can set out in the morning—with any luck you should be at Adam's holding by noon.'

'S-so soon?' Rose's stomach lurched. A white butterfly fluttered past them. A butterfly? They were nearing the harbour, Bosham harbour. She forced herself to look.

Black masts were sticking into the evening sky like pins in a pinholder. The Norman battle fleet. Dozen on dozen of ships at anchor—it must be the entire Norman navy. Beyond the fleet, Rose made out a wooden quayside and a harbour wall. A church tower glowed apricot in the evening sun. She saw the slow turning of a mill-wheel with the water running like liquid fire into the sea.

Clouds streaked across the sky, edged with pink and gold like the coverlet she had embroidered for Countess Muriel's daughter. It seemed a lifetime ago. As their ship drew up to the dockside, the sky began to darken, grey turning swiftly to black. One last streak of turquoise slashed violently across the sky; in moments it had darkened to purple.

Dusk was upon them, an English dusk. The rank smell of seaweed caught in her nostrils. Ropes snaked landwards; a man leaped on to the jetty; hawsers were looped round bollards. Too soon, Rose thought, throat tight with tears. We have reached Bosham too soon. Already Ben has left me and, in his mind at least, returned to Brittany.

After they had led the horses down the gang-plank, Ben found directions to an inn by making enquiries of two Norman lads who were tossing sticks into the millrace. 'It's probably best to avoid the docks,' he had said, 'if we don't wish to be plagued by sailors.'

It was hard to remember they had made landfall in England, with so many Normans about. Half Duke William's army—no, here in Wessex, Rose must remember he was *King* William, not Duke William as he was known back in Brittany—half King William's army had disgorged itself from the fleet.

They took the road indicated by the boys and rode past the church where the Saxon King Harold had once knelt to pray. The church stood as it had stood for centuries, looking out to sea. The small windows at the top of the tower were like eyes, eyes that must have observed the Norman fleet sail up the channel, eyes that now stared past the shifting masts, to the wider sea beyond. Plainsong was floating out of a studded oak door and past the yew trees in the churchyard. Rozenn shot a glance at Ben. Evensong in England sounded much like evensong in Brittany.

A big stone building lay in ruins by the roadside. The roof had been fired and stripped, charred roof timbers lay every which way. Half the stone walls had gone, but a few courses remained, enough to show the building's original size, otherwise it had been razed to the ground.

Rozenn's skin chilled. This was the first obvious evidence of the recent fighting. From the outline of the walls she judged the building to have been of some importance. Jet picked her way past a scatter of stones that the scavengers had missed. The last rays of sunlight fell on one that was shadowed with fine, deep carvings, fit for a palace.

'Ben?'

'Aye?'

'Harold Godwineson lived in Bosham, I think you said? The man who usurped the English Crown?'

'Aye.'

Rose gave the ruin a final look. It might have been the Saxon royal palace. No more. Duke William, no, *King* William, had brought war to this place along with his navy, and her brother Adam had ridden at his side. Shifting in her saddle, Rose glanced at a Saxon woman with a bundle of kindling strapped to her back. How much brutality had been employed in the conquering of this land? How would the native people regard her, a stranger from Brittany? She was only here because her brother had come in the conqueror's train....

The Buck's Head was pleasant enough. Its common chamber was clean and well appointed, with straw-filled mattresses aplenty, but, notwithstanding this, Rose didn't sleep a wink. All night, her mind kept turning, like the mill-wheel by Bosham church. Her mattress rustled as she shifted and tried to find sleep.

About her, muted conversations went on, in Norman French and in English. One Rose could understand; the other was a mystery. If she was to make her home here, she would learn English. She had arrived in Wessex, but her dreams of marrying a knight, of marrying Sir Richard, lay in tatters. She could not marry him when she pined for...someone else.

Perhaps Adam would offer her a permanent place in his hall instead; perhaps she could make her life with him? She had her skills, a few coins, her trading experience. Maybe Adam's new wife, Lady Cecily, would welcome a seamstress into her household.

Ben was lying in a pool of shadows an arm's length away. Yes, if she were to make her home here, she would learn English. And she would make England her home—there would be no going back to her old life. But Ben, oh, Ben...

Rozenn's throat constricted. Screwing her eyes shut, blocking out the sight of him, she struggled to hold back the tears. Ben was not for her. In a few days he would take his leave of Fulford. Ben must never know how much their parting cost her. For all his gallant pretence, for all his pretty shows of affection, Ben was not and never would be a marrying man. And love him though she might, she was not the woman to live the wanderer's life. Her love was doomed.

Her breast ached, it ached so much she would surely die of it. Curling her fingers viciously into her cut palm, so the fresh pain would distract her, Rose pressed her fist to her chest and dragged in a breath. No tears, Rose. Not tonight, not tomorrow, and certainly not when Ben bids you farewell. Tears would chain him, they might shackle him to some form of guilt and you must not, you shall not chain him in any way.

Ben is a free spirit.

The next day Ben rose and broke his fast before Rose had stirred. By the time she emerged from behind the sleeping curtain, and came to take her bread from the warming stone on the hearth, a Norman wine merchant had told him the quickest road to Fulford. Rose was wearing her blue gown, one on which she had embroidered a complicated Celtic pattern in white threads at the neck and cuffs. This morning her veil, like the embroidery, was white.

'Good morrow, mistress,' the innkeeper's wife said, in a stilted but recognisable version of Norman French. Ben watched as the woman waved Rose in the direction of a couple of platters laid out on one of the trestles. 'Do you care for ham with your bread?'

'No, thank you, but those pears look good.'

Ben took a place beside Rose to keep her company, and watched amused, as she sipped at the mug of local ale she was handed and tried, politely, not to wince. It was a very bitter brew. Rose had, Ben couldn't help but notice, dark circles under her eyes, as if she too had found it hard to rest. 'Only a short ride today—for an experienced horsewoman,' he said. 'So your muscles should not suffer too much.'

She tossed back her veil. 'Thank you, Ben, but I think I have grown accustomed. I have not had much stiffness since Josselin. You drove us at such a pace…'

Her words trailed off. She sounded, Ben thought, almost wistful. As if she too was regretting that their time together was almost at an end.

Ben was only too aware that they did not have much time left. They had one morning at most; and then there would be the excitement of seeing Adam again, and of meeting his wife, Cecily. And most damnable of all, Sir Richard of Asculf might be at Fulford. Richard knew nothing of Rose's expectations, but as Adam's good friend it was quite possible he was there. Christ. Should he tell her now, or enjoy their last few hours together without…?

'Ben? What's amiss?'

Ben dredged up a smile. *'De rien.* Nothing. But if you have finished playing with that pear, we can be on our way. Fulford awaits.'

Assuming the wine merchant was correct about the route, Ben calculated he would have about three more hours alone with Rose. And then?

Rose *must* be told.

The memory of the roles they had assumed on their journeying through Brittany rushed into his mind to taunt him. Rose had loved it when he had assumed the guise of a knight. Her eyes had shone and her whole body had seemed to melt, as she had surrendered utterly to her fantasy. Yes, no doubt of it, Rose wanted Sir Richard and she would never forgive Ben for deceiving her into making this journey.

About two hours to go. So why the devil was he wasting this time? Ben wondered, staring at Rose's back as she rode ahead of him.

They had followed the coast road before turning inland. With the sea on their left, the downs had risen up on their right and they had had occasional glimpses of great chalk cliffs, rearing up out of nowhere, or so it had seemed. The road had climbed and the land had gradually become wooded with beech and oak. Once the cliffs were left behind, it was not unlike parts of Brittany.

Rose's back was rigid. What was she thinking? Was she noting the similarities of the landscape in this foreign land? Or was she—this seemed more likely—dreaming of her chosen one, her knight?

They had not long left. Ben really ought to be talking to her, but it seemed he was losing his grip. He did not wish to spoil their last moments alone by shattering her illusions. *Merde.* He would have to shatter them soon.

He grimaced; there was a vile taste in his mouth. Christ, but that English ale was filthy, bitter stuff. His stomach was having a hard time digesting it. Guts griping, Ben plodded on, and half an hour later— only about an hour and a half to go, he reckoned— they passed a village with a wooden church.

A river meandered alongside the road. There were cress beds and fishponds and thickets of hazel. Brambles curled in and out of the hedgerows; the green fruits ripening in the warm July air.

The sun was shining, the skies were clear, it was a day for knowing happiness, but Ben felt…

The devil was clawing holes in his belly. Rose would loathe the sight of him when she discovered what he had done.

Estimating that it would take them about an hour to reach Fulford, Ben frowned. Surely the angle of the sunlight cutting through the leaves was wrong? He squinted skywards. The sun was shining through the overhanging branches of a beech tree and it seemed far higher than it should. His heart missed a beat, and he looked ahead to see another village, larger than the last. Fulford? *Already?*

There was a wooden hall with a wide green space in front of it—a grand wooden hall, with weathered thatch such as might have once belonged to a Saxon thane. Smoke drifted slowly out of the hall roof. A veiled woman sat on a bench outside the hall, spindle in hand, talking to a very small girl. He heard the honking of geese; the clanging of a smith; and the child's bright laughter. There was a mill and a cluster of outbuildings; a church…

Fulford.

Lord, their time was already at an end. Ben sank his heels into Piper's flanks and drew up alongside Jet.

'Are we here?' Rose shot him a sideways look, before swiftly turning away.

'It would appear so.' Ben reached out and urged her face back towards his. 'Rose, you've not been crying?' She gave him a lofty look that transported him back to Quimperlé and Countess Muriel—the Countess often used just such looks.

'Crying? Heavens, Ben, why should I do that?' She scrubbed her cheek with her sleeve. 'A midge flew into my eye, that is all.'

'I didn't see any midges.'

'Lucky you, I rode through a cloudful.'

Ben heard another gurgle of clear, childish laughter and there, tottering towards them on unsteady legs, was the girl from the hall. The woman looked across, dropped her spindle, and ran to scoop the child out from under the horses' hoofs.

Jet snorted. Ben slid from Piper's back and grabbed Rose's bridle.

Bosom heaving, veil aflutter, the woman—she was pregnant, Ben noted—put the girl on her hips and addressed them. In Anglo-Saxon.

Ben bowed. 'I am sorry, *madame,*' he said, using the few words of English that he knew. 'But please do speak slowly.'

A strand of shining flaxen hair had escaped the woman's veil and curled down past her waist. Her eyes were blue as cornflowers, and her features were fine and delicate. She was stunningly beautiful.

'My apologies.' The woman switched effortlessly to Norman French. 'May I help you?' Her accent was faultless.

'If you please. My name is Benedict Silvester, and this is Rozenn Kerber. We are looking for—'

But the woman's attention had gone straight to Rose. 'You… *You* are Rozenn?'

'Yes. And we are—'

Face alight, the woman surged towards her, child still on her hip. 'Oh, I am delighted to meet you! Adam will be overjoyed you have arrived!' The woman turned, started back to the hall, then whirled back again and laughingly indicated that they were to follow her. 'Please, come with me. Adam will be so happy when he returns, he is out in the practice field with the men.'

The woman's pleasure was so pure, Ben had to smile back. 'And you, *madame?* Are we to know your name?'

'My apologies, my manners! You caught me by surprise. I am Cecily, Cecily Wymark.' Her smile lost some of its force as her gaze met Rose's, as though she was suddenly unsure of what her reception might be. Unconsciously, protectively, her free hand came to rest on her rounded belly. 'Rozenn, I am your brother's wife.'

Following Lady Cecily, Ben led Rose to the hall entrance and helped her to dismount. He steeled himself to face the music. It could not be that bad, surely? He had had some practice at this, having lost Rose before, when she had married Per.

'Brian! Brian!' Lady Cecily called.

A lanky lad came to stand in the doorway, a fellow Breton from Quimperlé. Ben recognised him.

'Brian? Brian Herfu?' Rose smiled and flung her arms about him. 'I am right glad to see you!'

Reaching past her, Ben took Brian's hand and gripped it hard. 'Rose speaks for us both, Brian, it *is* good to see you.'

'My thanks.' Brian looked at Adam's wife. 'My lady, you want me to stable the horses?'

'If you please.'

The doorframe of Fulford Hall was deeply carved in the ancient style. Ben caught a glimpse of a winding snake, of trailing vines, of flowers, artfully entwined. Someone was moving about inside. Tension balled in his stomach like a steel fist. Rose would feel humiliated when she learned the truth, and as for himself, the guilt was killing him. He hated himself. In his life Ben had committed many sins, but guilt had never hit him so hard. He felt sick with it, physically sick. He hoped to God Sir Richard was absent.

Rose was smiling at the child on Lady Cecily's

hip, holding her arms out to her. The girl returned her smile and permitted Rose to take her.

Ben gripped Piper's reins and stared at Rose, drinking in that familiar profile. She had the prettiest smile in Christendom, the most tempting lips. And her dimples too, they were just begging to be kissed…

His heart felt cold as a stone.

'Benedict?' Hand outstretched to take Piper from him, Brian Herfu shot him a puzzled look. 'You can trust your horses to me. Adam taught me himself. I won't neglect them. I'll have your belongings sent in.'

'Yes, come inside, do.' Lady Cecily waved Brian away with a smile. 'You will want refreshments.'

Ben watched the horses go, but his feet did not seem to want to move in the direction of the hall.

'They are fine horses,' Lady Cecily said politely—no doubt she too was misconstruing his reluctance to enter as concern for Piper and Jet.

'Yes,' Rose put in eagerly. 'Ben's Piper was a gift from Duke Hoël.' The pride evident in her voice deepened Ben's sense of self-loathing.

'Your Breton duke?'

'Aye.'

Lady Cecily cast knowledgeable blue eyes over Jet as Brian led her out of sight round the corner of the building. 'That black has good lines to her too.'

'Jet is more placid than her appearance would lead you to believe, but she suits me. I cannot claim to have been born to the saddle.' Rose grimaced. The child perched on Rose's hip tugged experimentally at the edge of her veil. Rose laughed, the child giggled, and Ben felt as though the life was being squeezed out of him. 'Ben had to teach me to ride, when we first set out.'

Ben sensed Lady Cecily's eyes skim over him, as though she were measuring him. Briefly he wondered what her thoughts were. 'Your Jet is a fine animal.'

Rose nodded, and again the child tugged at her veil. More giggles. 'Oh, Jet does not belong to me,' Rose said. 'Ben hired her, I expect he will take her back when he leaves.'

Ben cleared his throat. 'No, *chérie*.' His voice was rusty, like an unoiled hinge. He did not seem to be able to control it. 'I thought you understood. Jet is yours, I bought her for you.'

Rose blinked. Her dimples vanished. 'But, Ben—'

Walking up to her, Ben fixed her with a look. 'We have been through this before, and you would not listen, Jet is *yours*.' The child stuck her thumb in her mouth and started to suck; she misliked his manner. For the child's sake, Ben gentled his voice and forced a smile. 'Accept her gracefully, little flower. Would I want to be trailing back to Quimperlé with a spare horse on a leading rein?'

Lady Cecily's expression was thoughtful. She laid a careful hand on Rose's arm. 'I think you should accept, Rose—if I may call you that. Rozenn seems very formal, and I am used to hearing Adam refer to you as Rose.'

'I… Oh, yes, of course you may.'

Lady Cecily smiled, and a delicate brow arched upwards. She looked from Ben to Rose. 'Well, do you accept this gift?'

Rose's brown eyes met his. Her dimples reappeared. 'I accept, of course I do. My thanks, Ben, you are more than generous.' Pressing a light kiss to his cheek, she surrendered to Lady Cecily's urging and went into the hall. 'He did mention it before,' she added confidingly, 'but I did not believe that he meant it.'

'Oh? Why so?'

Rose snorted. 'Because Ben is…Ben.' She hesitated, and lowered her voice and Ben found himself hurrying after them, practically tripping over the hem of her blue gown in order to catch the end of her sentence. 'When you get to know him, you will realise why. Ben… Ben is such a performer, such an entertainer, it is not always easy to find the truth in what he says.'

Ben took in the hall at a glance. Wooden walls,

plastered and limed, but stained with smoke from the central fire. Great beams arching overhead. A man and a woman sat talking in the light of one of the unshuttered windows.

A trestle was set up at the other end of the hall, under the overhanging ceiling of a loft room. It was set with flagons and a number of pottery cups on a tray. A loaf of bread sat on a board, partially covered in a cloth and a bowl of green apples seemed to glow in the square of light that fell through a shutter. Lady Cecily directed Rose towards the trestle. Ben followed. He felt as though he were walking to his execution. This did not feel right, this…

'Gudrun—' Lady Cecily gestured at the woman by the shutter '—come and meet Adam's sister, come all the way from Brittany. And this is their good friend…'

Ben nodded and smiled while the introductions were made, and hoped he said the right things. A small boy, scarcely more than a baby, was held up for his inspection. His name was Philip, apparently, and he was Lady Cecily's brother. As Ben gently touched the boy Philip's nose, he came to a decision.

Chapter Sixteen

'My thanks,' Ben said, accepting the cup of wine—*wine,* thank God, Fulford was civilised—that Gudrun pressed into his hand.

Rose turned to Adam's new wife. 'My lady?'

'Please, both of you, call me Cecily.'

'My thanks. Cecily, is Sir Richard on the practice field with Adam?'

Ben stopped breathing. *Oh, Lord, here we go.* This could be very awkward. Had Adam told Cecily that they had used Sir Richard to tempt Rose into this journey? He prayed not. However, he would say nothing, just yet. Ben had been in awkward situations before and sometimes the best course was to say nothing. In his line of work, discretion was often the better part of valour.

'I am sorry, Sir Richard is not here,' Cecily said. 'He was recalled to the garrison at Winchester. He left this morning.'

'This morning?' Frowning, Rose reached for the cross at her neck, twisting the chain round her forefinger. Round and round, round and round. 'We only missed him by a few hours?'

'Aye.'

Confusingly, Rose's brow cleared, as though she were relieved by this news. Relieved? 'And Sir Richard will not… He will not be returning?'

'I don't think so.' Cecily laid her hand on Rose's sleeve, her eyes conveying both concern and puzzlement. 'Was it important that you see him? I believe Sir Richard has new orders from the King, but I do not know, precisely. Maybe Adam will know more.'

Ben breathed again. It would appear that Adam had *not* let Cecily in on their plans.

'I see.' Rose let go of her cross and glanced across at Ben. And, yes, her expression had lightened, it had definitely lightened. Ben's heart began to thud. 'I hope my brother does not mind if I stay at Fulford until we may get word to Sir Richard.'

'Would you?' Genuine pleasure lit Lady Cecily's eyes. She gestured admiringly at the cut of Rose's gown and reached for her veil, tracing the embroidery that decorated the hem. 'You made these beautiful clothes yourself, did you not?'

'Yes.'

Lady Cecily smiled, and that curl of yellow hair

gleamed like gold in a beam of light. 'I would *love* it if you could make your home here. You see, Rose, I am not very accomplished in the—how shall I put it—in the ladylike arts. In truth, I make a sorry wife for your brother.'

Rose made a dismissive movement. 'I am sure that is not true.'

Lady Cecily's eyes shone. 'No, it *is* true. I spent many years in a convent, and my time there was spent helping the sisters in the herb garden. I know when the season is right for the sowing of seeds; I can train an apple tree along a wall; I can plant out herbs, manage a vegetable plot—but as to needlework…' She gave an expressive shudder, and laughed. 'Why, you will have seen for yourself, how quickly I laid aside my spindle when I saw you ride up. I was glad of the diversion, I assure you.' She let out a heavy sigh. 'And as for sewing… It is a great flaw in me, and it has never mattered until now…' she rested her hand on her stomach '…when I ought to be making clothes for our baby, but believe me, Rose, I cannot even hem swaddling bands. My maid is, I am afraid, equally unskilled and Gudrun is far too busy. Will you teach me?'

Rose's lips curved and her dimples, both of them, peeped out. 'Assuredly.'

'My thanks. I do want to be a good wife, you see.'

Ben's heart warmed towards Cecily of Fulford. It could not have been easy for her to become Adam's second wife, particularly when his first wife, Gwenn, had been so beloved. Seeing the conversation was turning to domestic matters, and that the danger appeared to be over for the moment, Ben turned away and wandered to the door. Half of his mind listened to Rose and Cecily, while the other half was busy giving thanks that they had indeed missed Sir Richard. He propped a shoulder on the carved doorpost and watched a couple of hens scratching about on the green in front of the hall. In the distance he heard the low rumble of the mill-wheel, and the cackling of geese.

Not here. Sir Richard was definitely not here. He bit back a smile. That gave him some time. He wondered how long he might need. He glanced over his shoulder at Rose, and picked out a phrase or two about the quality of linen best used for swaddling bands. He heard Lady Cecily exclaim as she noticed the cut on Rose's palm. And he realised with something of a jolt that he had not the faintest idea of what Rose felt about Sir Richard's absence.

She does not seem upset. She does not—a burst of laughter came from the trestle—*she does not appear to be pining for him.*

Women! What a mystery they were. And thank

God for it, he thought, a rueful smile twisting his lips as he shot another glance at Rose. She was unpinning her veil. Already she must feel at home. Her hair hung in its thick plait down her back and his fingers itched to loosen it for her. Even though Rose had her back to him, he knew her dimples would be in full view. His spirits lifted. He had liked Adam's Saxon wife on sight, and it would appear Rose agreed with him, which pleased him greatly. But he would have been hard put to define why that should be.

'Adam also told me,' Lady Cecily was saying, 'that you have designed huge wall-hangings for the castle at Quimperlé?'

Rose nodded, put her veil on the table and reached for an apple. Yes, she did indeed feel at home. Cecily was a clever, hospitable, *kind* woman.

Cecily was gesturing at the wall opposite the door, where a smoke-grimed tapestry was hanging. 'My grandmother made that but it is, I fear, past its best. Perhaps when your hand is fully healed and you have taught me to sew a straight seam, we could make a start on a replacement.'

While Ben waited for Adam to come in he listened and watched. He could not read Rose at all. The girl he had known most of his life was a stranger and he did not have the first idea of what she was thinking. His eyes were lingering on her womanly shape, were enjoying the narrowness of her waist and the gentle curve of her hips when a shadow filled the doorway.

Ben swung round, a smile at the ready, but it was not Adam. Brian was bringing in their packs.

Nodding at Ben, Brian hefted their belongings to the other end of the hall, placing them on a chest in what must be the general sleeping area. A series of looped-back curtains confirmed Ben's guess. At night, they would be drawn to form compartments for those wanting privacy.

Brian had put his lute on top of his pack. Startled to realise that Rose had him so abstracted he had left it on Piper's back, Ben wandered over and took it out of its bag. Sitting on a chest, he set about tuning it.

'Lady Cecily?' he said, trying out a note.

'Yes?'

'Is Maurice still with Adam?'

'Indeed, he is his squire.'

Ben smiled. 'I am glad of that.' He indicated his lute. 'I can play for you and your household this evening, if you wish.'

'That is very kind. But I do not want you to feel an obligation, I am certain you must be fatigued after your journey.'

'Not at all.'

'Then I shall be very glad to hear you play. But I should warn you, your reputation precedes you. Both Adam and Sir Richard have informed me that you are the best minstrel in Christendom. Indeed, Adam said that you were only to be rivalled by the Moorish slave-dancers that were stolen from Spain.'

Ben raised a brow. Adam had mentioned the Moorish dancers to his convent-bred wife? 'Adam thinks those dancers more entertaining than I? My lady, I am mortified.'

Rose giggled. Across the hall her eyes were alight with laughter.

Cecily picked up the wine flagon and brought it over. 'I have not seen the slave-girls, of course…' her lips twitched as she refilled his cup '…but I can imagine them. So tonight, you will just have to do your best. Perhaps Adam will change his mind, and rate you above the Moorish slave-girls.'

Ben grinned and, smiling his thanks for the wine, continued tuning his lute.

Rozenn was being shown round Fulford and Cecily had taken her into the cookhouse. Lufu the cook was cracking eggs into a wooden bowl when Rozenn heard a burst of men's laughter coming from the green outside.

'Do you think that is Adam?'

Cecily put down a basket of apples she had fetched from the storehouse, and peered through the doorway. Her face softened. 'Aye, it's Adam. He's by the millpond with the troop. He was not expecting you for a week or so—why don't you surprise him?'

Rozenn didn't need to be told twice and, smoothing down her skirts, she hurried out.

The sun was well past its zenith. The mill-wheel had been stopped and several men—they had doffed their armour, and were clad in simple tunics and cross-gartered trousers—were grouped round the millpond. Swallows and house martins were swooping low over the water and a couple of oversized wolfhounds were bouncing up and down by the reeds at the bank, whimpering with excitement. She saw splashes and heard another roar of laughter, but focused on the figures. Most of Adam's troop were familiar to her, or they had been when he had left Brittany to join Duke William. Yes, there was Maurice, and George, and Félix. And there at last, her brother Adam. Or, to be more precise, her adopted brother. Adam had his back to her, but that black hair and that strong soldier's stance were unmistakable.

'Adam!'

Adam turned. For a moment he looked blank, then his eyes lit up. 'Rose!' Striding over, he met her halfway, grabbed her by the waist and whirled her round exactly as he had done when she was a child. Fulford Hall, the church, the mill and the stables blurred dizzyingly into one.

'Put me down, you wretch!'

Grinning, Adam obliged and a lock of dark hair flopped over one eye. Reaching up to kiss his cheek, Rose smoothed it back.

'Let me look at you.' Adam gripped her by the shoulders and subjected her to a thorough scrutiny. 'You look well. You have caught the sun on your travels.'

'You also look to be in good health. Marriage to Lady Cecily must agree with you.'

'I cannot complain,' he said, in his serious voice, but she could see that he was having trouble hiding a smile.

It had been on the tip of Rozenn's tongue to ask Adam whether he still missed his first wife Gwenn, but Rozenn had seen how his eyes had warmed when she mentioned Lady Cecily. So too had Lady Cecily looked in the cookhouse when she had leaned out and seen that Adam was back from training his men. With something of a lurch, Rozenn realised that while her friend Gwenn would always hold a special place in her brother's memory, his heart was now in the keeping of a Saxon.

Something wet nuzzled her hand; the wolfhounds had bounded up and were vying for her attention. 'Yours?' she asked, drawing back a little. Count Remond had kept wolfhounds and she had learned to be wary of them.

Adam lifted a dark brow. 'They are. At least, I *think* they are.'

'Don't you know?'

'They were Thane Edgar's originally.'

'Cecily's father?'

'Aye.'

'And wolfhounds are usually faithful to one master?'

'Just so.' Adam grimaced. 'Let us say that they did not take to me at once, but I think I have won them over. It has been a long road.'

The dogs flopped into a sitting position, one at either hand, like sentries. Sentries with lolling wet tongues. Rozenn laughed. 'They look loyal now. Do they have names?'

'Rose, meet Greedy and Lightning.' Adam took her arm and turned towards the hall. Behind them, more laughter and splashing came from the pond. 'When did you arrive? Did Mother come with you?'

'No. I am very sorry, Adam,' Rozenn said, her steps slowing. 'Ivona sends you her best love. She filled a bag with gifts for you, but she said to tell you that she is too old and too set in her ways to undertake such a journey.'

Adam nodded, his expression thoughtful, but resigned. 'This is what I feared. Mother will stay in Quimperlé till her life's end, I think. But I am sorry. I would have had her here, so she might live out her remaining years with the honour that is her due.'

'Quimperlé is her home.'

'I see that.'

'Aye, it is what she knows and she is content.'

Adam tugged her braid. 'Whereas you, *ma belle,* you were not entirely happy there.'

Rose focused on the thatched roof of the hall. 'I was not aware that you had noticed.'

'I am not a complete blockhead.'

Rose sighed. 'I was the blockhead, Adam. I made a dreadful mistake with Per.'

'As did I,' came the quiet response. 'I have made a couple of bad mistakes where you are concerned, Rose, and I am more sorry that you can imagine.'

Rose blinked. What *was* Adam talking about?

He put his hand on her arm. 'But once I had word Per had died—'

'How did you hear? I have been wondering.'

'A trader in Winchester market, a Norseman. It turned out he was a distant cousin of Ketill Saffell.'

'The ship master who did business with Per?'

'The same. When this cousin learned that my

lady had married a Breton he struck up a conversation with her and…' Adam lifted his shoulders '…this world is smaller than we realise.'

'So news of Per's death travelled with the traders to England? How extraordinary.'

'Aye. And you may think very ill of me, but I was not exactly sorry when I heard.' He hesitated, his eyes full of sympathy. 'Rose, what of Per's debts?'

'Paid off!'

'Good girl, I am glad to hear it.'

Rose opened her mouth; she was bursting with questions—questions she was half-afraid of asking. Questions about Sir Richard, about whether he was returning; questions about his exact whereabouts, but no sooner had she begun to frame them… 'Adam, about Sir Rich—'

Ben strode round the corner of the cookhouse. *'Adam!'*

Rose snapped her mouth shut and watched as they exchanged greetings and slapped each other on the back in the casual way of men who had a profound fondness for one another. Frowning, she wondered what Ben had been doing; there had been no sign of him this past hour while she had been talking with Lady Cecily. It looked as though he had come direct from the armoury, but what business would Ben have in the armoury? No matter. He had probably been in the stables, checking up on Piper.

'Ben!' Adam was grinning from ear to ear. 'So you did escort Rose!'

What an odd thing for Adam to say. Rose felt confused. It sounded as though Adam had expected Ben to accompany her, but how could that be? They had had that falling out at around the time of her marriage to Per and she was not sure they had been in contact with each other since then. Still, here they were, embracing each other, exactly as though the quarrel had never taken place.

'Adam, let me tell you I have had the devil of a journey,' Ben said, rolling his eyes. 'Your sister…' And then to Rozenn's dismay, Ben reached out and tugged at her braid, as he had done on board the ship in Bosham harbour, as Adam had just done. As a brother would do, a *brother,* blast him. 'Your sister… Do you realise how sadly you neglected her education?'

'I neglected her education? How so?'

'She did not know one end of a horse from the other! Claimed never to have sat in a saddle.' Ben shook his head while Rose spluttered in indignation.

'I never said such a thing! Of course I had sat in a saddle! I just didn't like it.' Rozenn tossed her head, inwardly resigning herself to the fact that, since Ben had joined them, her questions would have to wait. Oddly, the questions no longer seemed so important. She found herself wanting to take Ben's hand. *That* seemed far more important. To prevent herself from doing anything so revealing in front of Adam, she edged away.

'And you the son of a horse-master, and a knight,' Ben was saying. 'Shame on you, Adam!'

'I can ride now,' Rose told Adam, with a touch of pride. 'I even have a horse.'

Adam lifted a brow.

'Yes, and she is beautiful. Her name is Jet and Ben gave her to me.' As she spoke, Rose was conscious of Ben's dark gaze on her. She shot him a glance, and something in his expression put her in mind of Adam when Cecily's name had been mentioned. Warmth surged into her cheeks, and she hastily renewed her interest in the pattern of the thatch along the roof ridge. *Wishful thinking,* she told herself, *wishful thinking.* 'I… I think I will leave you to catch up with your news,' she said, backing away. 'Cecily has promised me a tour of her herb garden.'

'It's that way.' Adam pointed. 'Out beyond the stables, just south of the orchard. You cannot miss it.'

'Oh, yes, I remember,' Rose said, and, picking up her skirts, she fled in the direction Adam had indicated.

Ben watched the gentle sway of Rose's hips as she crossed the sunlit grass and walked towards an arch in some wattle fencing. Behind the fencing, apple and pear trees were in full leaf.

Adam tipped his head to one side, a slow smile dawning. 'My thanks for bringing Rose,' he said. 'And it is good to see you in Wessex at last.'

'I would have come sooner, but the Duke bid me wait until your position here was secure.'

Adam's eyes narrowed. 'I am glad that he did so. But I would have you know that I would not have consented to your involving Rose or my mother for that matter, if my holding had been precarious. It is safer here than in Brittany, I think.'

'You may be right.'

'I confess I have missed little Rose greatly. My hope is that she will choose to stay. Does she know the truth?'

'No. And, Adam, I beg you to say nothing of Sir Richard just yet.'

Adam frowned. 'Why on earth not? The man is miles from here, but he never asked for her hand and this continuing deceit makes me uneasy. She was asking about him a moment ago.'

'And you said…?'

'Nothing, there was no time.' Adam grinned. 'You interrupted us at exactly the right moment. Which is probably a good thing, since I didn't have the first idea what to tell her. We need to discuss this, I don't want Rose hurt.'

'Neither do I, man, neither do I.'

'Then tell me your plans.'

'Aye, we must talk, but since what I have to say concerns the Duke, it needs privacy.'

'I understand.' Adam sighed. 'At least you brought Rose safely to Fulford. I owe you a debt of gratitude for that.' He jerked his head in the direction of the arch, where Rozenn had been joined by Cecily. Both women were smiling. 'I trust my wife will be a more congenial mistress than her majesty Countess Muriel.'

Ben watched, fascinated, as Adam's cheeks darkened. No question but that his friend was head over heels in love with his young wife. If Ben had not seen it for himself, he would never have believed it. Gwenn had been Adam's life, and he had thought Adam would never love again. How wrong he had been. Aloud he said, 'Aye, the Countess and Rose seldom saw eye to eye.' His gaze went back to the two women disappearing into the orchard. 'I hope they learn to like each other.'

'They will.'

'Your lady is not only beautiful; I can see she has a kind heart.'

'She has that.'

'And I hear I am to congratulate you. Already Cecily and Rose have been discussing the making of swaddling bands for your baby.'

Adam smiled. 'Have they indeed? Then you think Rose may stay?'

'You speak Norman French very well, my lady,' Rose said as her brother's wife led her along a scythed path between the fruit trees. The smell of the freshly cut grass was sweet and redolent of summer and the sun was warm on her back.

'I ought to, my mother was Norman.'

Rose blinked. 'So you… You are half-Frank?'

'Yes, it was my father who was wholly Saxon.'

'I see.' Rose's brow crinkled as she puzzled it out. 'I expect your knowledge of Norman French made it easier when you met Adam.'

They had reached the end of the orchard where a wattle gate led on to a small cultivated plot. Laughing, Cecily opened the gate and waved Rose through. 'Hardly. There was…' she hesitated '…some prejudice against him.'

'He was an invader,' Rose murmured, wondering at the nature of the relationship that had developed between her brother and his wife. She had yet to see them together, but Cecily's manner did not indicate that she was unhappy; on the contrary, her every word and gesture spoke of a woman who loved and who was loved in return. A pang of envy sliced through her. 'Yes, I see how it must have been—Adam's liege lord, William, killed your king. Adam was a conqueror. Did you see him as such?'

Cecily sighed. 'I did, I confess it. But once I had proposed to him—'

Rose's mouth fell open. 'You proposed to Adam?'

Cecily bent to pick a stalk of lavender and when she had straightened her cheeks were bright. 'Yes, shocking though that might be, I did. You see, my sister, Emma—Emma is older than me and by rights she should have been the one to marry your brother—Emma did not want Adam, and she gave him to me, and so I…I proposed to him. I was in the convent novitiate at the time, and…' noticing Rose's dumbfounded expression, she laughed and hung her head, but her eyes still sparkled '…yes, you are right, my behaviour was *most* unseemly. I was a novice and I married the man King William gave to my sister. Mother Aethelflaeda practically had me drummed out of the convent.' She lifted her head. 'But that is all in the past. Adam and I are happy now, and never more so now that you have come to join us. I am so glad you are here. Do you think you might stay? Adam would adore it if you made your home with us.'

Chapter Seventeen

Cecily took her hand, waiting for her answer, but Rose did not know how to respond. What about Sir Richard, whom she no longer wanted? What about Ben, whom she could not bear to lose? She reached for the cross and fiddled with the chain. 'I… I am in a slightly awkward situation,' she said. 'And I must confess I am slightly confused as to why Sir Richard is not at Fulford.'

Cecily stared. 'But why should Richard be here?'

'To meet *me!* He did send for me and he must have known I would come as quickly as I could.'

Cecily's gaze rested briefly on the cross Rose was twisting between her thumb and forefinger, and she frowned. 'Sir Richard sent for you?' Firmly, she shook her head. 'I think not, it was Adam who wanted you here.'

Rose's cheeks warmed. 'No, Cecily, you don't

understand. Adam's message… He told me that Sir Richard has asked for my hand.'

'He did?'

'Yes. And I thought I wanted to marry him, but the trouble is that now…that now…'

Cecily was eyeing her cross again, with a puzzled expression. 'Sir Richard asked to marry you? Truly?'

Rose lifted her chin. She did not want to marry the man, not any more, but it was rather galling not to be believed. 'Yes, yes, according to Adam, he did.'

Gentle fingers reached out, lightly touching the cross. 'Sir Richard gave you this, I am guessing, some years ago?'

Impatiently, Rose nodded. 'Yes, Sir Richard and I have known each other a number of years, but I fail to see what—'

Cecily sent Rose a soft smile. 'Rose, you are not the only woman to receive such a cross from Sir Richard.'

Rose blinked. 'Wh-what?'

'I have seen one that is the twin of yours. It is lying at the bottom of Adam's travelling chest. Apparently, Richard gave it to Gwenn when she married Adam.'

'He… He did?' *Two* crosses? There were *two* such crosses? If true, then Rose's cross was not a particular mark of affection as she had assumed. Her heart lifted.

'Yes. It was simply a gesture of friendship.' Cecily's eyes were thoughtful. 'I do not know why Adam should deceive you in this way, Rose, but it is my belief that you have been misled. It is unforgivable of him, but I can only think that he wanted you here and was prepared to use any means at his disposal to lure you.'

'You think there has been no offer from Sir Richard?' A smile began to tug at the corners of Rose's mouth.

'No. I… I am sorry, Rose… *Rose?* You are not angry?'

Laughing, Rose shook her head. Her relief was such that for a moment she could not speak. Her mind whirled.

Adam had sent for her, Adam alone! Her brother had wanted her to come to Fulford, while Sir Richard… Why, Richard of Asculf probably did not even know Adam had summoned her! Rose took a moment to examine her feelings. She might have expected to feel hurt at this revelation; it was something of blow to discover that the man she had been dreaming about had probably not spared her a thought since he had left Brittany. Sir Richard was not, and most likely never had been, the least bit interested in suing for her hand.

How odd. There was no hurt, no frustration, no sense of injured pride, only a deep underlying relief, as though a terrible storm had passed her by. Except…a sense of dread lingered. One particular storm may have moved elsewhere, but other more threatening clouds were massing on the horizon.

Rose gazed through the gate and across the orchard towards the millpond. Several fruit-laden boughs obscured sight of either Adam or Ben, but she heard a great shout. Then came a cheer, swiftly followed by a gust of laughter. Rose did not have to see to know what must be happening. Ben would be playing to the gallery, as usual. And no doubt in a moment Adam would toss Ben in the pond, and Ben would return the favour. Horseplay. Exactly as though they were boys again. It was good to see that they had put their disagreement behind them.

'You are thinking of Benedict, I think,' said a soft voice at her elbow.

'I… I… Yes. I am sorry, my lady, you were asking me something?'

'Cecily, please. I was expressing the hope that you will make your home with us. I do not expect you to answer at once of course, but promise to consider it, for Adam's sake.'

'I will. Yes, of course I will—and I do thank you.' Rose forced a smile, but it was hard work, because suddenly one thought dominated and it was not a happy one. She did not want to stay anywhere unless Ben was at her side. Yes, Ben had escorted her here, and, yes, he might stay a while. A week maybe, a month at most, since this was Adam's holding and they were no longer at odds with one another. But after that Ben would shoulder his lute and climb on Piper's back and…

Briefly, she closed her eyes—she would have to arm herself against that day. She would try to be ready, yes, indeed she would. When she looked again, Cecily's face was full of concern.

'Rozenn? You are fatigued after your journey, you need to rest. Come, let me take you somewhere quiet where you may lie down for a while.' Taking her elbow, Cecily made as if to lead her from the herb garden.

'No, I am fine, thank you,' Rose said. She glanced pointedly about her, seeing the herb garden properly for the first time. It was laid out in neat sections, with low lavender hedging, and the whole plot was surrounded and sheltered by hazel fencing. 'I should like you to show me your garden, if you please.' Anything, she thought, anything to distract me from the thought of bidding Ben farewell. 'It looks to have been recently planted.'

Cecily's face lit up. 'It has; the old one, the one my mother ordered, had run wild. Adam had this one dug for me, and most of the planting was done just before Lent. See, this bay tree has taken well, and this rosemary too.' She gave a little laugh. 'You will have to excuse my enthusiasm, I am a much keener gardener than I am a needlewoman.'

'What I know about gardening would not fit on the head of a pin.'

'Perhaps we could teach each other,' Cecily suggested.

Rose did not know what to say. Cecily's friendliness was warming, but Rose realised that if she committed to settling in Fulford she would be settling on her own. Ben would not be with her. Sick at heart, Rose chewed the inside of her mouth, for the moment oblivious of Cecily, who was awaiting her response. How could Ben stay here? A wandering minstrel could not put down roots. No, if Rose made her home in Fulford, she might see him occasionally, for he would doubtless add Fulford to his regular itinerary. But would a yearly visit be enough?

Her vision blurred. A yearly visit? To see Ben but once a year? What kind of a life would that be?

Blindly, she turned her face towards the woman who had married Adam. 'Cecily…' Her voice cracked and Rose knew her decision had been made. When Ben announced his departure there was only one course open to her…

'Come, Rose,' Cecily said, in her kind voice, and, taking her hand, she led her to a bench by a rosemary bush. 'We scarcely know each other, but I can see you are troubled. I would be honoured if you would consider me your friend and confide in me.' A white butterfly flew past, and Cecily's gaze fastened on it. 'You could begin, perhaps, by explaining your feelings for the charming Benedict Silvester...' Rose threw Cecily a startled look, but Cecily merely smiled and continued. 'I am a trifle confused, but it strikes me that you are in love with him.'

Rose gulped, and found herself confessing. 'Yes, I… I am.'

Cecily tilted her head to one side. 'He loves you too, I think.'

'No, no, there you are wrong. He is fond of me, but Ben loves only his music, that and the road. And he has a secret life, I think—important enough for him to conceal it from me—some kind of work for the Duke of Brittany. But I should not have said that!'

'Well, about Ben himself, I think you are the one who is in the wrong. He loves you.'

As Rose stared, Cecily gave an emphatic nod and her veil shifted. 'Assuredly. But one thing puzzles me greatly, and that is this business concerning Sir Richard of Asculf.'

Rose sighed. It was so complicated. The truth, she must tell Adam's wife the truth. She was not sure whether it was due to the years that Cecily had spent in the convent, but Cecily seemed to deserve only the truth. 'When I was young, I had a dream of how my life would be,' Rose said softly. 'It was rather like one of Ben's ballads.' Catching Cecily's sympathetic gaze on her, she smiled. 'You will have heard similar ballads, I am sure. A young maiden meets a handsome young knight and falls in love with him. He falls in love with her and comes to carry her off on the back of his white charger. He takes her to his castle and...'

'That was your dream? That you should marry a knight?' Cecily's blue eyes were confused. 'Adam told me you married a merchant.'

'Yes, I did. It was a mistake. My husband and I...we were not...compatible.'

'I see.' It was a brief response, but in it lay a world of understanding.

'Also, Per was improvident. He had many debts. So after his death, while I was working to pay them off, the old dream returned. I thought if I married a knight, I would never have to worry about money, I would never feel shame again.' Rose hung her head. 'The... The circumstances of my birth are...shadowy, to say the least.'

A warm hand pressed hers. 'Adam said you were abandoned and that his mother adopted you. He has always been thankful for that.'

'Adam is a good man. Would that he were my brother in truth.'

'He is, Rose, in all the ways that count.' Cecily grimaced. 'Though I could wish that he had not deceived you in this matter of Sir Richard.'

Rose straightened her shoulders. 'Adam knew my dream of old, he knew what I wanted. So when his message reached me, telling me that Sir Richard was proposing marriage, I wanted to believe it. Let us say that I was looking for an escape from Quimperlé, and Adam's message came at the right time…' Her voice trailed off and she found herself staring at a bee as it lurched from one lavender flower to the next. 'I was very foolish, it seems.'

An airy hand dismissed Rose's follies as of no account. 'The important thing is that you love Benedict Silvester.'

'I always have, I think.'

'I am certain that he loves you.'

'Would that that were true, but I am equally certain you are wrong. Because if Ben did love me, he would…' Rose frowned '…he would at least *ask* me, and that he has never done.'

Cecily's eyes sparkled. 'You want him to carry you off on the back of that white charger.'

'Yes, yes, I do! It does not matter that he has no title or castle, I would marry him in rags if needs be.'

'Would you be content to share his wandering life?'

'I used to think that such a life would kill me. I wanted a house of my own.' She gestured about her. 'Perhaps even a garden like this.'

'You have changed, I think.'

'Now a life with Ben…' Rose sighed. 'I am no traveller, but I would journey to Jerusalem and back, if it meant I could be with him.'

'Yes, that is love.' Cecily would have said more, but at that moment two boys rushed into the herb garden, and pounded up to the bench.

'Lady Cecily, Lady Cecily!' the tallest boy got out. His chest was heaving so much he could barely speak. 'We have a message from Matty—'

'Calm yourself, Harold, catch your breath. Rose, these are the miller's boys, Harold and Carl. My maid Matty is their sister. Harold, what is it?'

'It's Matty. She…she…' the boy mumbled and scuffed a leg of the bench with his boot.

'I beg your pardon?'

Harold squared his shoulders. 'Matty gave me a message for you, my lady.'

Cecily blinked. 'Why on earth can't she give it to me herself?' Her brow cleared. 'I have it! She has forgotten to buy the thread we need in Winchester.'

Carl stepped forwards, a cloth-wrapped package

in his hands, he thrust it at Cecily. 'No, my lady, here are the things you asked for.'

Cecily opened the package; it contained several bobbins of thread and a roll of unbleached linen with a supply of needles threaded through it— good, sharp needles judging by the way they flashed to white fire in the sunlight. Her clear brow furrowed and her gaze went from one boy to the other. 'I don't understand, why won't Matty give me these herself?'

A small silence fell. No, not silence, there was a backcloth of noise: the drone of bees in the flowers; sparrows chirruping in the orchard; a wren chattering in an apple tree; and, out by the millpond, the sound of men's laughter. Ben had taught Rose that silence was rarely complete— how right he was.

Harold continued to scuff the bench leg with his toe. Carl seemed fascinated with a patch of mint. At length, Harold took a deep breath. 'Matty's message—she says to thank you for all you did—'

'For taking her on as your maid,' Carl interjected.

Harold nodded. 'That's it. But Matty also said that she is very sorry, but—she will not be coming back.'

'Not for a while, anyways,' Carl finished.

Cecily's hand went to her brow. 'I'm sorry,

boys, I seem to be particularly slow-witted this afternoon. It must be the heat. You say Matty is not returning?'

'No, my lady. She said to say she is staying in Winchester tonight at Evie's new house. And after that…after that…'

Slowly, Cecily rose to her feet. 'It's Sir Richard, isn't it? You are trying to tell me that Matty is going to follow Sir Richard?'

'Yes, my lady,' Carl said. 'That's exactly what she's doing, she's going to follow Sir Richard.'

'And tonight?' Cecily caught Carl's arm. 'You are certain she is not alone?'

'Quite sure, my lady. She's with Evie and Leofwine in Winchester.'

The tension left Cecily's body. 'Praise the Lord, they will talk sense into her, and then we will send someone to fetch her back here where she belongs.'

'Yes, my lady. Thank you, my lady.'

As the boys bowed and left the herb garden, Cecily sank back on to the bench, hand on her belly. Lifting an eyebrow at Rose, she shook her head and muttered under her breath.

'Cecily?'

'Oh, sweet Lord.' Cecily's blue eyes brimmed with laughter. 'The ballads that these minstrels sing would seem to bear much responsibility.'

* * *

The next morning, after breaking his fast, Ben followed Adam to the stables. On the previous night they had taken time to discuss Duke Hoël's business, talking into the small hours, but this morning Ben had a personal favour to ask. Finding a leather bucket, he wandered out to the water trough, yawning.

'Too early for you?' Adam grinned. Beating Ben to the trough, he dipped his bucket into the water.

Ben rolled his shoulders and grunted. He had not slept well in Adam's hall, but neither the hall nor the pallet were to blame. He had been ushered to a place behind the curtain in the unmarried men's sleeping area while Rose, as an unmarried woman, had made her bed on the other side of it. Though Ben had known she was nearby, he had missed her. He had missed her scent; he had missed her warmth; he had missed her softness. Damn it, he had missed talking to her. Without Rose at his side, the night was empty and dark and the few yards between them had yawned like a chasm. In a fever of yearning, he had tossed and turned for hours; dawn had been a long time coming.

Adam's gaze was speculative. 'Pallet too hard? Or was it the late night?' As Adam's grin broadened, Ben realised that Adam had drawn his own conclusions as to why Ben was bleary-eyed. Adam was doubtless recalling that Ben had once offered for Rose and knew Ben wanted her close.

Scooping water into his bucket, Ben thought about the favour he was about to ask and repressed the urge to toss the contents into Adam's face. Instead, he marched back into the stables. Setting the bucket down, he propped himself against a wall and watched thoughtfully as Adam backed Flame, his chestnut destrier, out of his stall. Flame was magnificent, a worthy mount for a knight high in the favour of his king. Adam motioned at a lad to begin mucking out.

'You were snug in that sleeping loft with your lady,' Ben said, leaving Piper and Jet in their stalls as he followed Adam and Flame into the yard. 'But you might spare a thought for me wedged in between Brian and Maurice. They were singing a nightmare of a duet and I swear it lasted the night through.'

The sun was rising above the roof of Fulford Hall and another boy was harnessing a mule to a cart. A couple of scythes and a pitchfork gleamed in the morning light. It would be another hot day; they would probably be haymaking as soon as the sun had burned away the dew.

'Brian and Maurice? They were snoring again? Bad luck.'

'Bad luck? I tell you another night like that and I'm off.'

Adam laughed and stroked Flame's neck. 'You can't, at least not for a while. As you explained it, the Duke's business demands that you remain here. Besides, Fulford could do with a minstrel now Sir Richard has left.'

Ben folded his arms across his chest. 'He played for you?'

'On occasion.' Adam's glance in his direction was swift, but keen. 'Richard has improved considerably since you last heard him at the White Bird.'

Ben smothered a curse and did not reply. He had heard enough of Sir Richard of Asculf to last him a lifetime, and he did not want Adam of all people to start singing his praises.

Across Flame's neck Adam's eyes were watchful. 'You are not happy.'

'What is happiness?' Ben responded, and even to his own ears he sounded bitter. 'It comes, it goes...' He shrugged. 'However, I have plans...'

When Adam stopped stroking Flame's neck, Flame tossed his head and butted him in the side. 'It's Rose, isn't it? Whatever was between you— it has flared up again. I thought—no, I will admit it, I *hoped* this might happen. In all truth, that was the main reason I agreed to your involving Rose in the first place. Do you...' He gave Ben another penetrating glance. 'Do you want to try for her hand?'

Ben shook his head. 'I'll not ask again.'

Adam frowned. 'You are certain? I made a mistake when I refused you before—I would not make the same mistake twice.'

'No, I shall not be asking for her hand. However, there is something I would discuss with you.'

Adam rested his arms against Flame's back and looked at him. 'And that is?'

'As far as Rose is concerned, I am not ready to withdraw from the lists.'

'I am right glad to hear it.'

'Rose wants a hearth and a home, Rose wants stability.' Ben grimaced, waving his arm to encompass Fulford. 'But how the hell does a minstrel provide the likes of this for her when the longest he spends in any place is twelve nights? And that is at Duke Hoël's Christmas court in Rennes. Believe me, Adam, the court is hardly the place to set up hearth and home.'

Adam nodded. 'I remember Rennes vividly and I agree Rose would hate it. But, Ben, I am sure that Duke Hoël—'

'What I need,' Ben continued, 'and what Rose needs, is a house somewhere, a cottage, even—it need not be large. And then I could...' Shaking his head, he rubbed at the back of his neck. 'But what lord would give a minstrel a house if he knew he was likely to vanish on his errant way whenever the need took him?'

Adam held Ben's gaze a moment, and said, quietly, 'You're looking at him.'

Ben's heart thudded. 'Eh?'

'You heard me perfectly well, Benedict,' Adam said, lips curving. He jerked his head in the direction of the green. 'You will be needing a base in Wessex and I have a cottage that just might suit. It is next to the church and we have spent the spring repairing it. I thought to house my mother and Rose there, but since the Duke has commanded you get established here…'

Ben took a couple of involuntary paces across the yard, hesitated, and looked back. 'Adam? You mean this?'

Looping Flame's reins around a hook, Adam slung an arm across Ben's shoulders and began walking him past the hall and across the grass. 'Of course I mean it. Rose is my sister and I want her to stay, if she chooses to, naturally.' His smile was lopsided. 'Had I known offering her a place would mean you remaining with her, I may not have been so keen!'

'My thanks.' Ben let Adam's teasing pass over his head, because he was staring at a cottage facing the green that could have been built with Rose in mind. It was wooden, built with wide, seasoned planking, and it had a sturdy door and two shuttered windows at either side. The windows were large enough to admit plenty of light, so a woman could sit by the fire in winter to do her sewing and not get too cold…

The thatch had been patched. It still needed repairing in parts, but… As Ben stared, a house martin darted in under the eaves. House martins! Exactly as there had been at her house in Quimperlé. He could picture Rose in that cottage, he really could. Rose and him. Together. They would not be penniless, for the Duke paid him well, but with Ben needing to continue the pretence that he was merely the Duke's favourite minstrel, he had not been able to work out how to get Rose a settled home.

However, if it were made known that Rose's *brother* had provided for her…

Swallowing hard, Ben looked at his friend. 'Adam.' He could barely speak for the rush of emotion. Firmly, he gripped his hand. 'My thanks. You are the answer to many prayers. I would have been hard pushed to achieve this for her without endangering my work for the Duke.'

Adam grinned. 'Ben, you are my greatest friend. Besides, you are not the only man who wishes to support Brittany's interests in England.'

'Adam, Cecily has given me an idea and I need a favour.'

'What, *another* favour?'

Ben grinned. 'Actually, *two...*'

'Yes?'

'One, I shall need to borrow Flame...'

'*Flame?* Good God, man, what else might you want—my back teeth and my right arm, perhaps?'

'No, you may hang on to those, but I will also be needing your hauberk and helm.'

'That's *three* things!'

'So it is. Well? What do you say?'

Chapter Eighteen

Rose was walking some yards behind Harold and Carl's haycart when the bell for vespers began to ring. She had spent the day exploring the village, testing her resolution, and had come to a conclusion that was both happy and painful. If she could choose a place in which to make her home, it would be Fulford.

A lone figure in her blue gown, Rose was wearing a pair of kid shoes that Cecily had given her. The thin soles were no protection against the hardness of the dried-out ruts in the road, but Rose was very glad of the shoes, it was far too hot for her clunky travelling boots. Earlier, when watching Harold and Carl scything the hayfield, Rose had removed her veil and tucked it into her girdle with her headband. As she neared the church, the cream lawn fluttered at her side, like a knight's pennant.

The boys and the cart, their mule, the freshly cut hay, indeed the whole of the village was bathed in a golden glow. While the boys' cart rattled and bumped to a halt outside the church, Rose glanced westwards. The sunset was breathtaking. If only she could replicate those exact colours in a tapestry: that clear blue above the dark line of trees on the hill, a blue that somehow gave life to those wild splashes of apricot in the clouds, to those dazzling bronze edges. Though the sun itself had lost most of its power and dusk was fast creeping up on them, the sky was so bright, so glorious, it almost hurt to look at it.

A house martin hurtled across the village green and whisked under the eaves of a cottage next to the church. For a moment time seemed to stop. A wolfhound bayed once, twice and, from the other side of the hall, Rose heard the chink of chainmail and the soft neighing of a horse. Perfect. Fulford was perfect. If it were not for one thing…

The glow in the sky intensified. And then, even as a horse clattered out of the stable yard and on to the green behind her, the flush of pinks and apricots were blending with deeper colours, with madder red, with oxblood. Sinister hues, but none the less heartbreakingly beautiful. Rose gazed, memorising the colours, determined to get them on canvas.

Behind her, the horse broke into a trot.

Her instincts awoke. Those hoofbeats were too loud, the horse must almost be upon her. Frowning, but not unduly alarmed, Rose turned. The road was wide enough, and surely no horseman from Adam's stables would ride their lord's sister down…

She froze. A warhorse was thundering right at her, the knight's face hidden by the noseguard of his helmet. Something did not fit, but there was no time to ponder on what that might be. Heartbeat matching the pounding of those great hoofs, Rose leapt to one side. The warhorse swerved. Nostrils flaring, it headed straight for her, churning up a cloud of dust.

Dimly, Rose heard shouting by the stables. Adam, she thought she recognised Adam's voice, but she must not look in that direction, she must watch the destrier as it barrelled towards her, mane and tail flying. She lurched towards the ditch. Leather creaked, the knight—he was oddly familiar—leaned towards her, acrobatic as a tumbler on a performing horse. A tanned hand stretched out and gripped her by the girdle. No chain-mail. This knight was wearing only a leather gambeson over a kingfisher-blue tunic. And surely she knew that hand as well as her own…

Gripping the crupper of his saddle, he hauled at

her so violently her breath was jerked from her body. If she did not help him, she, and possibly he, would land in the ditch or, worse, they might fall under those drumming hoofs. Clutching at his outstretched arm—*Ben,* it was *Ben!*—Rose found his foot with hers and pushed. The clasp of her girdle gave way with a pop. Her cream veil fell between the horse's legs, was pounded into the ground. She did not see what happened to her headband. Ben grunted, she squealed, he hauled and twisted, and then somehow she landed ungracefully behind him on the back of the saddle and could breathe again. Her skirt was about her hips, the side seam had ripped.

'Hold hard!' Ben said, guiding her hands about his waist. She heard more shouting from the stables and the sound of running feet. Laughter. Adam's.

Of course! This was Adam's warhorse, Flame. Ben kicked his flanks and gave him his head, one hand firmly gripping hers. Rose clung for her life.

Fulford mill, the fishponds and the hayfield raced by. They careered on, up the hill that led, or so Rose had been told, to the woods and thence to the downland where they grazed the sheep. Ben let the great horse slow when they reached a line of beech trees that stretched for the sky. He turned, and his helmet and the leaf canopy behind him were both silhouetted against the sunset.

Her heart was pounding, but Rose smiled. She was not afraid because this knight had deep brown eyes, with green-and-grey flecks in them. His lashes were long and dark, like the knight she had ached for, the knight that had never existed. 'What in God's name is this, Benedict Silvester?'

'I'm carrying you off. Got the idea from Cecily.' Tugging off the helmet, Ben looped it round the pommel. His hair stuck out in all directions.

Without thinking, Rose lifted her hand and combed her fingers through it. When he raised an eyebrow and grinned, she slid her hand down to rest on his shoulder, which was clad in Adam's leather gambeson. It was slightly too large for him. 'No chain-mail?'

Ben dismissed chain-mail with a grimace. He was breathing hard. 'Tried it, too restricting. Was afraid I would drop or bruise you. Thought we should do better without it.'

'Real knights wear chain-mail,' she said softly, absurdly pleased that he had gone to all this trouble.

'I know it. But I am not a real knight, and never will be. However, *I am going to keep you.*'

And then Ben faced forward and Flame plodded on up the hill. The horse's chest was heaving too from his recent exertion.

Happiness blooming within her, Rose leaned

her cheek against Ben's leather-clad back and sighed. 'Keep me? What do you mean?'

'Just that. I am not going to let you go. You are my prisoner, little flower.'

She lifted her head. 'Don't you think we should have this conversation on the ground? The back of this saddle is fiendishly uncomfortable.'

'No.' Twisting his head, he flung her a smile. He had never looked so handsome. 'I have gone to a lot of trouble to put you at a disadvantage, and I am going to keep you there until you have agreed.'

'Agreed? Agreed to what?'

'Rose, you are going to marry me.'

'I am?' More happiness, it flooded her whole being.

'Yes, you are. As soon as possible.'

'It is customary,' Rose said, 'for a knight to go down on bended knee, for a knight to ask—'

His head jerked round; he was scowling. 'Rose, I asked you before and you refused me—'

'I refused you? Ben, what *are* you talking about?'

Dark brown eyes gazed intently at her. 'You refused me, Rose, don't try to deny it.'

'Ben, I am not trying to deny anything, but I have to say I don't know what you are talking about.'

'Back in Quimperlé, before you married Per…I asked for your hand. Adam said—'

There was pain in his eyes. Seeing it, Rose touched his cheek. 'Ben, I never knew.'

'Adam never told you?'

'No, no, he didn't.' Rose brought her brows together. 'But yesterday, when we arrived Adam did mutter something about having made some bad mistakes as far as I was concerned. At the time I did not know what he was talking about.'

'Truly, you never knew I wanted to marry you?'

'No.'

'Well, there will be no arguments today. You *will* marry me.'

'Will I, indeed?'

'*Yes.*'

Rose swallowed and her arms tightened about his waist. Her lips curved—she could not stop them. 'Th-that sounds very domineering,' she said, aglow with happiness, because she had picked up on a slight uncertainty in his voice. Ben would never force her into anything unless he knew that in her heart she wanted it. Which in this case she did. It was not the most sensible of matches, but she loved him and wanted to marry him, wherever that might take them.

'You will agree?'

'There is one condition.'

'Condition?'

'Ben, there must be no secrets between us. If

you are some kind of undercover agent for Duke Hoël, I want to know about it.'

'You know?' His voice was startled. 'You know I work for the Duke?'

'I became certain after we had left Josselin.' She maintained her grip about his waist. 'I know your work is dangerous, Ben, and I would never betray you. But I do need to know that there are no secrets between us. We must trust each other. Fully.'

'I agree,' Ben said, and his brow cleared as he pressed a swift, hard kiss to her cheek. It was not enough, but already he had turned back to the road. They had reached a fork and he urged Flame down the left-hand track.

'Ben?'

'Mmm?'

'Where are we going?'

'You will see.' His voice had a smile in it.

'I think we should return to Fulford.'

'Wait and see.'

'But my things, Ben, I have left my things behind. I did pack but…oh! What about Jet and Piper! Ben, we can't leave our horses behind!'

'We are not going to leave anything behind,' Ben said. He pointed ahead. 'Look, little flower.'

Rozenn blinked. Ahead of them was Fulford mill, or its exact match, flaming in the evening sun. But, no, it *was* Fulford. There was the church, the green and the hall, bathed in the last rays of the sunset.

He drew rein outside the cottage next to the church and dismounted. When he reached for her, his eyes were laughing. 'We turned round a ways back.'

Taking his hand, Rose slid from the saddle and let herself stand within the circle of his arms. 'Oh.' She would have felt stupid if it were not for the light in Ben's eyes. He was insisting she married him, as if he did not realise that her ambitions to marry Sir Richard had been left behind in Brittany. To herself she was at last able to acknowledge that her happiness lay in Ben's hands; she would follow him to the ends of the earth. She would tell him as much, once they were married.

'Come on, *chérie.*' Ben led her to the door of the cottage as a house martin arrowed past them and vanished under the eaves. In their nest, its babies twittered and cheeped.

'Ben?' He pushed open the cottage door and bowed her in. Bemused, Rose stepped over the threshold.

The fire in the central hearth had been lit and water was bubbling in a cauldron hanging from a chain in the rafters. The light angling through the shutters fell on a scrubbed wooden table upon which stood a couple of candles, beeswax by the look of them, and a tray with a wine-pitcher and two goblets. Some food too, Rose guessed, covered by a cloth. There was a posy of wild roses in an earthenware jug.

A wide box-bed was set to one side of the cottage, in the gable end. It had been made up with white linen, which Rose recognised because Cecily had shown it to her earlier that day, when she had asked her opinion of its quality. It was of the finest. Another spray of wild roses, prettily bound with streamers of cherry-coloured ribbon, was nailed to the beam above the bed. The flowers put her in mind of Mikaela. Rozenn's eyes filled.

Ben was watching her, a smile on his lips. 'You like it?'

'Of course I do. I *love* it, all of it. But I don't understand. Is this Adam's guest-house? Are we to rest here while we are in Fulford?'

Hands on her waist, he drew her close. 'It is ours, *ma belle*. Welcome to our home.'

He would have kissed her, but she drew back, bemused. 'Ours? But how can that be? It will be empty most of the year, while we are travelling.'

Nuzzling her ear, Ben gave it a slight nip. 'No, it won't,' he murmured, breath warm on her cheek. 'We won't be travelling. Rose, Fulford can be our home. For one thing, Adam has a need of a minstrel—'

'He can't afford you every day!'

'No, but his reeve is getting on in years, and Adam wants someone to take over from him. And Cecily likes you and she tells me there is great need of someone in Fulford who can sew a straight seam. Her maid has run off and lord knows when she will be back and…' Ben sighed and looked into her eyes as his hand wandered to her hips and his fingers began edging up her skirts. Hot blood rose to her cheeks, her heart thudded. 'Can't this wait, *ma belle?* You know you want to live here.'

'And the other thing?'

'The Duke has commanded me to ensure that a base is established in England for his supporters to… Rose, can't this wait?'

Stunned, Rose steadied her weakening knees and reached up to caress his cheek. Dusk hid his expression. 'You… You are prepared to settle in one place? *You?*' She had accepted him; she had made him promise there would be no secrets, but this she had not expected.

Turning his head, he kissed the cut on her palm. 'Yes, since you will marry me and be at my side. I think that I have always loved you. It is just that after you refused me—'

'Ben, I told you, I never refused you.'

'Adam thought me unsuitable.' He gave a

dramatic sigh. 'Genevieve's bathhouse, now there was a place…'

'You'll not be visiting Genevieve's again, I hope.'

He nuzzled her ear. 'It was never as bad as Adam thought. I only went there on the Duke's business.'

Rose put her hands on her hips and tapped her foot. 'Ben?'

He grinned. 'Never again, I swear.'

Rose's heart swelled. Sliding her hand into his hair, she drew his head down and their lips met. As she pulled him close, closer, the scent of him, familiar and beguiling, filled her nostrils and her mind. The warmth of his lips moving over hers was the only warmth she would ever want. This was Ben, and he was hers at last. The hard length of his body pressed against hers was demanding a response and for a moment she gave it before tearing her lips free. 'You must love me.'

'Always, little flower.' His grin was crooked, an eyebrow lifted, and the love in his eyes brought her hands round his neck.

Ben's love. It had been there for years and had she not been blinkered by ambition and fear, she might have known it. She caressed the silky dark hair at the nape of his neck, almost swooning with lust when he groaned.

'Rose, I do love you.' His voice was husky, his expression intent. 'I will *never* abandon you.'

He was thinking about her mother, she realised, remembering how he had found her abandoned by the wayside. He was reassuring her because he knew that deep down she had always felt insecure. 'So this cottage—' she pulled herself out of his arms '—is truly ours.'

'Indeed.'

Joy bursting out of her, Rozenn evaded his hands and danced towards the door. 'Our house. *Our* house.' Reaching for the latch, she grinned. 'Let me fetch my things, I won't be a moment.'

'No, you don't.' He came swiftly towards her and squashed her to the door with his body. His head came down and he touched his lips to her neck, breathing into her ear. 'Later, little flower, fetch your things later.'

'But…' Under Ben's gentle but determined on-slaught Rose's thought processes were muddled. Her insides were melting, but there was some-thing she must tell him. 'It will only take a moment—I was ready to leave Fulford so every-thing is packed.'

'Packed?' His eyes were as dark with passion as she knew hers must be. 'You were ready to leave?'

She twined her fingers in dark hair that was soft as silk and nodded. 'Certainly I was, at a moment's notice.'

Now it was he who was drawing back, holding

her above the elbows. There was hunger in his eyes, definite hunger. 'Rose?'

'You know why,' she mumbled, flushing. Suddenly shy, she would have looked away, but he caught her by the chin.

'Rose? Why were you packed and ready to leave?'

She could not wait till they were married to tell him—he needed to know at once, the intensity of his gaze made that quite clear. 'Didn't want to get left behind when you left.'

His mouth fell open. It was the first time in her life she had seen Ben do anything as inelegant. 'You… *You* were ready to come with me? To abandon hearth and home? To be my woman?'

She shrugged. 'To share your life, if that was what you wanted.' Her eyes met his and she grinned. 'I did hope that you might marry me, but thought perhaps that I might have to be the one to ask, as Cecily did with Adam.'

'What happened to your desire for a knight?'

She reached up on her toes and kissed his cheek, smiling as his arms snaked round to hold her snug against him. 'Oh, that? Nothing but a young girl's dream. It was the Duke's lute-player I really wanted.' Half-heartedly, she struggled to free herself. 'But do let me fetch my pack. If this cottage is going to be ours, I would like my things brought over from the hall.'

'Not a chance. You can fetch your things later, we have waited long enough.' Ben's grip shifted and, holding her one-handedly, he flipped the shutters closed and shot the bolts home. Before Rose could blink she was being picked up, warm lips were pressed to hers and the hot blood surged in her veins. He set her down by the bed, fingers busy at the lacings of her gown. Abruptly, his fingers stilled. 'But first, you have something to say to me, I think.'

Rose reached for the buckle on his gambeson. As it fell away, she opened her eyes wide. 'And what might that be?'

'Don't you flash those dimples at me, you know very well what I mean. Say it, Rose, for pity's sake.'

Placing her hands on his chest, Rose held his eyes with hers. 'I love you, Benedict Silvester. Please marry me and…and never ever leave me.'

Face transfigured, he caught her to him and they tumbled, limbs tangling and fingers caressing, on to the fine white linen.

'Rose.' Ben's voice was choked. He had stopped kissing her and was running his hand over her breast, and a fiery longing such as Rose had never felt in her life shot from her breast to her core. 'Squire for me?' His other hand was tugging at the hem of her gown.

'No, my love, I'll never do that,' Rose said, even as she was lifting her hips to help him ease her gown up to her waist. 'Never again.'

Ben drew back and his eyes, dark with need and cloudy with confusion, met hers. 'Little flower?'

Smiling, she took the opportunity to pull his tunic and shirt over his head. Placing her hands on his chest, she ran them up and over the muscles of his shoulders. Lifting her head, she pressed a kiss in the centre of his chest. 'Beautiful,' she murmured. 'Beautiful Benedict.' His shudder went through her, as did his half-suppressed groan. Briefly she wondered if his insides felt molten, as hers did. 'I will not squire you because that game belongs in the past. I am marrying a lute-player and lute-players—even the Duke's own lute-player—do not have squires.'

'I am still the Duke's man,' Ben muttered, pressing kisses on her neck. 'He needs eyes and ears in Wessex. There's Winchester and…'

Rose yanked at the ties of his hose and pushed them impatiently down over his buttocks. And then there were no more words for Ben's mouth came down on hers, confident, possessive. His tongue slipped between her lips, in imitation of that last, final intimacy that they had never shared.

All thought, all reason fled. His fingers slid over

her belly, down farther, found her ready. Both of them groaned, both were breathing fast.

Now, Rose thought, as he positioned himself over her. *Now.*

He gave a single thrust and then he was inside her. For an instant, he froze. Rose felt no soreness, only a delightful sensation of fullness. But, of course, this was Ben, he would feel right inside her.

'No pain?' he managed.

'No.' She ran her fingers over his cheekbone. 'I… I'm not too small?'

A startled laugh. 'Never. You…' withdrawing a fraction, he pushed a shade deeper '…are…' quivering, he repeated the movement '…perfect.' And then he was driving into her hard and fast, and she was helping him, holding him to her, gripping his buttocks with her nails, panting his name over and over.

Faster and faster. There was only this—Ben's body over hers; Ben, inside her; Ben and a magical tension that wound tighter and tighter with his every thrust. She wanted nothing but this. He shifted on to his elbows. He was watching her, and that dark, beloved face was taut with passion. Hands holding her head, hands she was astonished to feel were trembling, he buried his face in her neck, thrusting deeper, more frantically with every stroke. 'Little flower,' he muttered.

And then it happened. It felt as though she had been flung into the stars as something tightened inside and she throbbed and pulsed around him.

Ben groaned, gave one final, shuddering thrust and collapsed on top of her, panting.

Cradling his head, Rose swallowed and watched as though from another world. Her breathing slowed, her heartbeat steadied. 'So that,' she said, at last, clearing her throat, 'is what the washer-women in Quimperlé were talking about!'

Rolling to his side, Ben eased his weight off her. 'Hmm?' He pulled her head onto his shoulder. 'What's that?'

The firelight was shining in his eyes. Smiling, Rose ran her hand along his jawbone and brought his lips back to hers. 'I wonder if you can make it happen every time…'

* * * * *

HISTORICAL

LARGE PRINT

SCANDALISING THE TON

Diane Gaston

Lydia, Lady Wexin has been abandoned by her family and friends, and creditors hound her. Her husband's scandalous death has left her impoverished, and the gossip-mongering press is whipped into a frenzy of speculation when it becomes clear the widow is with child. Who is the father? Only one man knows: Adrian Pomroy, Viscount Cavanley…

HER CINDERELLA SEASON

Deb Marlowe

Lily Beecham has been taught that pleasure is sinful – now she is determined to find out for herself! Freed from dowdy gowns and worthy reading, Lily charms Society – except for the cold, aloof and wildly handsome Mr Jack Alden. At the end of the Season Lily must return to normality – unless the wicked Mr Alden can save her from a future of good behaviour…

THE WARRIOR'S PRINCESS BRIDE

Meriel Fuller

Benois le Vallieres, legendary Commander of the North, is ruthless in battle. But when he rescues Tavia of Mowerby, a feisty yet vulnerable maid, she gets under his skin like no woman before… When her royal blood is discovered, Tavia has his protection and his passionate desire – but will she ever melt his frozen heart?

MILLS & BOON®
Pure reading pleasure™

HIST0209 LP

HISTORICAL

LARGE PRINT

SCANDALOUS SECRET, DEFIANT BRIDE

Helen Dickson

Some call Christina Thornton spoilt, others simply call her beautiful. But one thing's for certain: she's a young woman firmly in charge of her destiny – or so she thinks! But when the dark-hearted Count Marchesi rides into town, it is to claim Miss Thornton as his bride. Her future is in the hands of this brooding Italian…

A QUESTION OF IMPROPRIETY

Michelle Styles

Diana Clare has had enough of London – the balls, the rakes you can never trust. Having returned home in disgrace, she is trying to forget what drove her from the *ton*. But rake and gambler Brett Farnham, Earl of Coltonby, seems intent on making Diana remember *exactly* what it was like to be seduced by the glint in your partner's eye…

CONQUERING KNIGHT, CAPTIVE LADY

Anne O'Brien

There is no way Lady Rosamund de Longspey has escaped an arranged marriage only to be conquered by a rogue. But Lord Gervase Fitz Osbern, weary of war and wanton women, will fight for what rightfully belongs to him. A warrior to his fingertips, he'll claim his castle – and just maybe a bride!

MILLS & BOON®
Pure reading pleasure™

HIST0309 LP

HISTORICAL

LARGE PRINT

MISS WINBOLT AND THE FORTUNE HUNTER

Sylvia Andrew

Respected spinster Miss Emily Winbolt, so cool and cynical with would-be suitors, puts her reputation at risk after tumbling into a stranger's arms. Her rescuer is none other than Sir William Ashenden, a man of some distinction. He needs to marry – and Emily yearns to believe that he wants her not for her fortune but for herself…

CAPTAIN FAWLEY'S INNOCENT BRIDE

Annie Burrows

Battle-scarred Captain Robert Fawley was under no illusion that women found him attractive. None would ever agree to marry him – except perhaps Miss Deborah Gillies, a woman so down on her luck that a convenient marriage might improve her circumstances. Deborah accepted his pragmatic proposal – because she was already halfway to falling in love with him…

THE RAKE'S REBELLIOUS LADY

Anne Herries

Tomboy Caroline Holbrook is used to running riot, and can't imagine settling into a dull, respectable marriage. But her zest for life and alluring innocence draw the attention of Sir Frederick Rathbone – who is far from dull! In fact, he's the most exciting man Caroline has ever met. But should she resist the attentions of this rakish bachelor…?

MILLS & BOON®
Pure reading pleasure™

HIST0409 LP

HISTORICAL

LARGE PRINT

THE CAPTAIN'S FORBIDDEN MISS

Margaret McPhee

Captain Pierre Dammartin is a man of honour, but his captive, Josephine Mallington, is the daughter of his sworn enemy… She is the one woman he should hate, yet her innocence brings hope to his battle-weary heart. As the Peninsular War rages on, can the strength of their love conquer all that divides them?

THE EARL AND THE HOYDEN

Mary Nichols

Miss Charlotte Cartwright has never forgotten Roland Temple's contemptuous rejection of her hand in marriage. And she's not about to forgive, either – even if Roland, the new Earl of Amerleigh, is now older, wiser and ten times more handsome! But Roland is determined to right the wrongs of the past – and this time the hoyden will be his bride…

FROM GOVERNESS TO SOCIETY BRIDE

Helen Dickson

Lord Lucas Stainton is in need of a governess. The man is ruthless, rude beyond belief, and Eve Brody wishes him to the devil – but the position is hers if she'll accept… As sparks fly between Eve and the magnificent man of the house she learns that the dark-hearted Lord is carrying the weight of ruin on his broad shoulders. So she offers him a proposal…

MILLS & BOON®

Pure reading pleasure™

HIST0509 LP